STORY AND ART BY
HIDEKI GOTO

Volume 2
VIZ Media Edition

Story and Art by
Hideki Goto

Translation **Tetsuichiro Miyaki**
English Adaptation **Bryant Turnage**
Lettering **John Hunt**
Design **Kam Li**
Editor **Joel Enos**

TM & © 2020 Nintendo. All rights reserved.

SPLATOON IKASU KIDS 4KOMA FES Vol. 2 by Hideki GOTO
© 2018 Hideki GOTO
All rights reserved.
Original Japanese edition published by SHOGAKUKAN.
English translation rights in the United States of America, Canada, the United
Kingdom, Ireland, Australia and New Zealand arranged with SHOGAKUKAN.

Original Design vol.ONE

Printed in the U.S.A.

Published by VIZ Media, LLC
P.O. Box 77010
San Francisco, CA 94107

10 9 8 7 6 5 4 3 2 1
First Printing, November 2020

PARENTAL ADVISORY
SPLATOON: SQUID KIDS
COMEDY SHOW is rated A and
is suitable for readers of all ages.

Splatoon
SQUID KIDS
COMEDY SHOW

2

STORY AND ART BY
HIDEKI GOTO

Characters

Maika
A city girl who uses Dualies.

Kou
An elite boy with three big advantages going for him—he's tall, rich and smart.

Hit
A boy from the countryside who came to the city to become a cool squid kid!

Contents

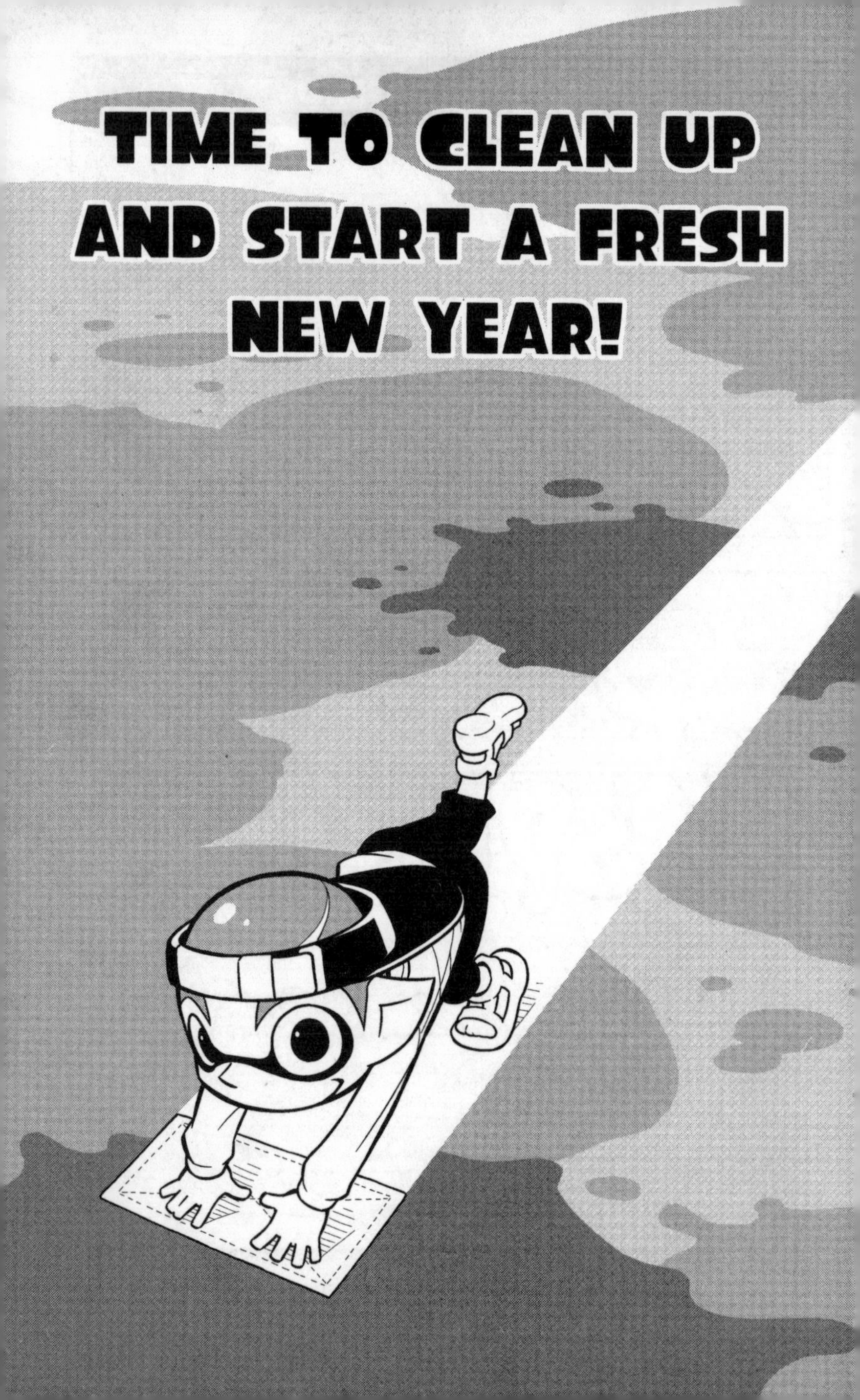
TIME TO CLEAN UP AND START A FRESH NEW YEAR!

HUGE CLEANUP

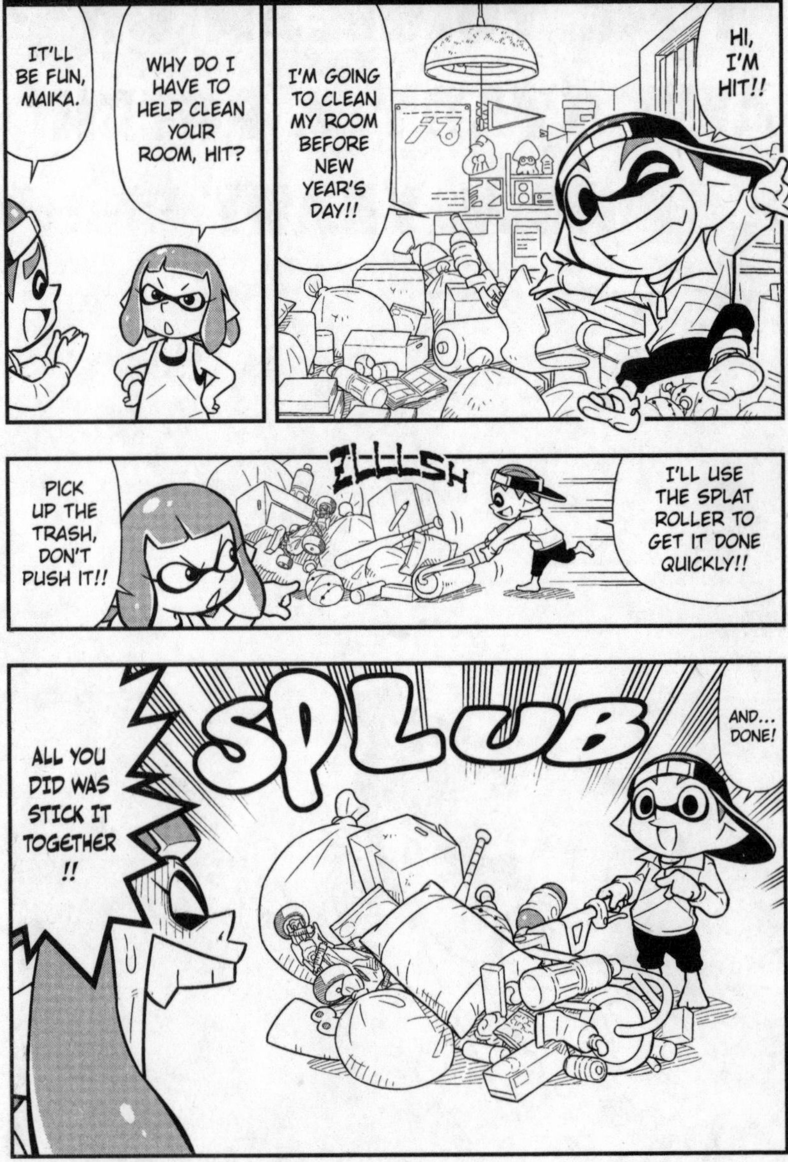
HI, I'M HIT!!
I'M GOING TO CLEAN MY ROOM BEFORE NEW YEAR'S DAY!!
WHY DO I HAVE TO HELP CLEAN YOUR ROOM, HIT?
IT'LL BE FUN, MAIKA.
I'LL USE THE SPLAT ROLLER TO GET IT DONE QUICKLY!!
ZLLLSH
PICK UP THE TRASH, DON'T PUSH IT!!
AND... DONE!
SPLUB
ALL YOU DID WAS STICK IT TOGETHER!!

LAUNDRY

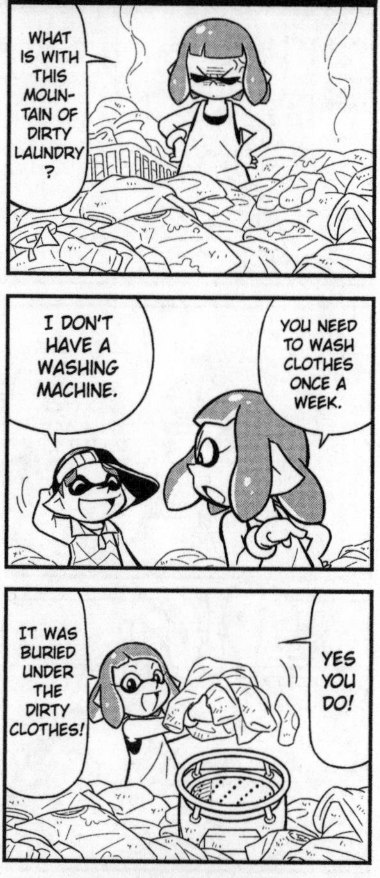
WHAT IS WITH THIS MOUNTAIN OF DIRTY LAUNDRY?
YOU NEED TO WASH CLOTHES ONCE A WEEK.
I DON'T HAVE A WASHING MACHINE.
YES YOU DO!
IT WAS BURIED UNDER THE DIRTY CLOTHES!
SLOSHING MACHINE
GWOOSH!
THAT'S A WEAPON THAT SPITS OUT INK!!

BROOM

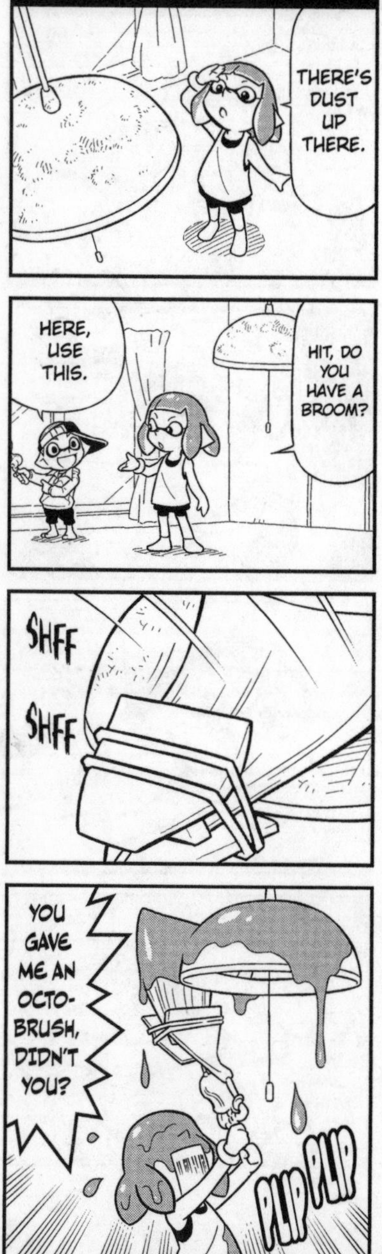
THERE'S DUST UP THERE.
HIT, DO YOU HAVE A BROOM?
HERE, USE THIS.
SHFF
SHFF
YOU GAVE ME AN OCTO-BRUSH, DIDN'T YOU?
PLIP PLIP

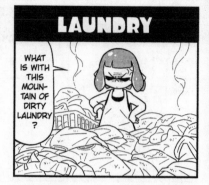

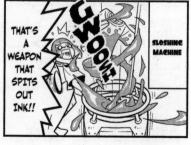

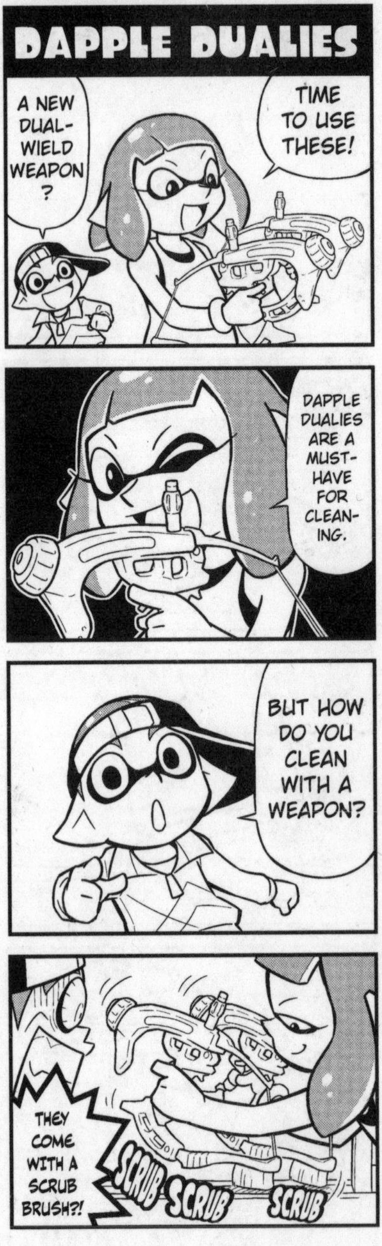
DAPPLE DUALIES
TIME TO USE THESE!
A NEW DUAL-WIELD WEAPON?
DAPPLE DUALIES ARE A MUST-HAVE FOR CLEANING.
BUT HOW DO YOU CLEAN WITH A WEAPON?
SCRUB SCRUB SCRUB
THEY COME WITH A SCRUB BRUSH?!

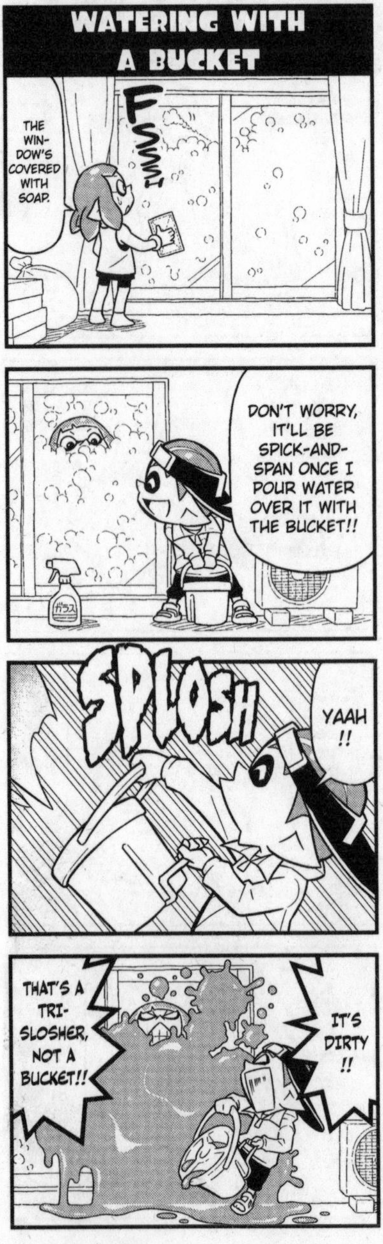
WATERING WITH A BUCKET
FSSSH
THE WINDOW'S COVERED WITH SOAP.
DON'T WORRY, IT'LL BE SPICK-AND-SPAN ONCE I POUR WATER OVER IT WITH THE BUCKET!!
ガラス
SPLOSH
YAAH!!
IT'S DIRTY!!
THAT'S A TRI-SLOSHER, NOT A BUCKET!!

EXPLODE

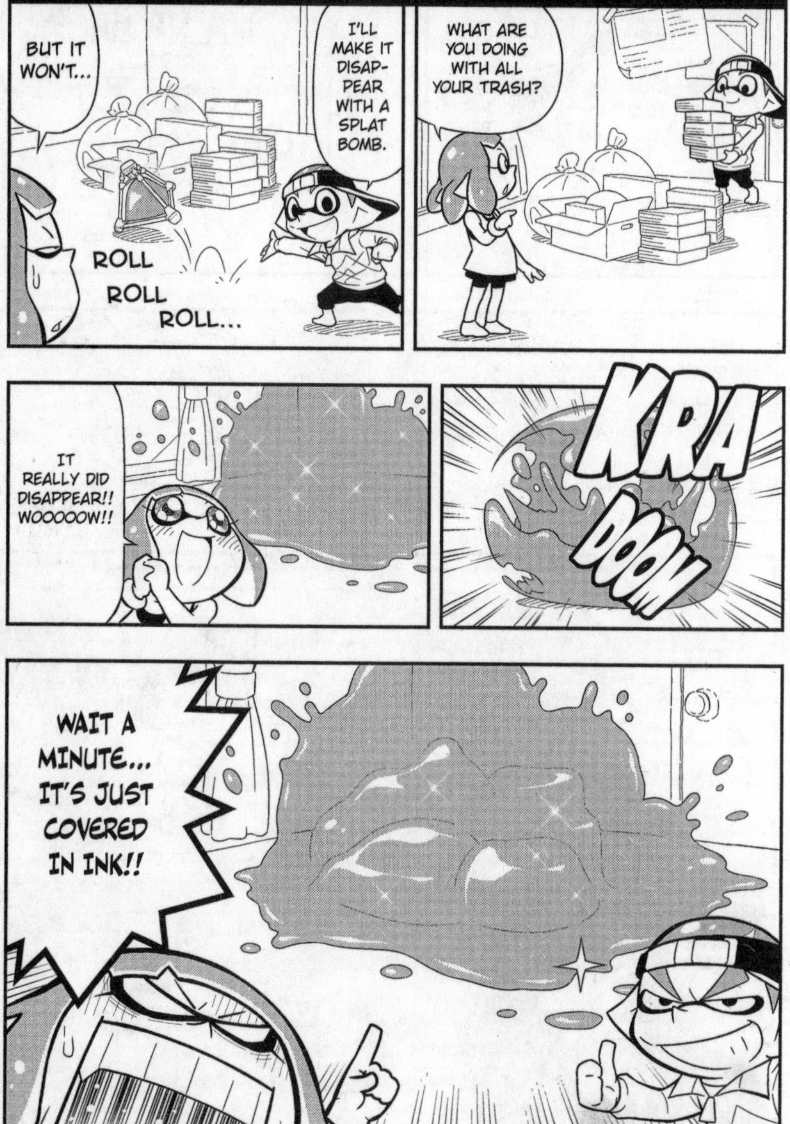
WHAT ARE YOU DOING WITH ALL YOUR TRASH?
I'LL MAKE IT DISAPPEAR WITH A SPLAT BOMB.
BUT IT WON'T...
ROLL ROLL ROLL...
KRA DOOM
IT REALLY DID DISAPPEAR!! WOOOOOW!!
WAIT A MINUTE... IT'S JUST COVERED IN INK!!

ROBOT VACUUM CLEANER

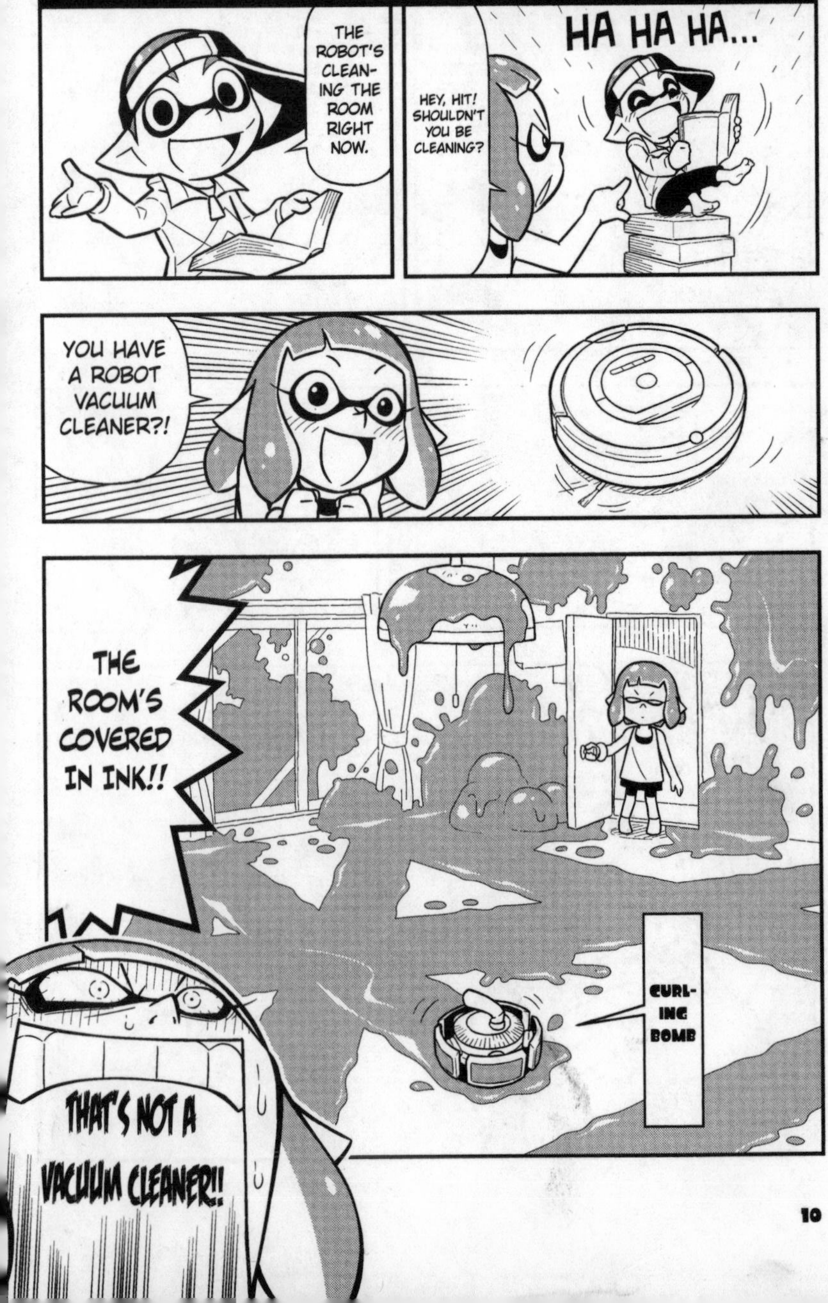
HEY, HIT! SHOULDN'T YOU BE CLEANING?
HA HA HA...
THE ROBOT'S CLEAN-ING THE ROOM RIGHT NOW.
YOU HAVE A ROBOT VACUUM CLEANER?!
CURL-ING BOMB
THE ROOM'S COVERED IN INK!!
THAT'S NOT A VACUUM CLEANER!!

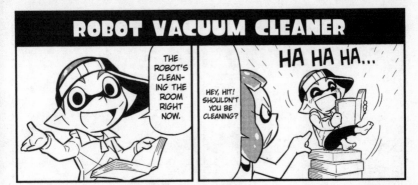

TIME TO REACT TO THE NEW YEAR'S JOKES!

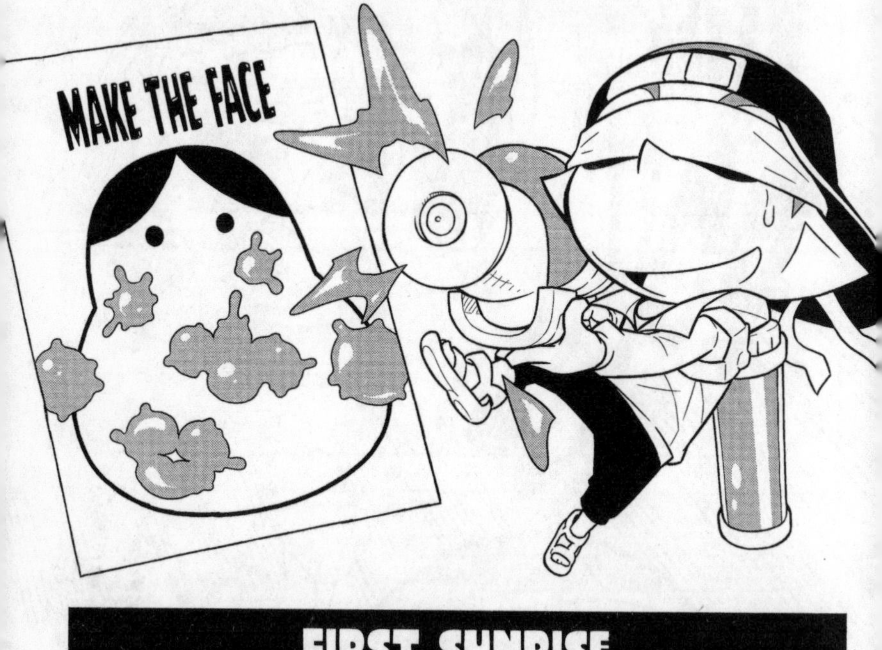
MAKE THE FACE

FIRST SUNRISE

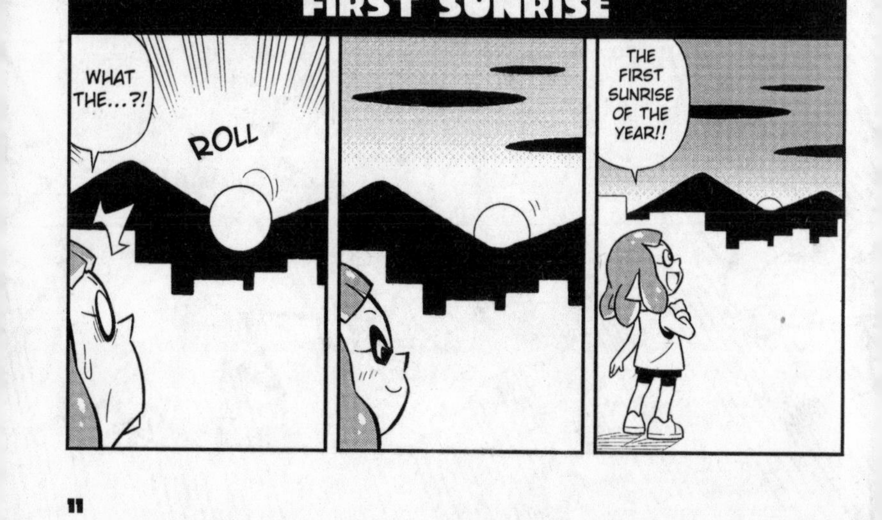
THE FIRST SUNRISE OF THE YEAR!!
WHAT THE...?!
ROLL

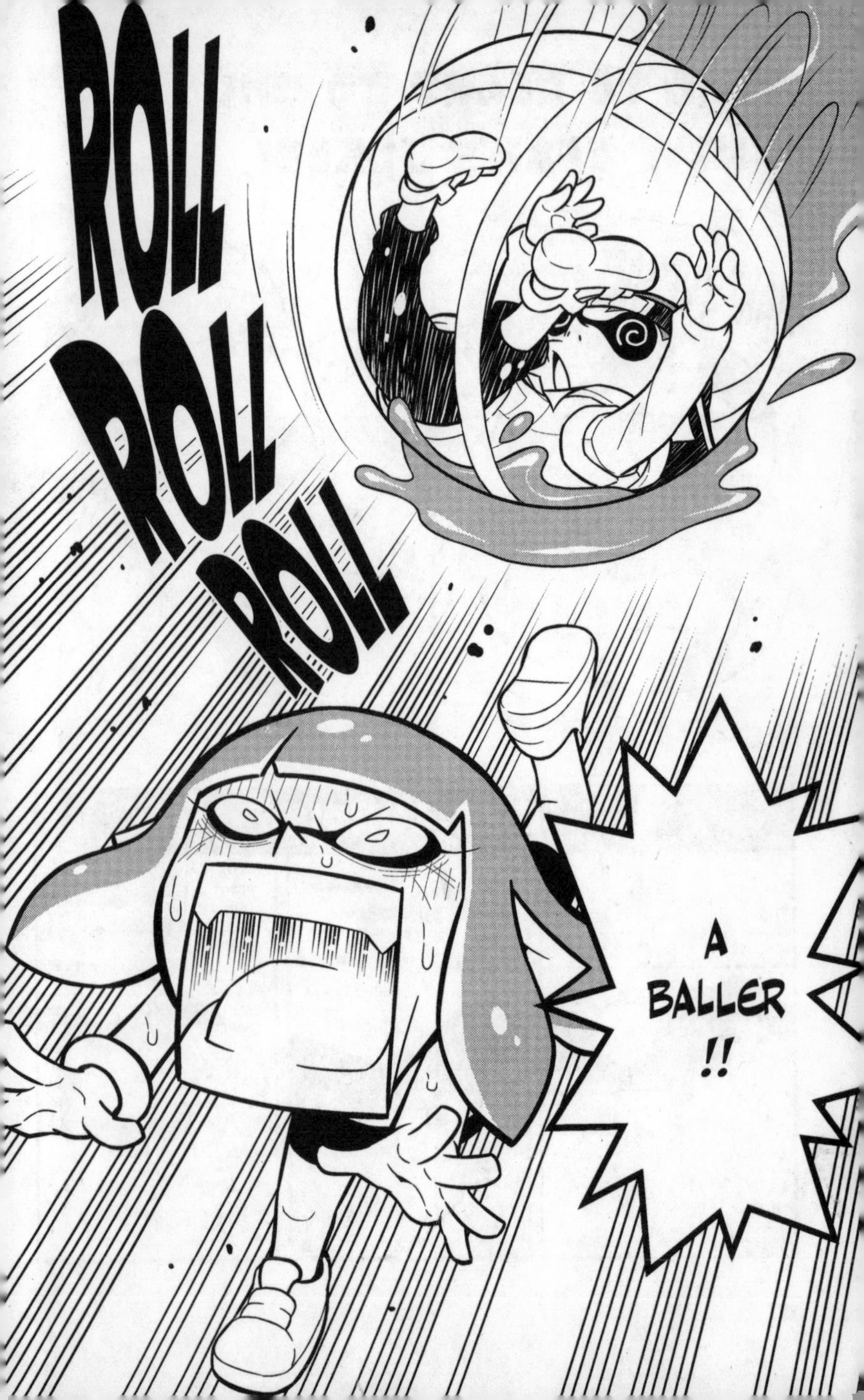
ROLL ROLL ROLL
A BALLER !!

NEW YEAR RICE CAKE

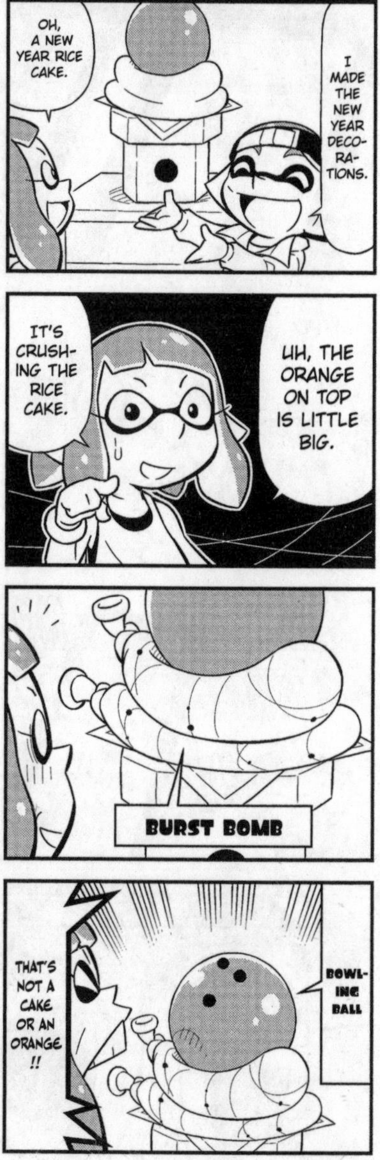
I MADE THE NEW YEAR DECO-RA-TIONS.
OH, A NEW YEAR RICE CAKE.
UH, THE ORANGE ON TOP IS LITTLE BIG.
IT'S CRUSH-ING THE RICE CAKE.
BURST BOMB
BOWL-ING BALL
THAT'S NOT A CAKE OR AN ORANGE !!

FLYING KITES

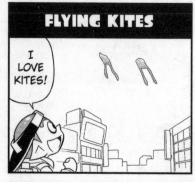

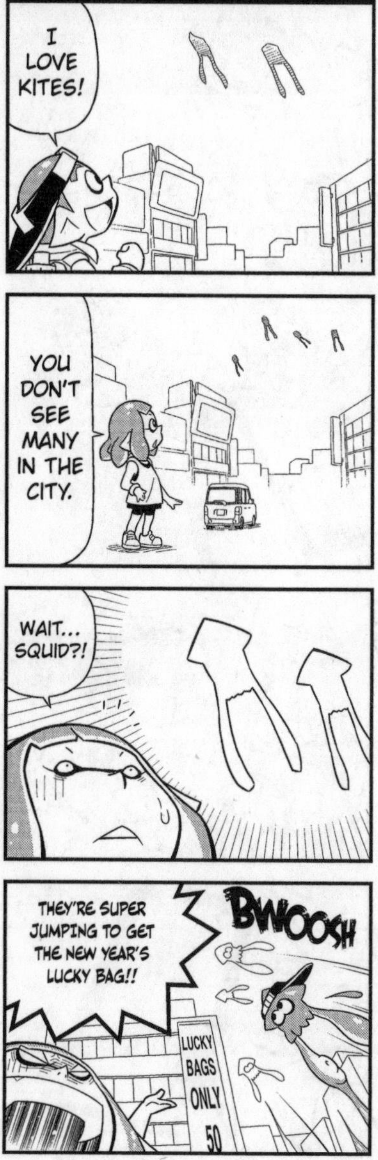
I LOVE KITES!
YOU DON'T SEE MANY IN THE CITY.
WAIT... SQUID?!
BWOOSH
THEY'RE SUPER JUMPING TO GET THE NEW YEAR'S LUCKY BAG!!
LUCKY BAGS ONLY 50

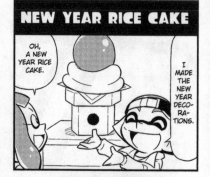

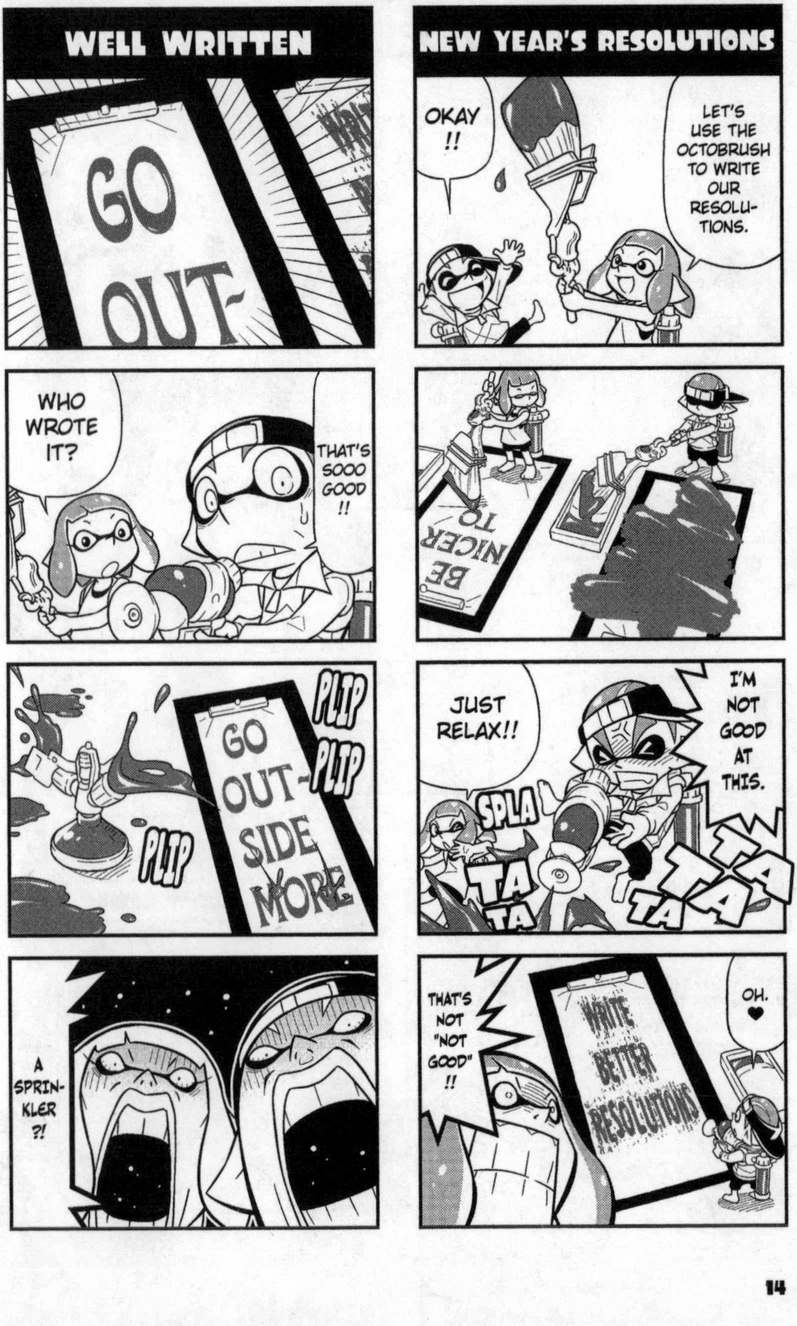
NEW YEAR'S RESOLUTIONS
LET'S USE THE OCTOBRUSH TO WRITE OUR RESOLU-TIONS.
OKAY!!
BE NICER TO
I'M NOT GOOD AT THIS.
JUST RELAX!!
SPLA
TA TA TA TA
TA TA
OH. ♥
WRITE BETTER RESOLUTIONS
THAT'S NOT "NOT GOOD"!!
WELL WRITTEN
GO OUT-
THAT'S SOOO GOOD!!
WHO WROTE IT?
PLIP
PLIP
GO OUT-SIDE MORE
PLIP
A SPRIN-KLER?!

NEW YEAR'S SHRINE VISIT

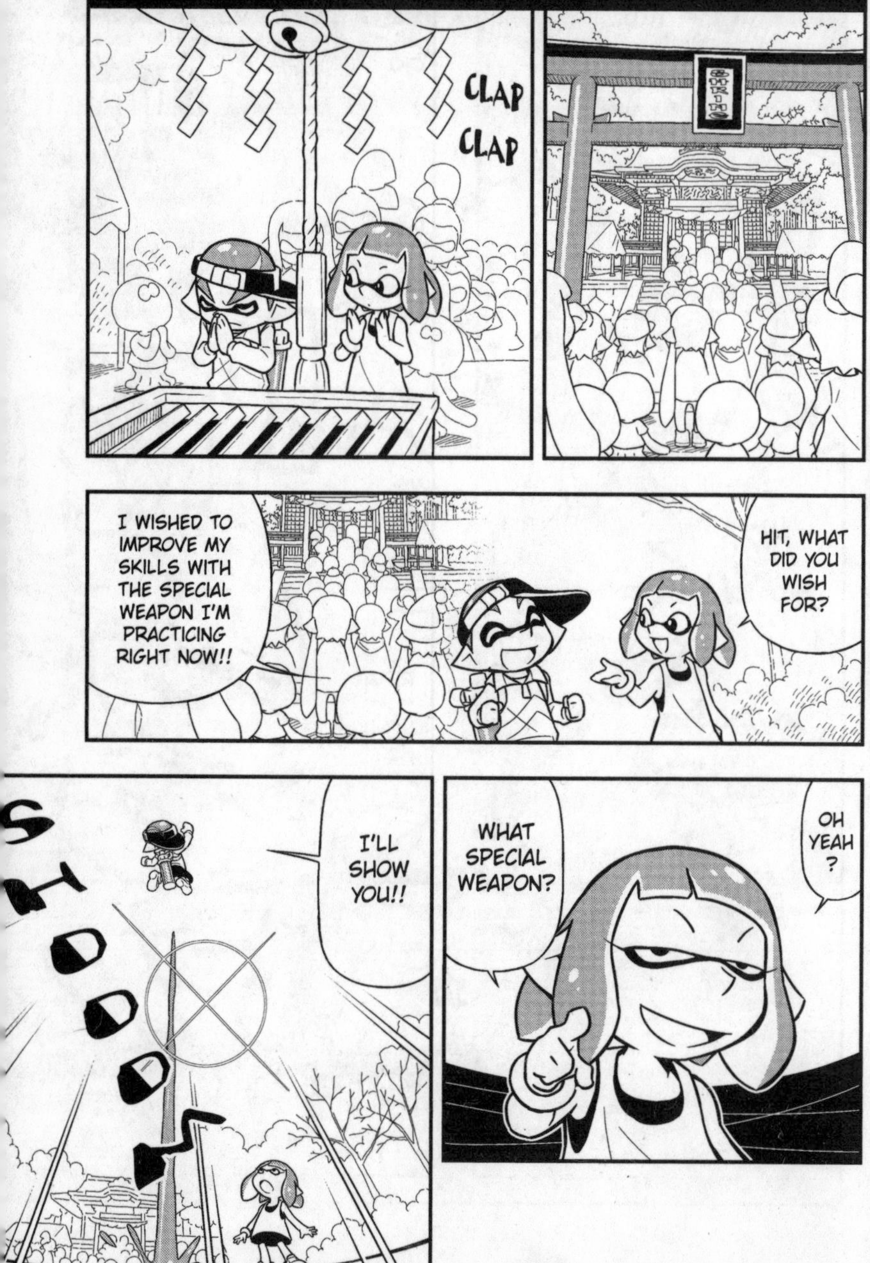

CLAP
CLAP
HIT, WHAT DID YOU WISH FOR?
I WISHED TO IMPROVE MY SKILLS WITH THE SPECIAL WEAPON I'M PRACTICING RIGHT NOW!!
OH YEAH?
WHAT SPECIAL WEAPON?
I'LL SHOW YOU!!

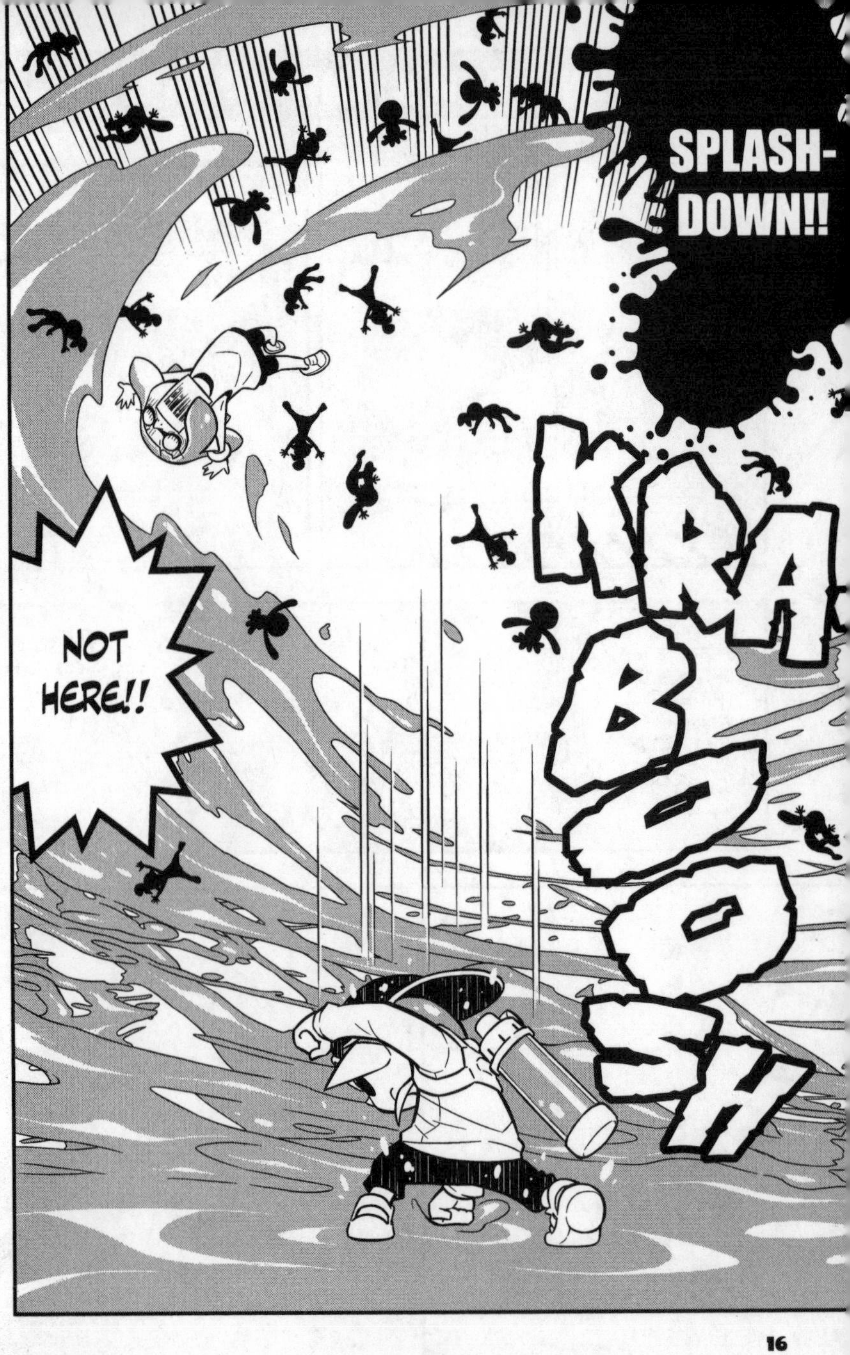
SPLASH-
DOWN!!
KRA
BOOSH
NOT HERE!!

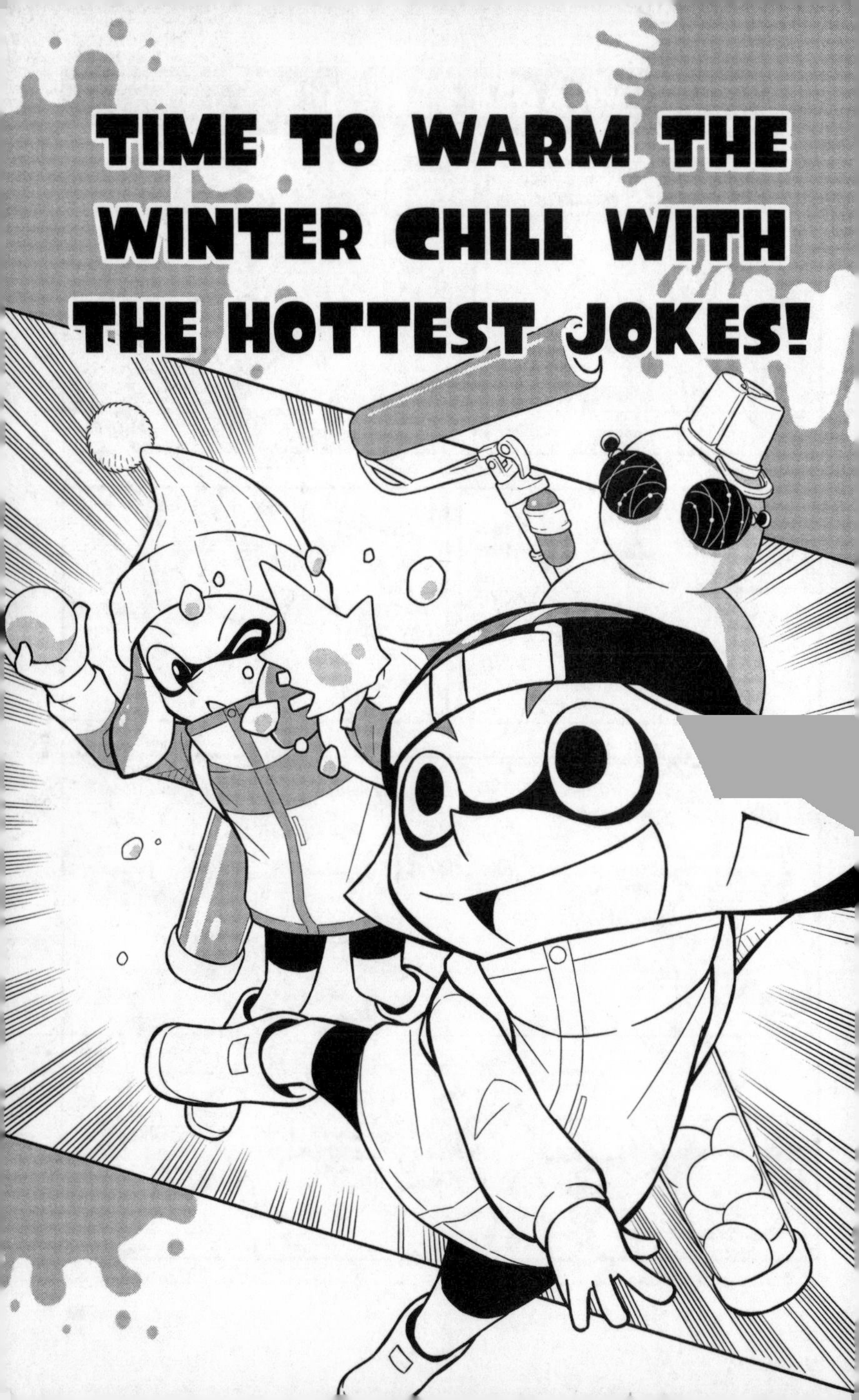
TIME TO WARM THE WINTER CHILL WITH THE HOTTEST JOKES!

WARM CLOTHES

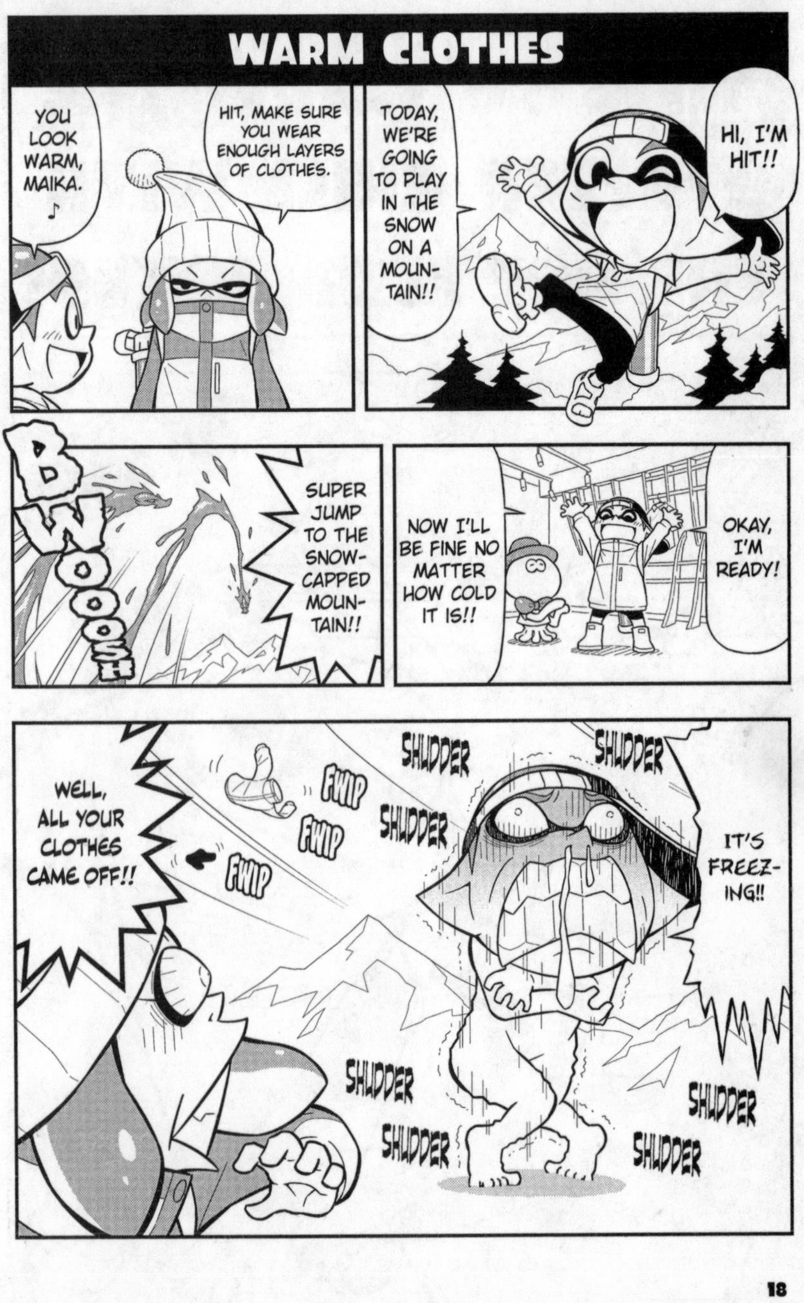
HI, I'M HIT!!
TODAY, WE'RE GOING TO PLAY IN THE SNOW ON A MOUNTAIN!!
HIT, MAKE SURE YOU WEAR ENOUGH LAYERS OF CLOTHES.
YOU LOOK WARM, MAIKA. ♪
OKAY, I'M READY!
NOW I'LL BE FINE NO MATTER HOW COLD IT IS!!
SUPER JUMP TO THE SNOW-CAPPED MOUNTAIN!!
BWOOOOSH
IT'S FREEZING!!
SHUDDER
SHUDDER
SHUDDER
SHUDDER
SHUDDER
SHUDDER
SHUDDER
FWIP
FWIP
FWIP
WELL, ALL YOUR CLOTHES CAME OFF!!

SNOWBALL FIGHT

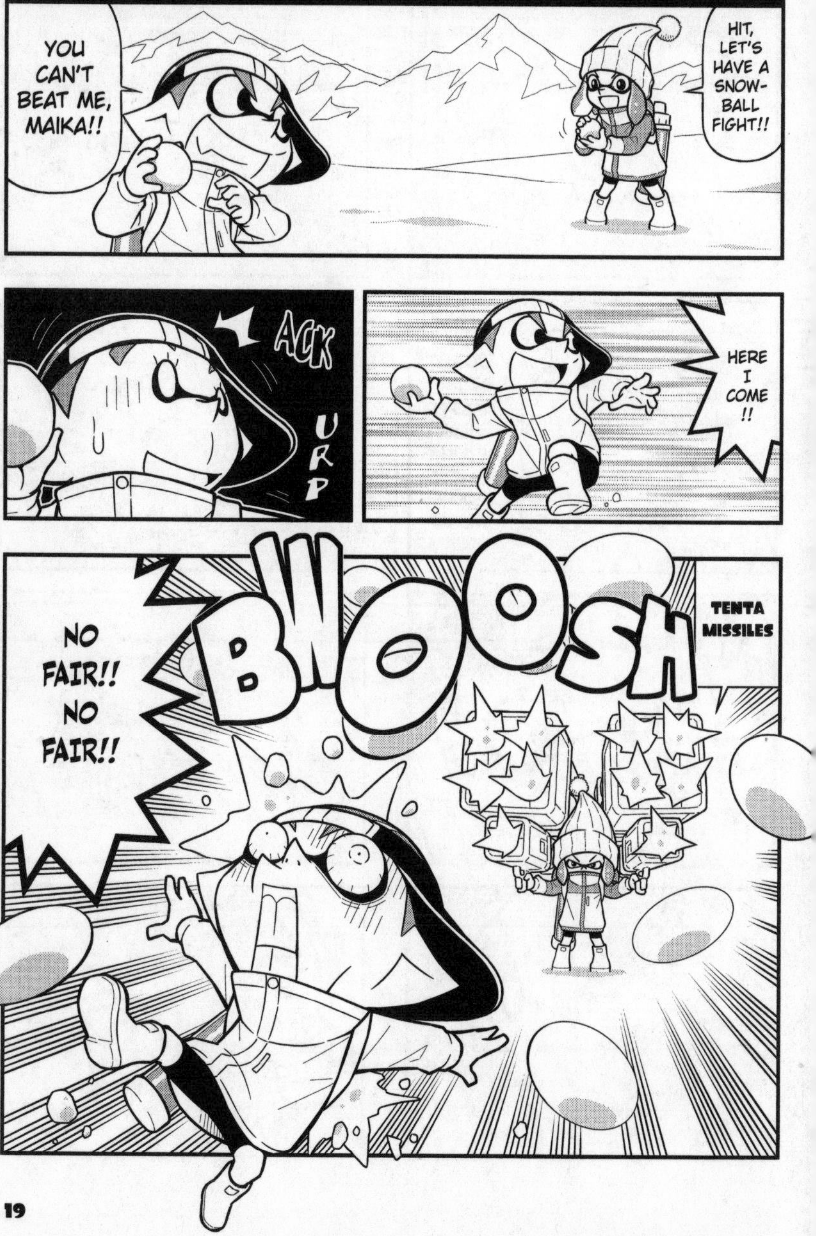

HIT, LET'S HAVE A SNOW-BALL FIGHT!!
YOU CAN'T BEAT ME, MAIKA!!
HERE I COME!!
ACK
URP
BWOOSH
TENTA MISSILES
NO FAIR!! NO FAIR!!

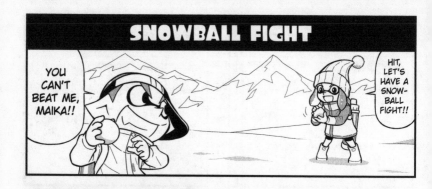

WALL

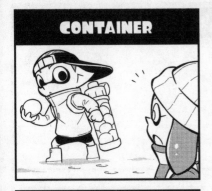

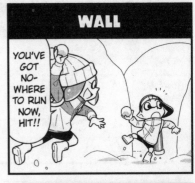

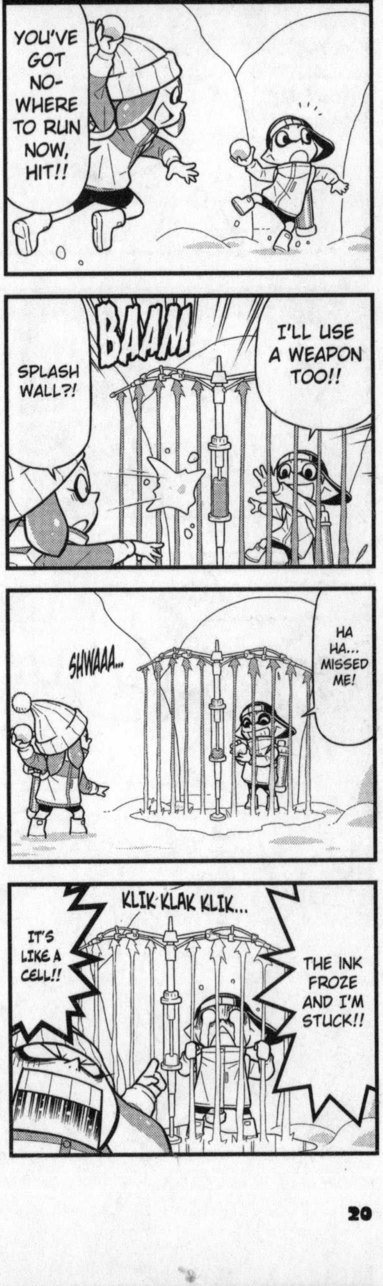
YOU'VE GOT NO-WHERE TO RUN NOW, HIT!!
I'LL USE A WEAPON TOO!!
BAAM
SPLASH WALL?!
HA HA... MISSED ME!
SHWAAA...
KLIK KLAK KLIK...
THE INK FROZE AND I'M STUCK!!
IT'S LIKE A CELL!!

CONTAINER

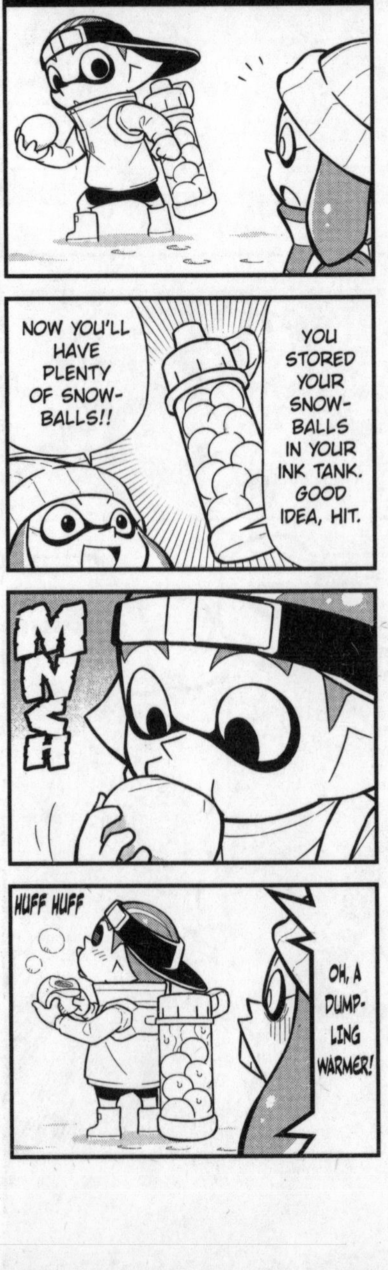
YOU STORED YOUR SNOW-BALLS IN YOUR INK TANK. GOOD IDEA, HIT.
NOW YOU'LL HAVE PLENTY OF SNOW-BALLS!!
MNSH
OH, A DUMP-LING WARMER!
HUFF HUFF

SNOWDOWN

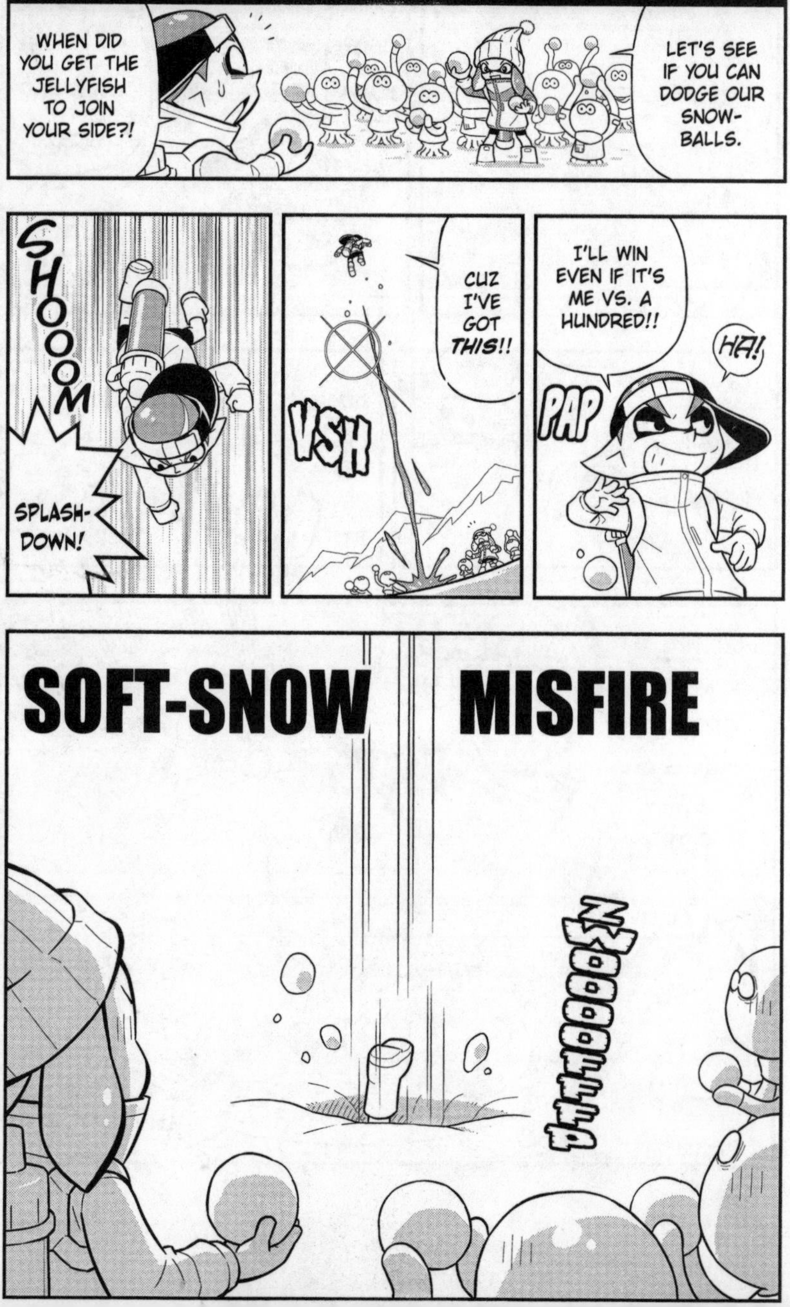
LET'S SEE IF YOU CAN DODGE OUR SNOW-BALLS.
WHEN DID YOU GET THE JELLYFISH TO JOIN YOUR SIDE?!
I'LL WIN EVEN IF IT'S ME VS. A HUNDRED!!
HA!
PAP
CUZ I'VE GOT THIS!!
VSH
SHOOOOM
SPLASH-DOWN!
SOFT-SNOW MISFIRE

HOT SPRING IN WINTER

WE PLAYED FOR SO LONG AND NOW I'M COLD.
SHUDDER SHUDDER SHUDDER...
I NEED TO WARM UP.
GO AHEAD AND USE THIS.
A HOT SPRING IN AN IGLOO?!
OOOH, ITS SOOOOO WARM.
AHHHH...
SAL-MONIDS USE HOT SPRINGS TOO?
BLUB BLUB
IT'S NOT A SPRING... IT'S A STEW POT!!
BLUB BLUB

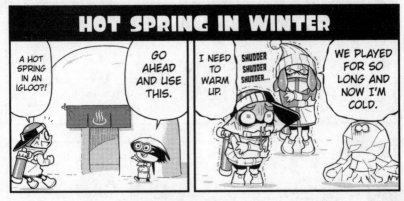

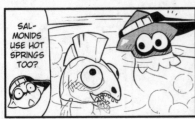

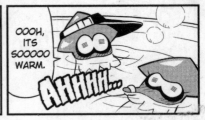

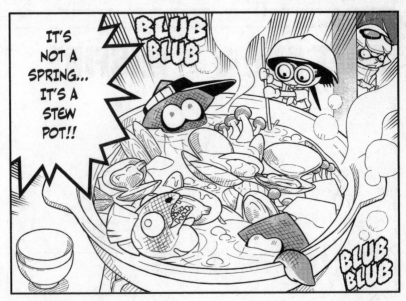

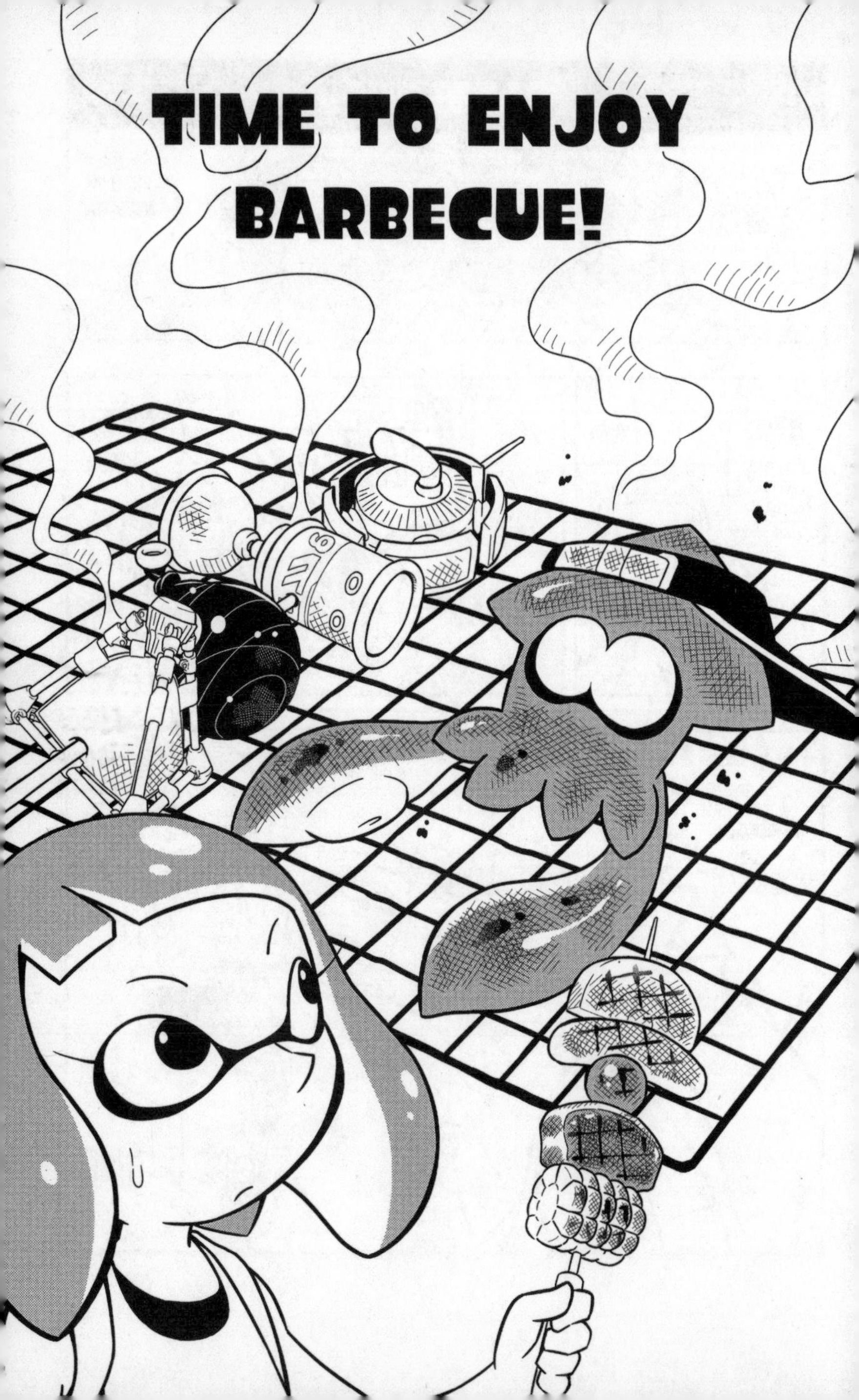
TIME TO ENJOY BARBECUE!

BARBECUE

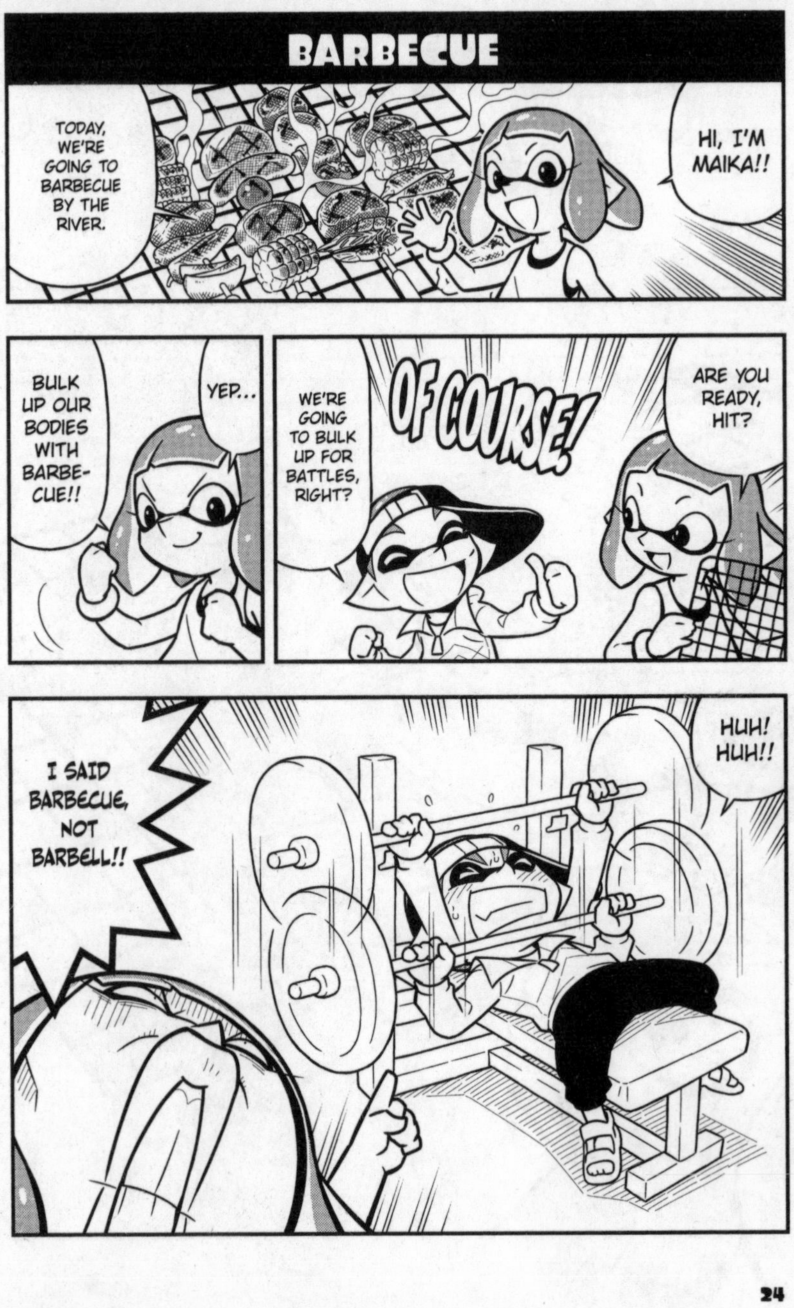
HI, I'M MAIKA!!
TODAY, WE'RE GOING TO BARBECUE BY THE RIVER.
ARE YOU READY, HIT?
OF COURSE!
WE'RE GOING TO BULK UP FOR BATTLES, RIGHT?
YEP...
BULK UP OUR BODIES WITH BARBE-CUE!!
HUH! HUH!!
I SAID BARBECUE, NOT BARBELL!!

ROCKS

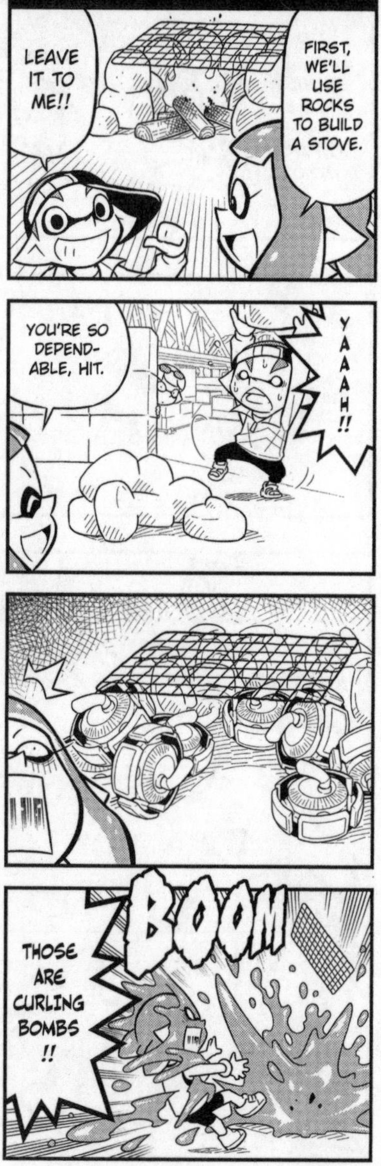

FIRST, WE'LL USE ROCKS TO BUILD A STOVE.
LEAVE IT TO ME!!
YAAAAH!!
YOU'RE SO DEPEND-ABLE, HIT.
BOOM
THOSE ARE CURLING BOMBS!!

COB

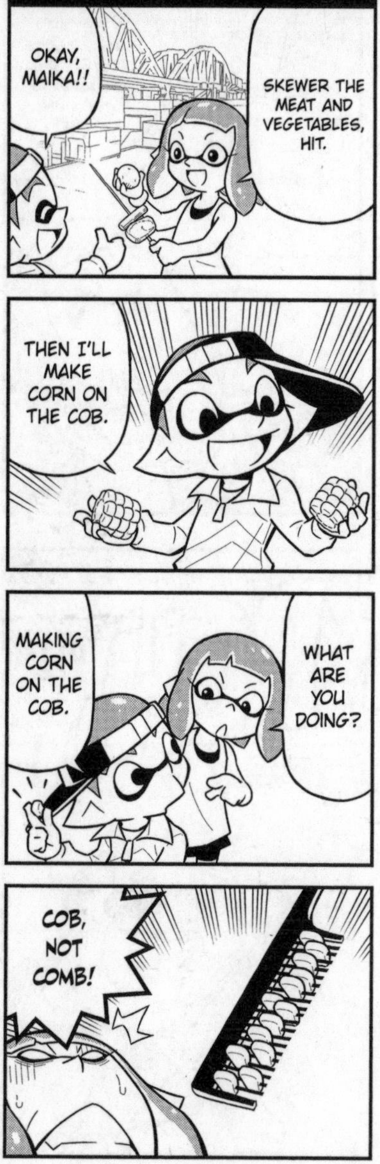

SKEWER THE MEAT AND VEGETABLES, HIT.
OKAY, MAIKA!!
THEN I'LL MAKE CORN ON THE COB.
WHAT ARE YOU DOING?
MAKING CORN ON THE COB.
COB, NOT COMB!

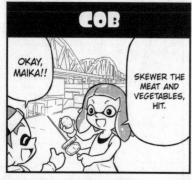

LONG SKEWER

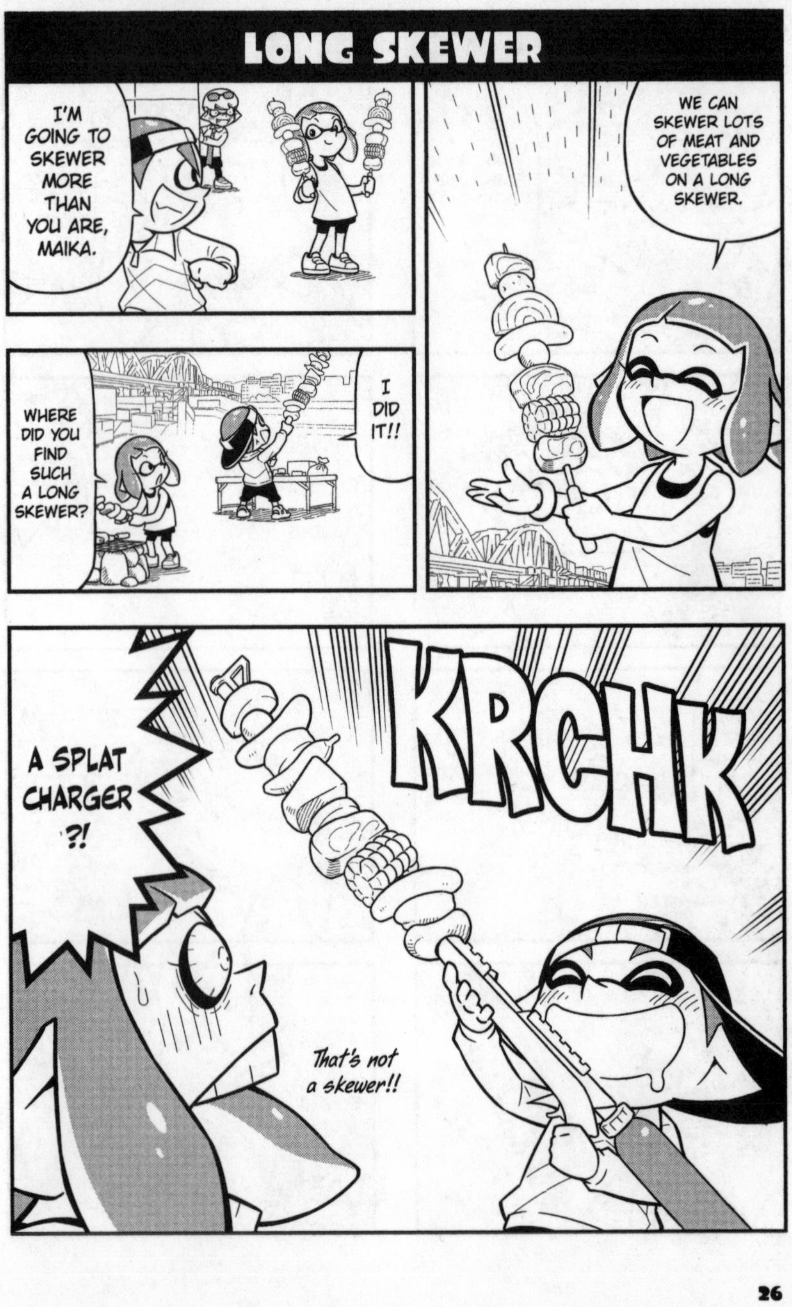
WE CAN SKEWER LOTS OF MEAT AND VEGETABLES ON A LONG SKEWER.
I'M GOING TO SKEWER MORE THAN YOU ARE, MAIKA.
I DID IT!!
WHERE DID YOU FIND SUCH A LONG SKEWER?
KRCHK
A SPLAT CHARGER ?!
That's not a skewer!!

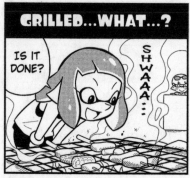

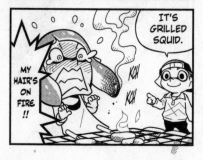

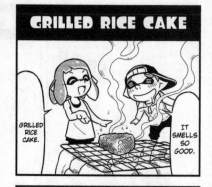

GRILLED RICE CAKE

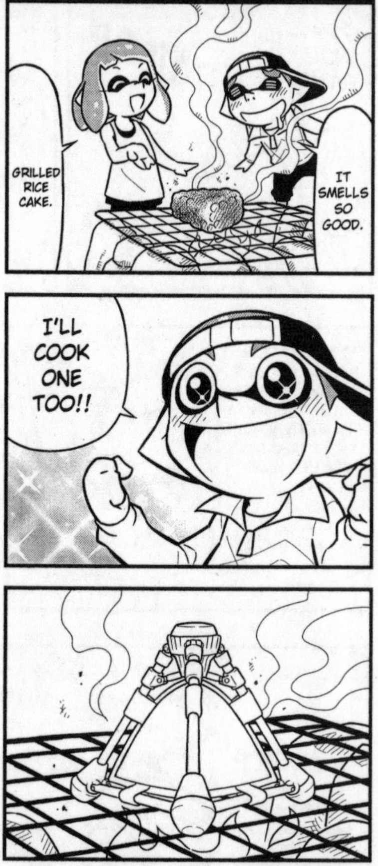

IT SMELLS SO GOOD.
GRILLED RICE CAKE.
I'LL COOK ONE TOO!!
BOOM
NOT WITH A SPLAT BOMB!!

GRILLED...WHAT...?

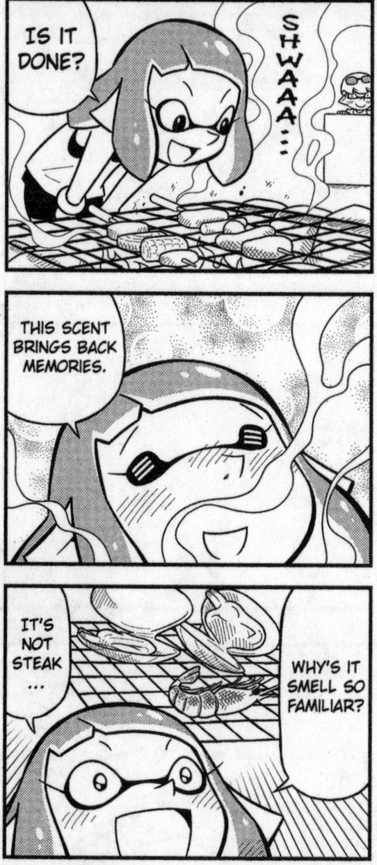

SHWAAAA...
IS IT DONE?
THIS SCENT BRINGS BACK MEMORIES.
WHY'S IT SMELL SO FAMILIAR?
IT'S NOT STEAK...
IT'S GRILLED SQUID.
KCH
KCH
MY HAIR'S ON FIRE!!

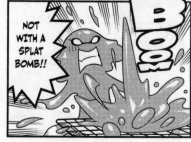

DREAM GUY KOU

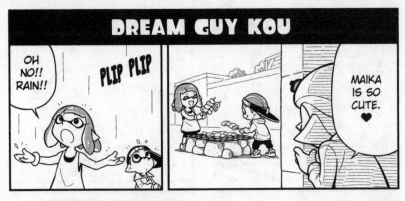

MAIKA IS SO CUTE. ♥
OH NO!! RAIN!!
PLIP PLIP
YOUNG LADY, YOU CAN STAND NEXT TO ME.
I'M KOU!! I'M BASICALLY YOUR DREAM GUY! IF YOUR DREAM IS A GUY WITH THE THREE D'S! I'M DEBONAIR, DAPPER AND HAVE LOTS OF DOLLARS! NICE TO MEET YOU!
THANKS, I'M HIT... WITH ONE H...FOR "HIT."
I WASN'T TALKING TO YOU!!

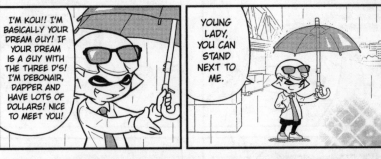

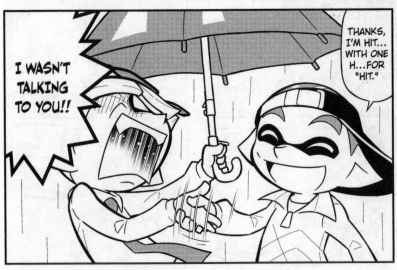

BRELLA

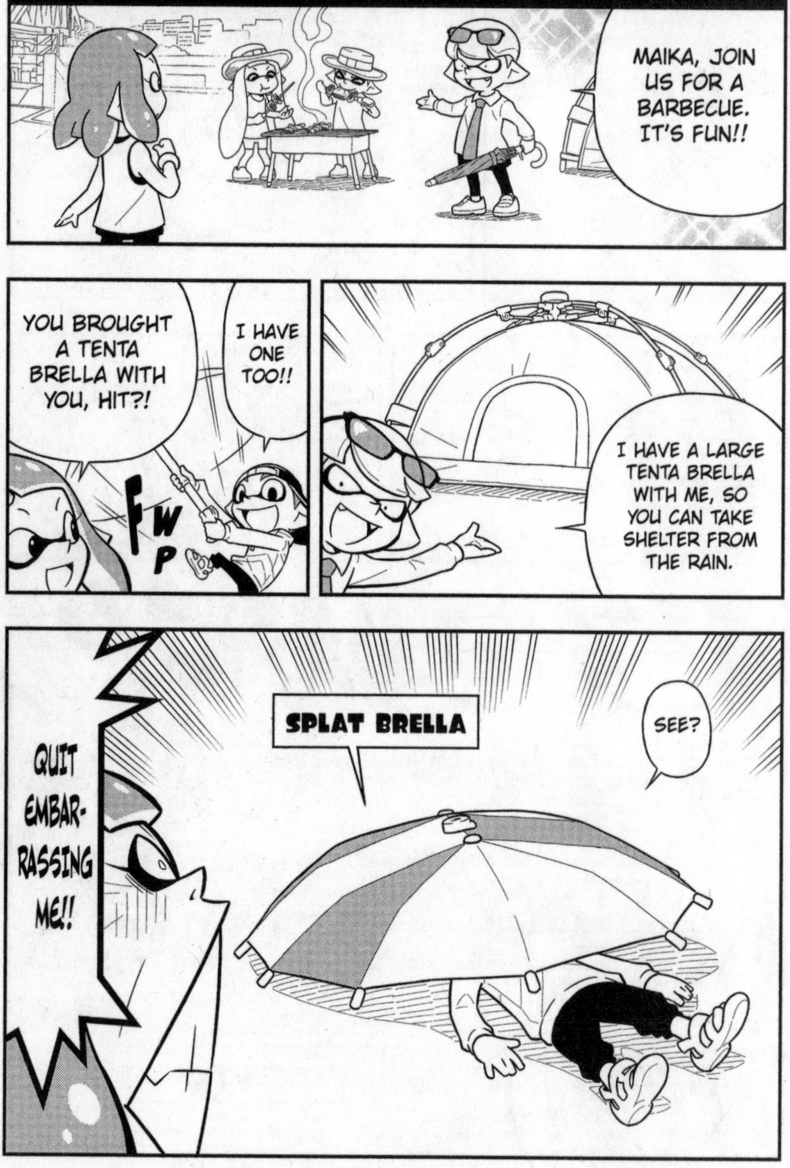
MAIKA, JOIN US FOR A BARBECUE. IT'S FUN!!
I HAVE A LARGE TENTA BRELLA WITH ME, SO YOU CAN TAKE SHELTER FROM THE RAIN.
I HAVE ONE TOO!!
YOU BROUGHT A TENTA BRELLA WITH YOU, HIT?!
FWP
SEE?
SPLAT BRELLA
QUIT EMBAR-RASSING ME!!

SHOOT-OUT

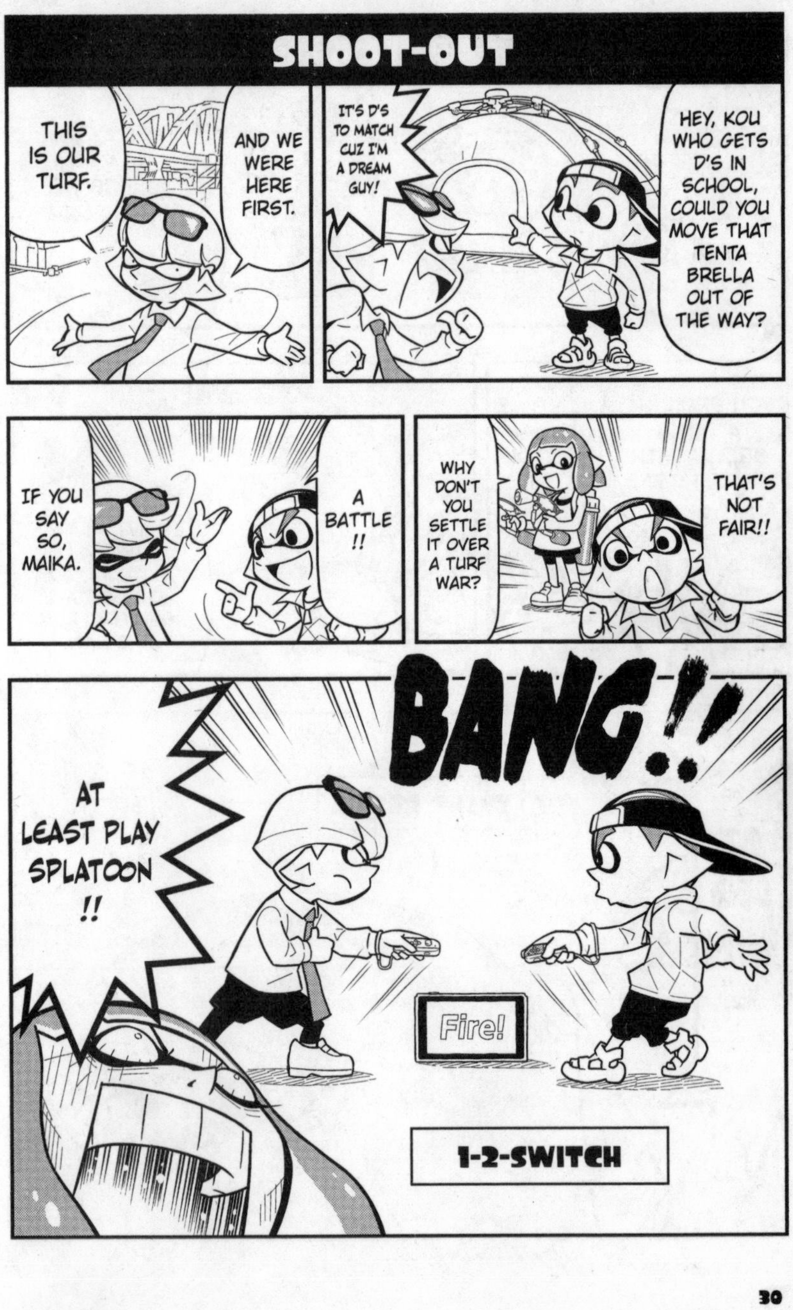
HEY, KOU WHO GETS D'S IN SCHOOL, COULD YOU MOVE THAT TENTA BRELLA OUT OF THE WAY?
IT'S D'S TO MATCH CUZ I'M A DREAM GUY!
AND WE WERE HERE FIRST.
THIS IS OUR TURF.
THAT'S NOT FAIR!!
WHY DON'T YOU SETTLE IT OVER A TURF WAR?
A BATTLE !!
IF YOU SAY SO, MAIKA.
BANG!!
AT LEAST PLAY SPLATOON !!
Fire!
1-2-SWITCH

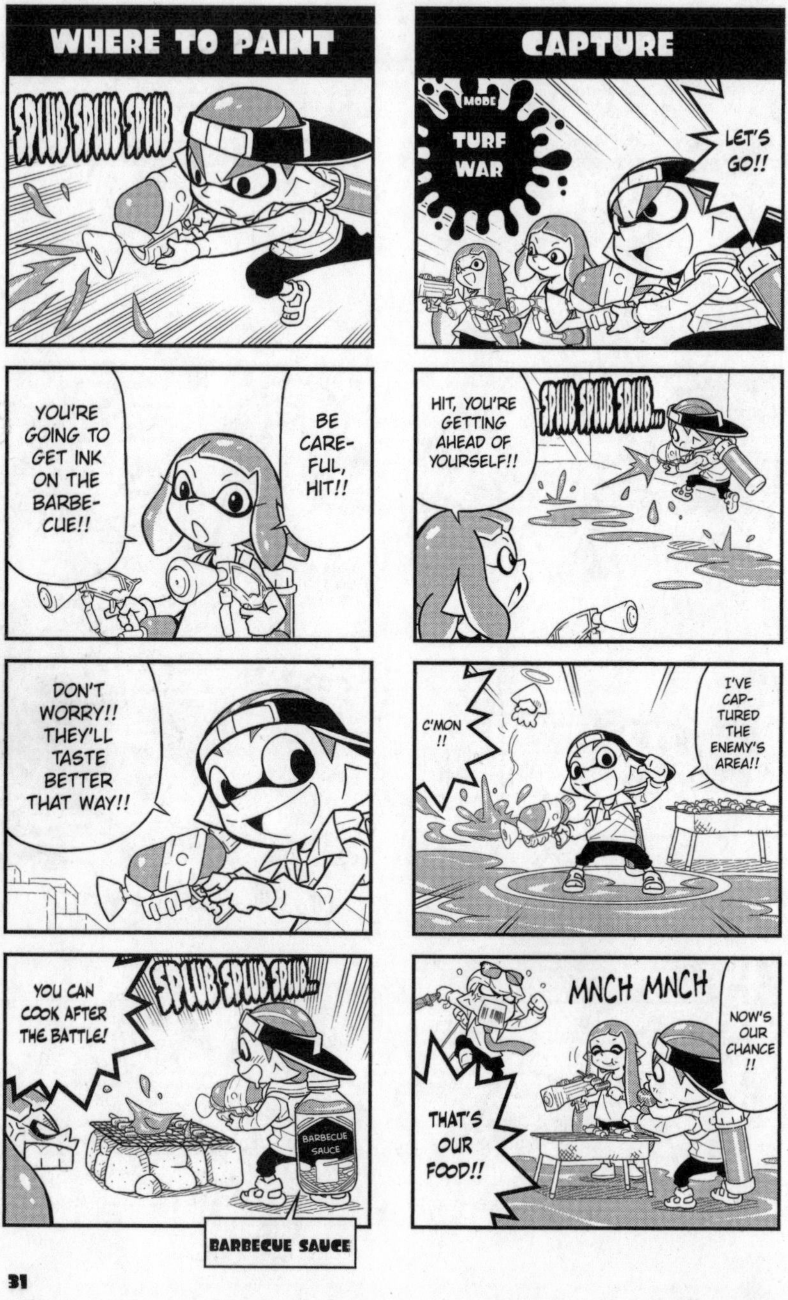
CAPTURE
MODE
TURF WAR
LET'S GO!!
SPLUB SPLUB SPLUB...
HIT, YOU'RE GETTING AHEAD OF YOURSELF!!
I'VE CAPTURED THE ENEMY'S AREA!!
C'MON!!
NOW'S OUR CHANCE!!
MNCH MNCH
THAT'S OUR FOOD!!
WHERE TO PAINT
SPLUB SPLUB SPLUB
BE CAREFUL, HIT!!
YOU'RE GOING TO GET INK ON THE BARBECUE!!
DON'T WORRY!! THEY'LL TASTE BETTER THAT WAY!!
SPLUB SPLUB SPLUB...
YOU CAN COOK AFTER THE BATTLE!
BARBECUE SAUCE
BARBECUE SAUCE

VEGETABLE INK

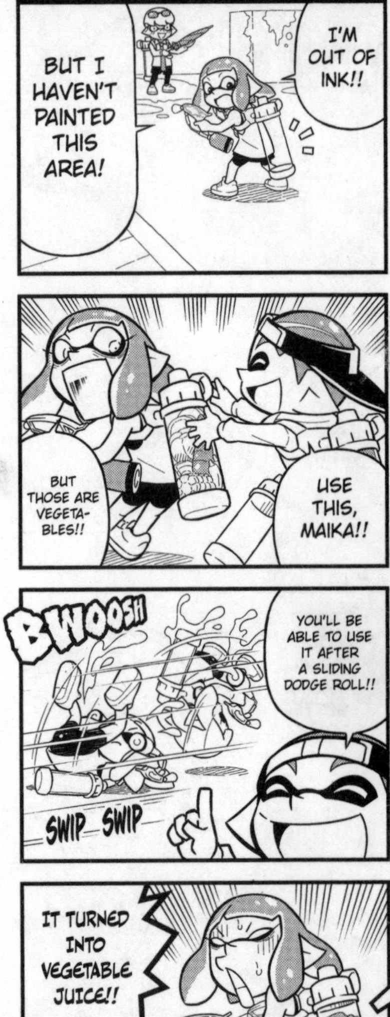
I'M OUT OF INK!!
BUT I HAVEN'T PAINTED THIS AREA!
USE THIS, MAIKA!!
BUT THOSE ARE VEGETA-BLES!!
YOU'LL BE ABLE TO USE IT AFTER A SLIDING DODGE ROLL!!
BWOOSH
SWIP SWIP
IT TURNED INTO VEGETABLE JUICE!!
SPLUB SPLUB

SHOW-OFF

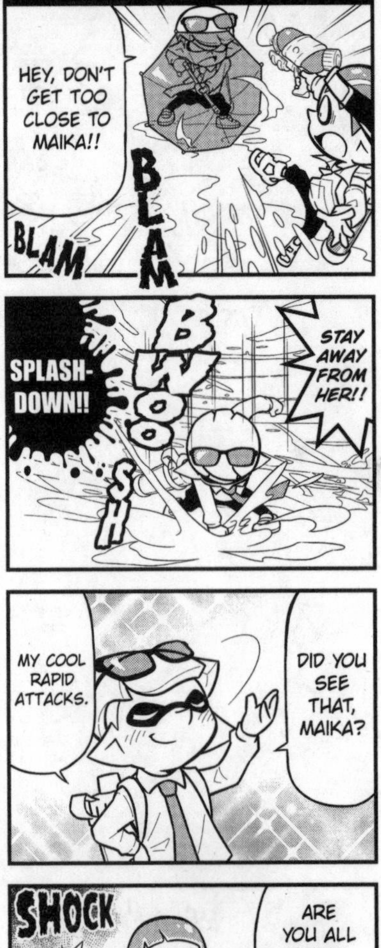
BLAM
HEY, DON'T GET TOO CLOSE TO MAIKA!!
BLAM
STAY AWAY FROM HER!!
BWOOSH
SPLASH-DOWN!!
DID YOU SEE THAT, MAIKA?
MY COOL RAPID ATTACKS.
ARE YOU ALL RIGHT, HIT?
SHOCK

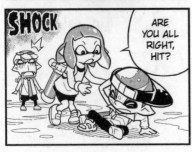

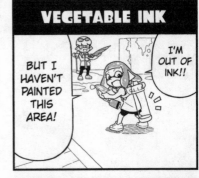

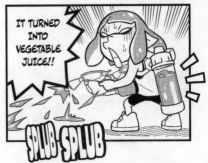

THE END AND BEGINNING

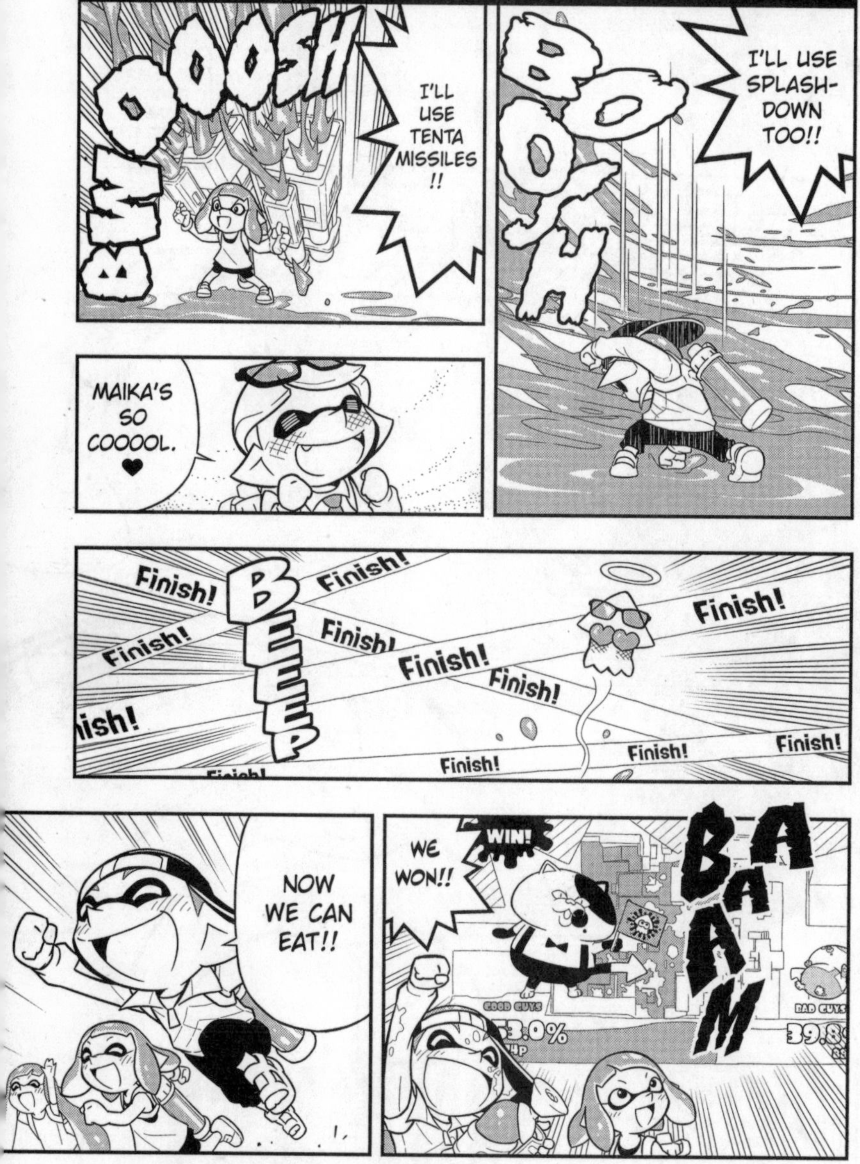
BOOH
I'LL USE SPLASH-DOWN TOO!!
BWOOOOSH
I'LL USE TENTA MISSILES!!
MAIKA'S SO COOOOL. ❤
Finish!
Finish!
Finish!
Finish!
Finish!
Finish!
Finish!
Finish!
Finish!
BEEEP
BAAAM
WIN!
WE WON!!
GOOD GUYS
BAD GUYS
NOW WE CAN EAT!!

←IT'S FINALLY TIME TO ENJOY THE BARBECUE!!

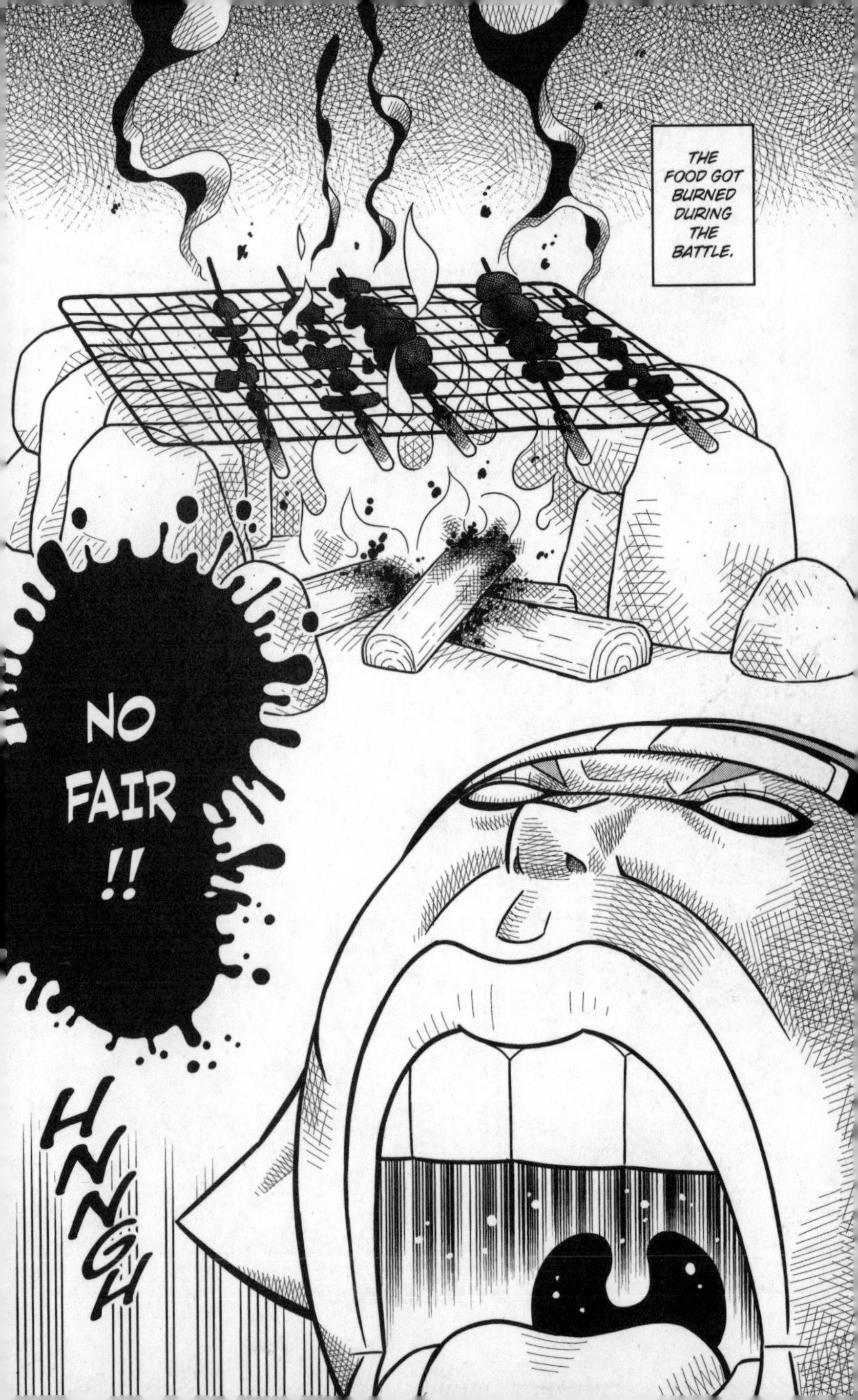
THE FOOD GOT BURNED DURING THE BATTLE.
NO FAIR!!
HNNGH

TIME FOR AN EXCITING BATTLE ON THE SOCCER FIELD!

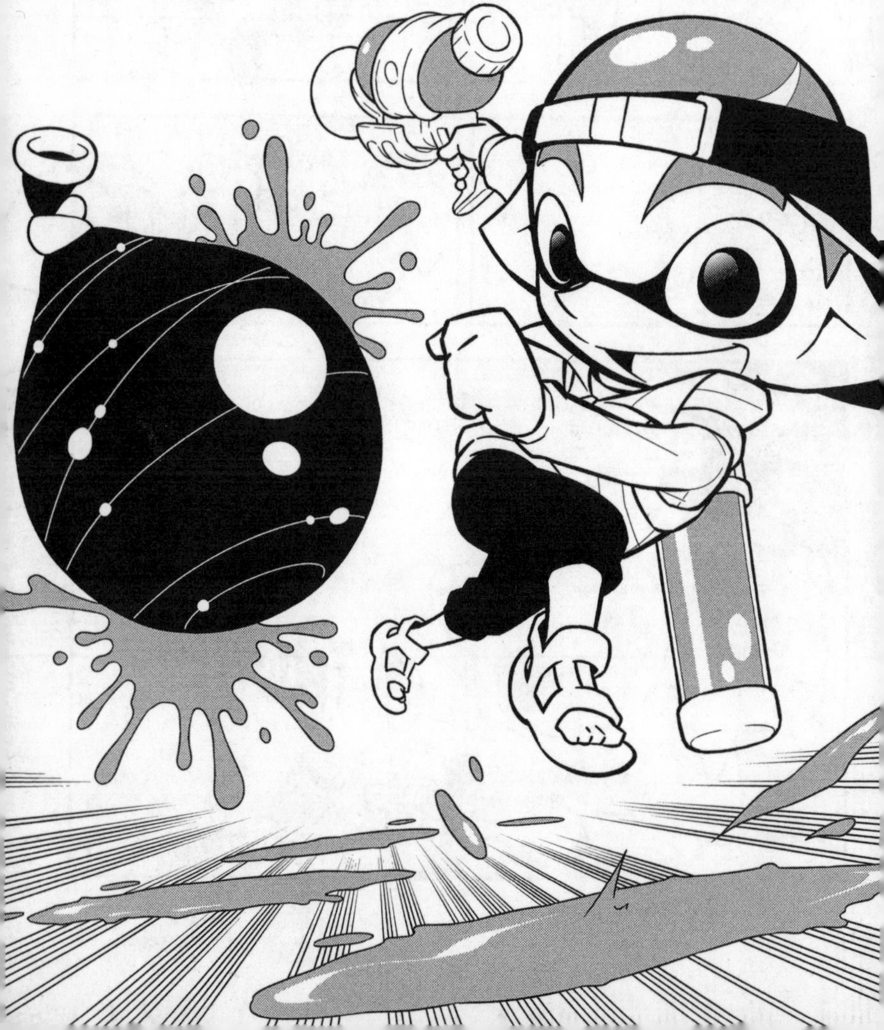

SPECIAL STAGE?!

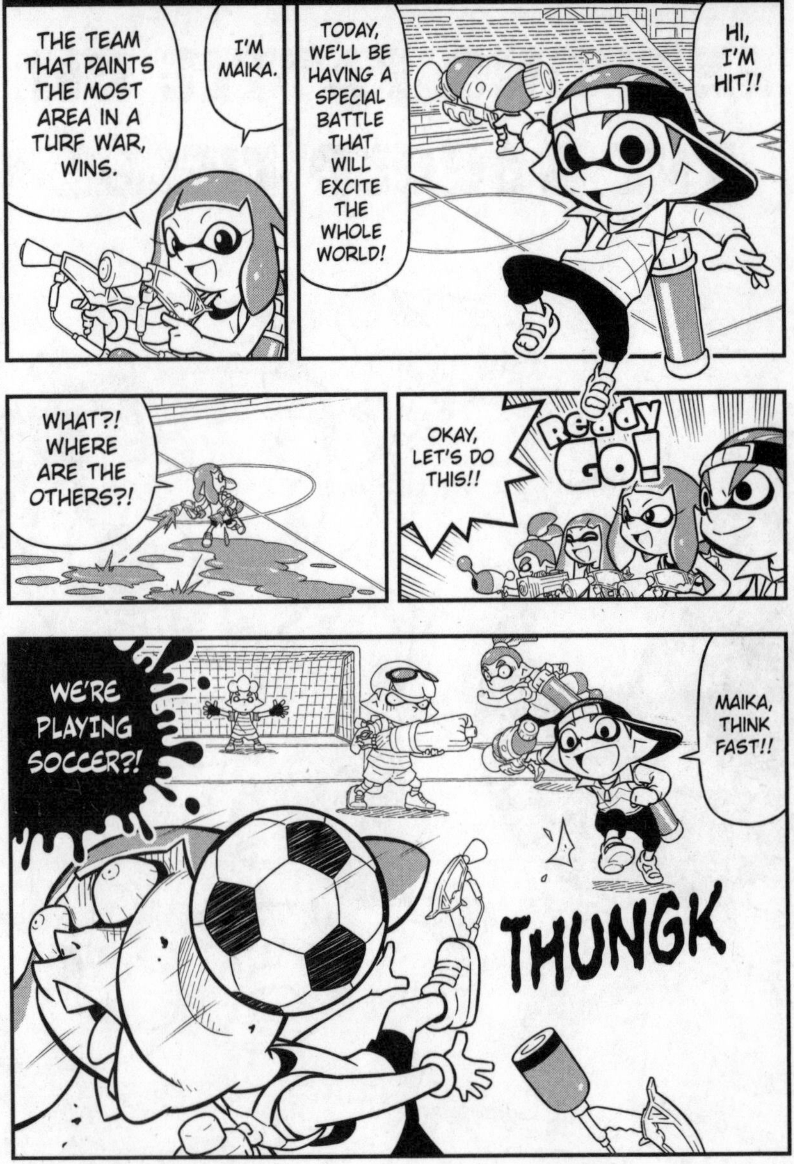
HI, I'M HIT!!
TODAY, WE'LL BE HAVING A SPECIAL BATTLE THAT WILL EXCITE THE WHOLE WORLD!
I'M MAIKA.
THE TEAM THAT PAINTS THE MOST AREA IN A TURF WAR, WINS.
Ready GO!
OKAY, LET'S DO THIS!!
WHAT?! WHERE ARE THE OTHERS?!
MAIKA, THINK FAST!!
WE'RE PLAYING SOCCER?!
THUNGK

AIMING THE BALL

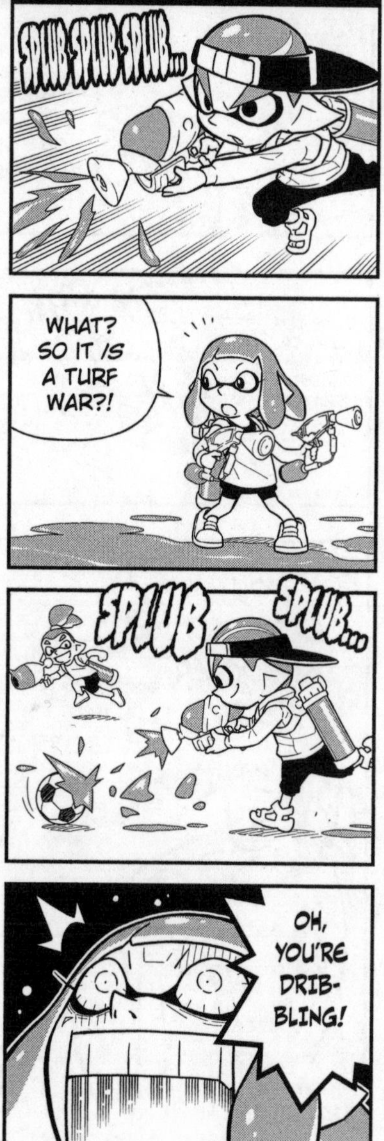
SPLUB SPLUB SPLUB...
WHAT? SO IT IS A TURF WAR?!
SPLUB SPLUB...
OH, YOU'RE DRIB-BLING!

ACE PLAYER

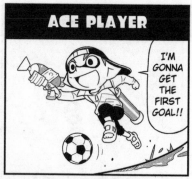

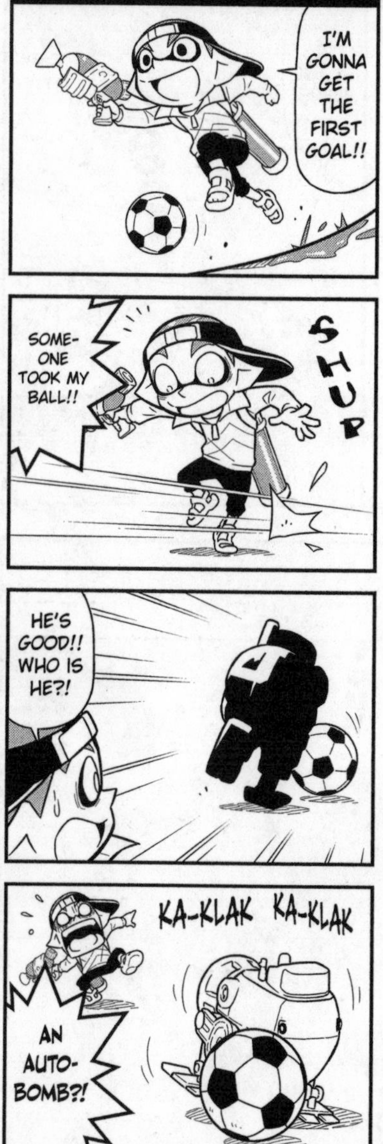
I'M GONNA GET THE FIRST GOAL!!
SOME-ONE TOOK MY BALL!!
SHUP
HE'S GOOD!! WHO IS HE?!
KA-KLAK KA-KLAK
AN AUTO-BOMB?!

LONG PASS

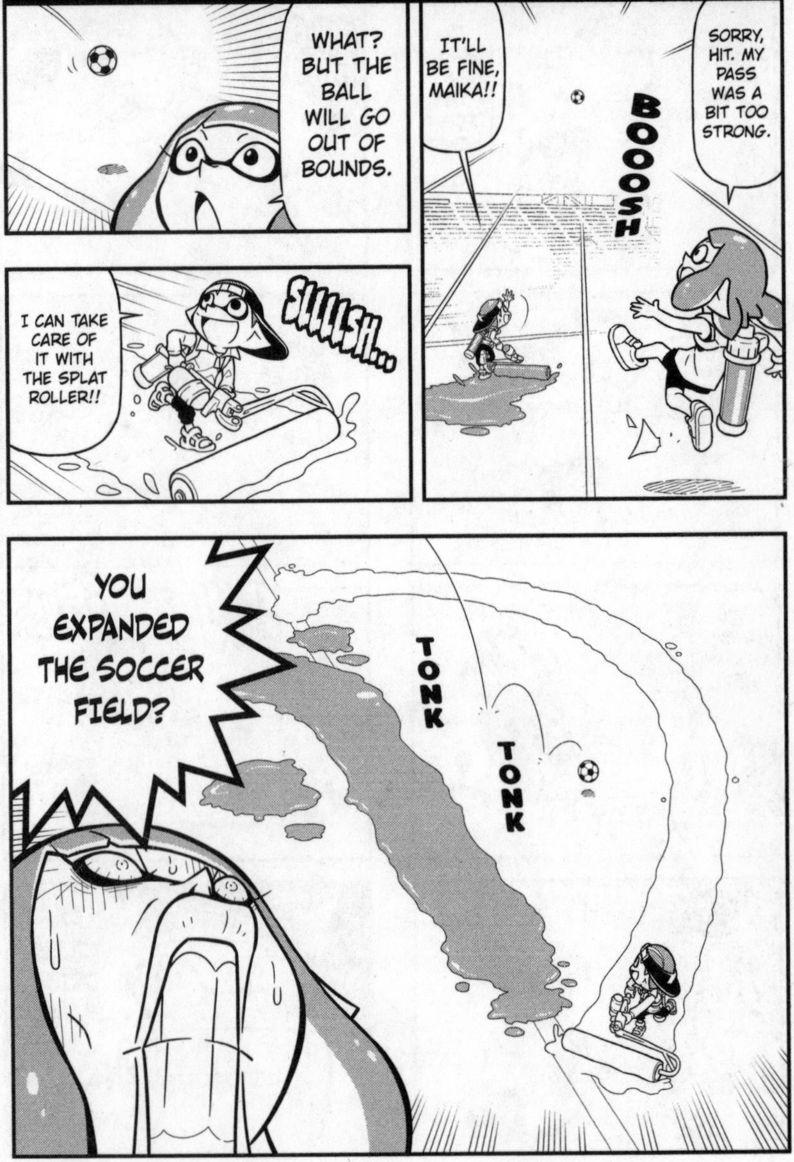
SORRY, HIT. MY PASS WAS A BIT TOO STRONG.
BOOOOSH
IT'LL BE FINE, MAIKA!!
WHAT? BUT THE BALL WILL GO OUT OF BOUNDS.
I CAN TAKE CARE OF IT WITH THE SPLAT ROLLER!!
SLLLLSH...
YOU EXPANDED THE SOCCER FIELD?
TONK
TONK

ROLLER USER

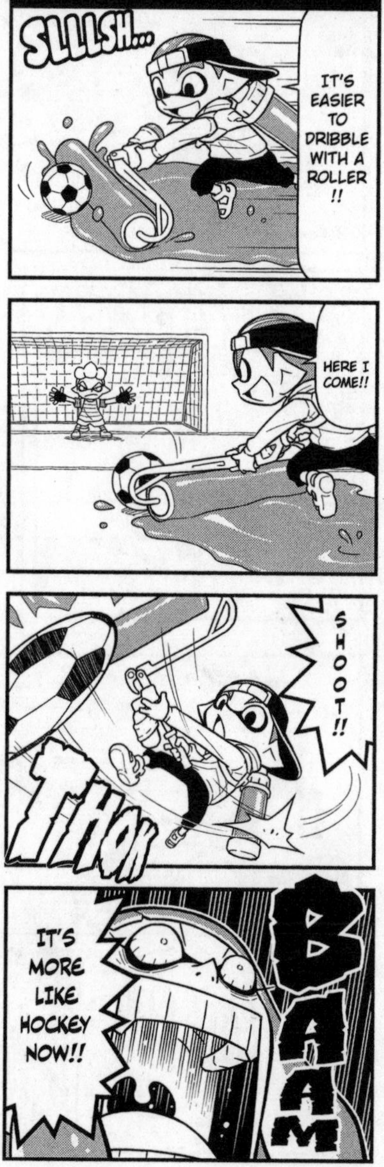
SLLLSH...
IT'S EASIER TO DRIBBLE WITH A ROLLER!!
HERE I COME!!
SHOOT!!
THOK
IT'S MORE LIKE HOCKEY NOW!!
BAAAM

HIGH-PRESSURE SHOT

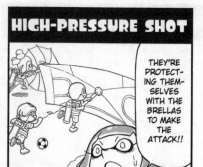

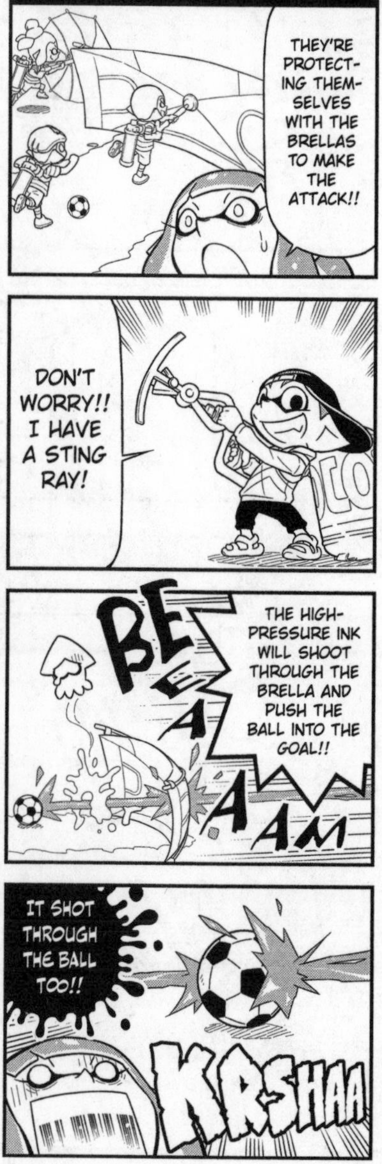
THEY'RE PROTECTING THEMSELVES WITH THE BRELLAS TO MAKE THE ATTACK!!
DON'T WORRY!! I HAVE A STING RAY!
THE HIGH-PRESSURE INK WILL SHOOT THROUGH THE BRELLA AND PUSH THE BALL INTO THE GOAL!!
BEEAAAM
IT SHOT THROUGH THE BALL TOO!!
KRSHAA

THE GOAL-LINE WALL

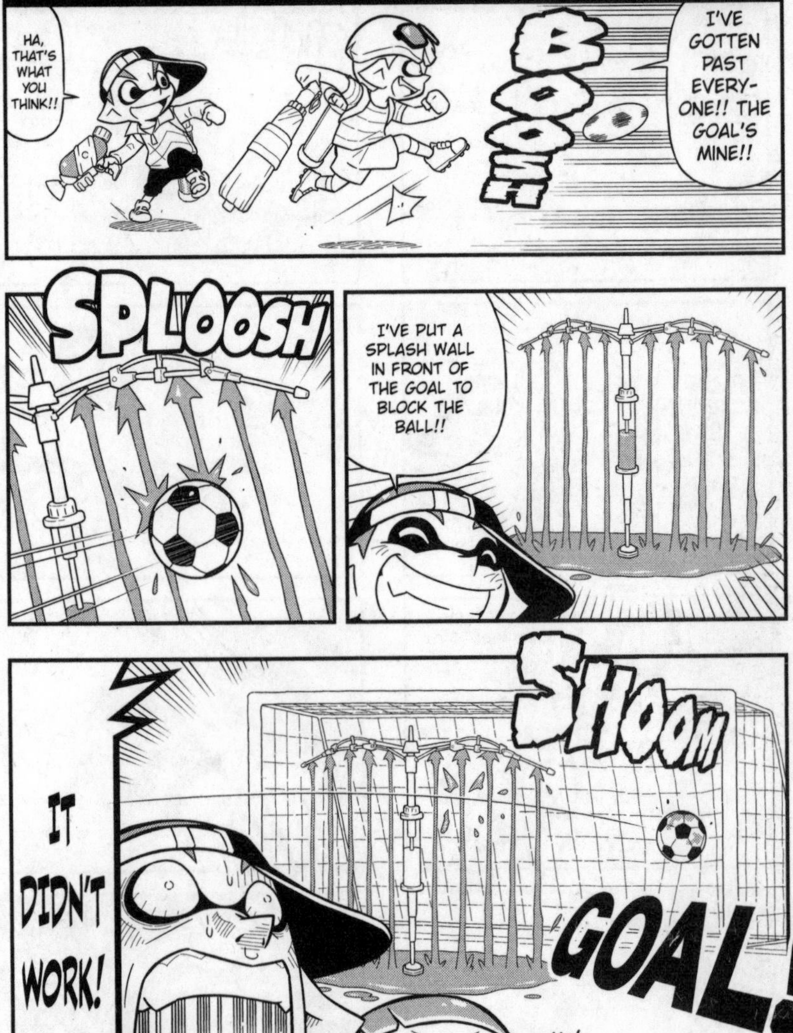

I'VE GOTTEN PAST EVERYONE!! THE GOAL'S MINE!!
BOOM!!
HA, THAT'S WHAT YOU THINK!!
I'VE PUT A SPLASH WALL IN FRONT OF THE GOAL TO BLOCK THE BALL!!
SPLOOSH
SHOOM
GOAL!
Ugh.
IT DIDN'T WORK!

BALLER DRIBBLE

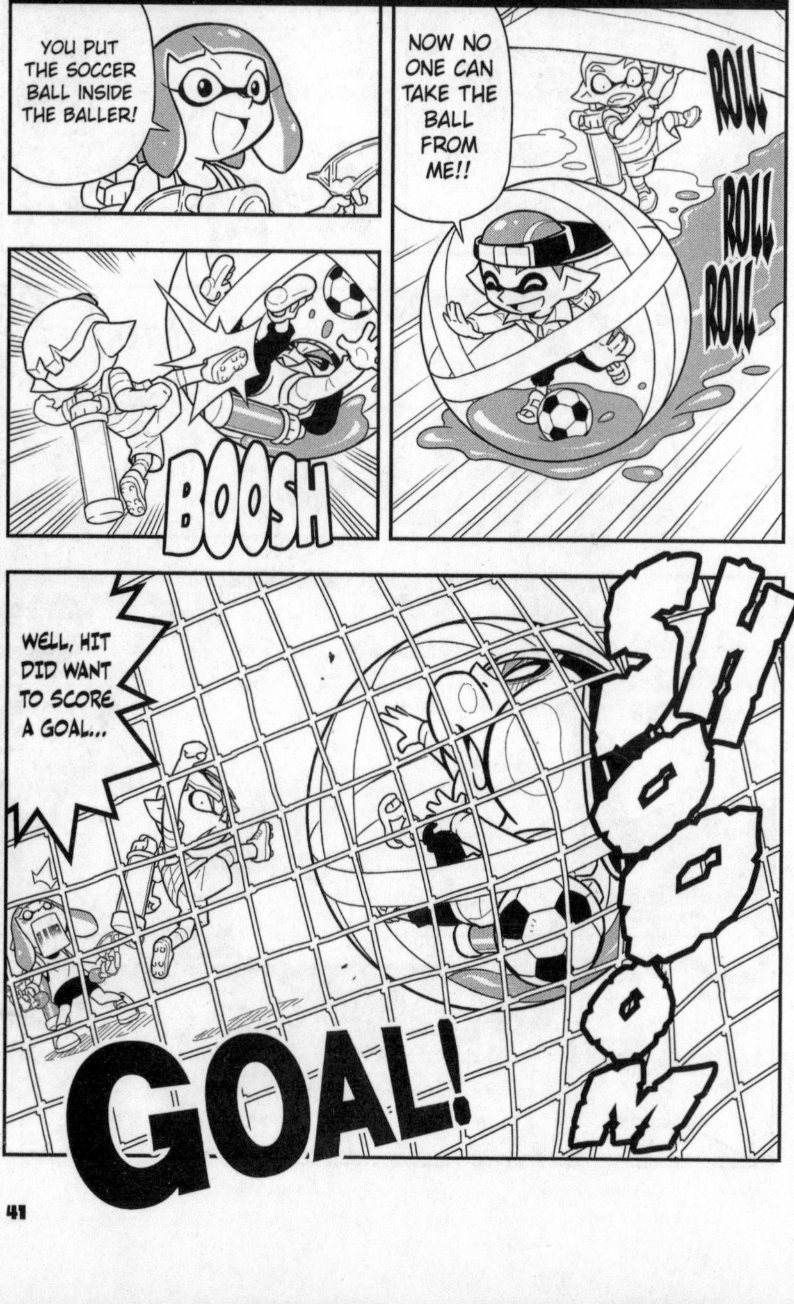
NOW NO ONE CAN TAKE THE BALL FROM ME!!
ROLL
ROLL
ROLL
YOU PUT THE SOCCER BALL INSIDE THE BALLER!
BOOSH
SHOOOM
WELL, HIT DID WANT TO SCORE A GOAL...
GOAL!

HUGE COMEBACK

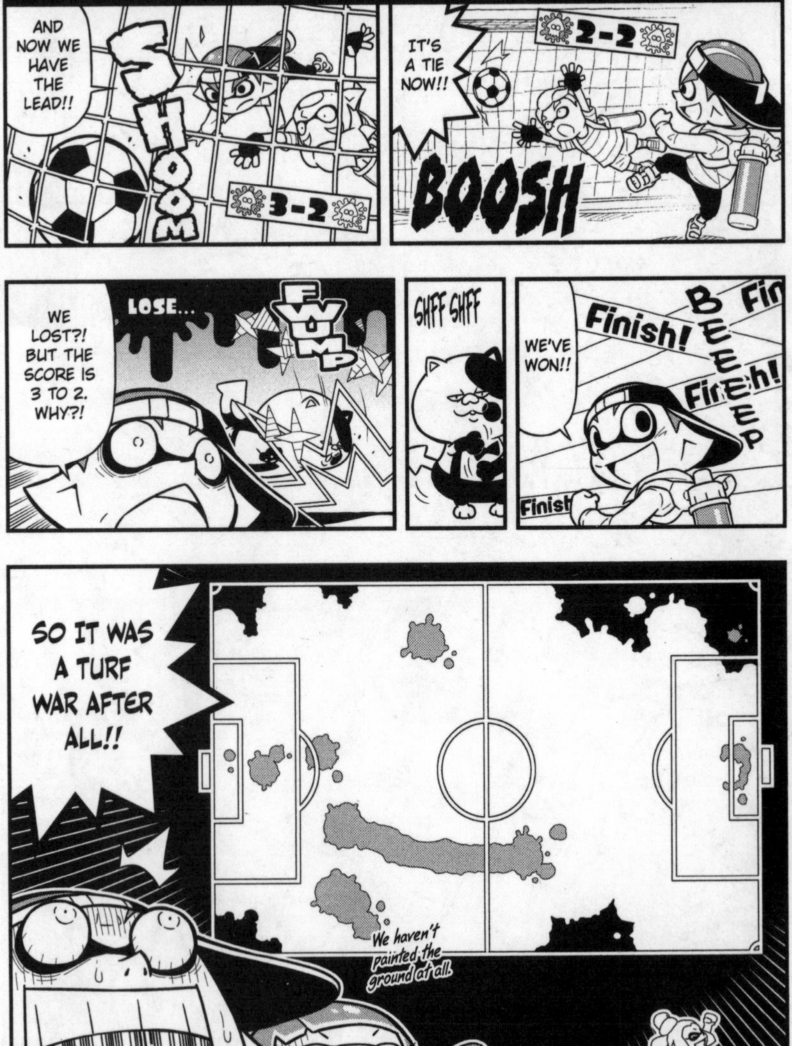

IT'S A TIE NOW!!
2-2
BOOSH
AND NOW WE HAVE THE LEAD!!
SHOOM
3-2
WE'VE WON!!
Finish!
BEEEEEP
Finish!
Finish
SHFF SHFF
WE LOST?! BUT THE SCORE IS 3 TO 2. WHY?!
LOSE...
FWUMP
SO IT WAS A TURF WAR AFTER ALL!!
We haven't painted the ground at all.

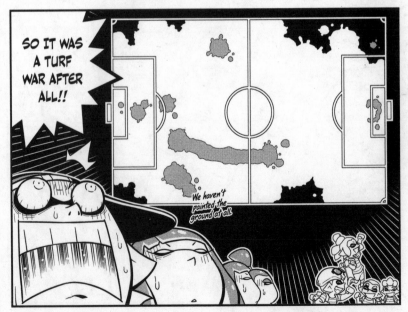

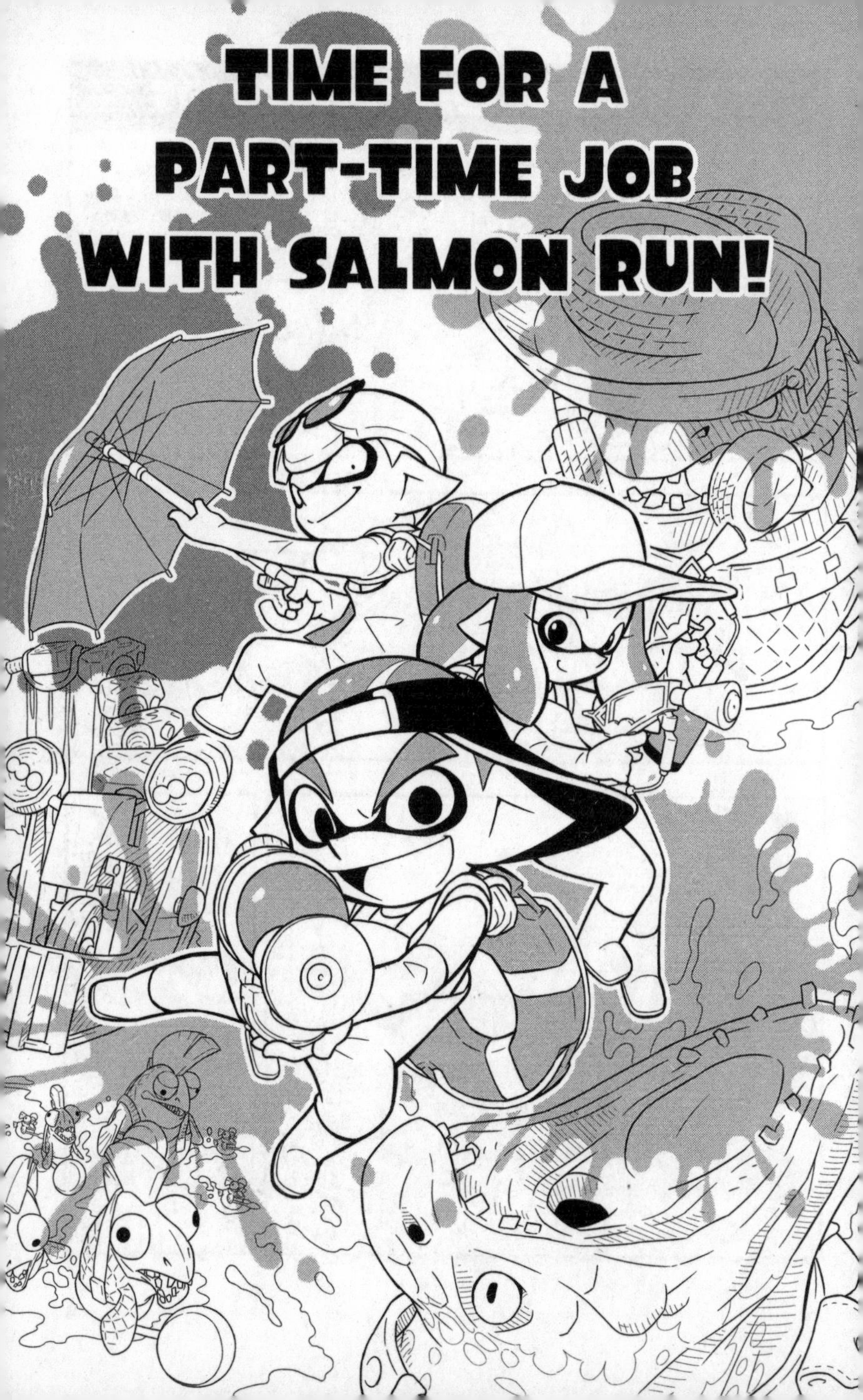
TIME FOR A
PART-TIME JOB
WITH SALMON RUN!

PART-TIME JOB COWORKERS

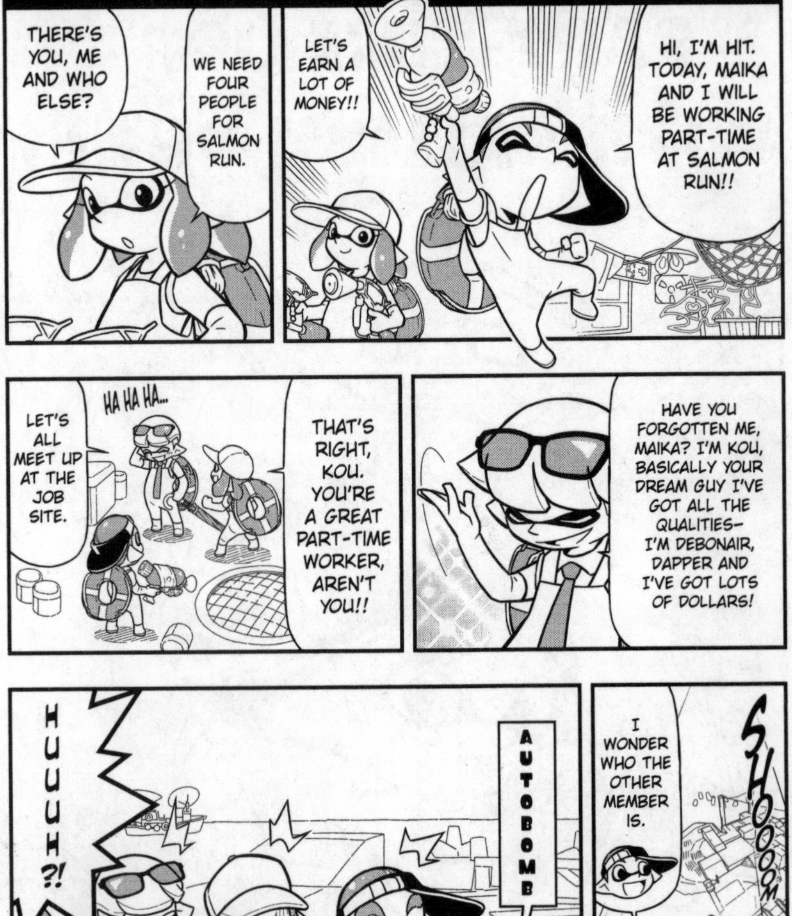
HI, I'M HIT. TODAY, MAIKA AND I WILL BE WORKING PART-TIME AT SALMON RUN!!
LET'S EARN A LOT OF MONEY!!
WE NEED FOUR PEOPLE FOR SALMON RUN.
THERE'S YOU, ME AND WHO ELSE?
HAVE YOU FORGOTTEN ME, MAIKA? I'M KOU, BASICALLY YOUR DREAM GUY I'VE GOT ALL THE QUALITIES– I'M DEBONAIR, DAPPER AND I'VE GOT LOTS OF DOLLARS!
THAT'S RIGHT, KOU. YOU'RE A GREAT PART-TIME WORKER, AREN'T YOU!!
HA HA HA...
LET'S ALL MEET UP AT THE JOB SITE.
SHOOOOM
I WONDER WHO THE OTHER MEMBER IS.
AUTOBOMB
HUUUUH?!

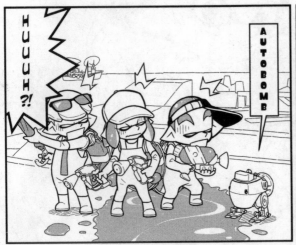

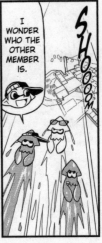

SURROUNDING SALMONIDS

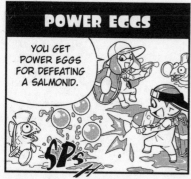

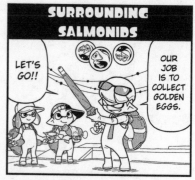

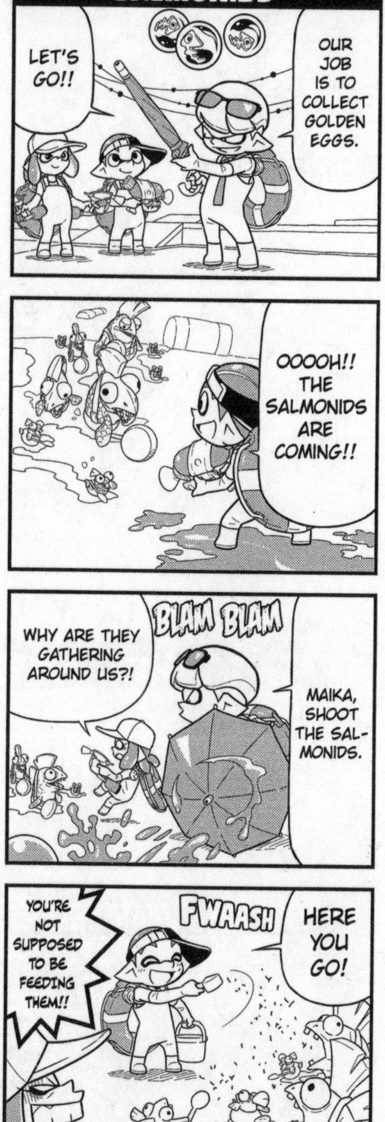
OUR JOB IS TO COLLECT GOLDEN EGGS.
LET'S GO!!
OOOOH!! THE SALMONIDS ARE COMING!!
BLAM BLAM
MAIKA, SHOOT THE SAL-MONIDS.
WHY ARE THEY GATHERING AROUND US?!
HERE YOU GO!
FWAASH
YOU'RE NOT SUPPOSED TO BE FEEDING THEM!!

POWER EGGS

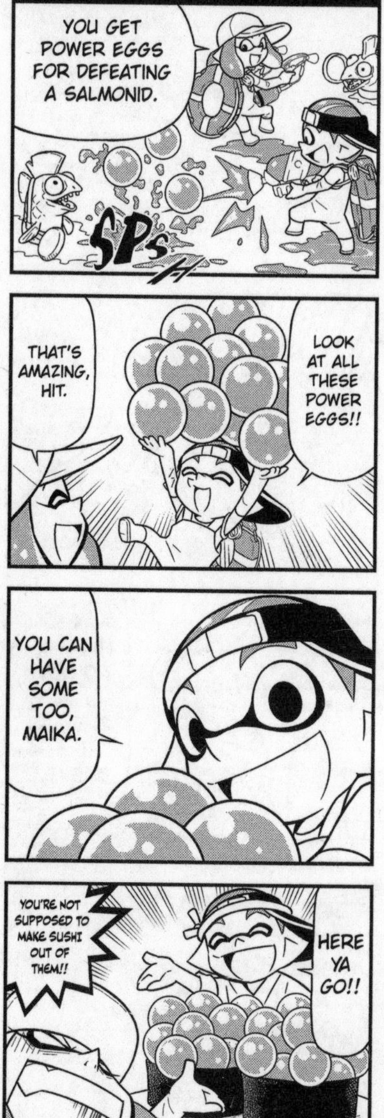
YOU GET POWER EGGS FOR DEFEATING A SALMONID.
LOOK AT ALL THESE POWER EGGS!!
THAT'S AMAZING, HIT.
YOU CAN HAVE SOME TOO, MAIKA.
HERE YA GO!!
YOU'RE NOT SUPPOSED TO MAKE SUSHI OUT OF THEM!!

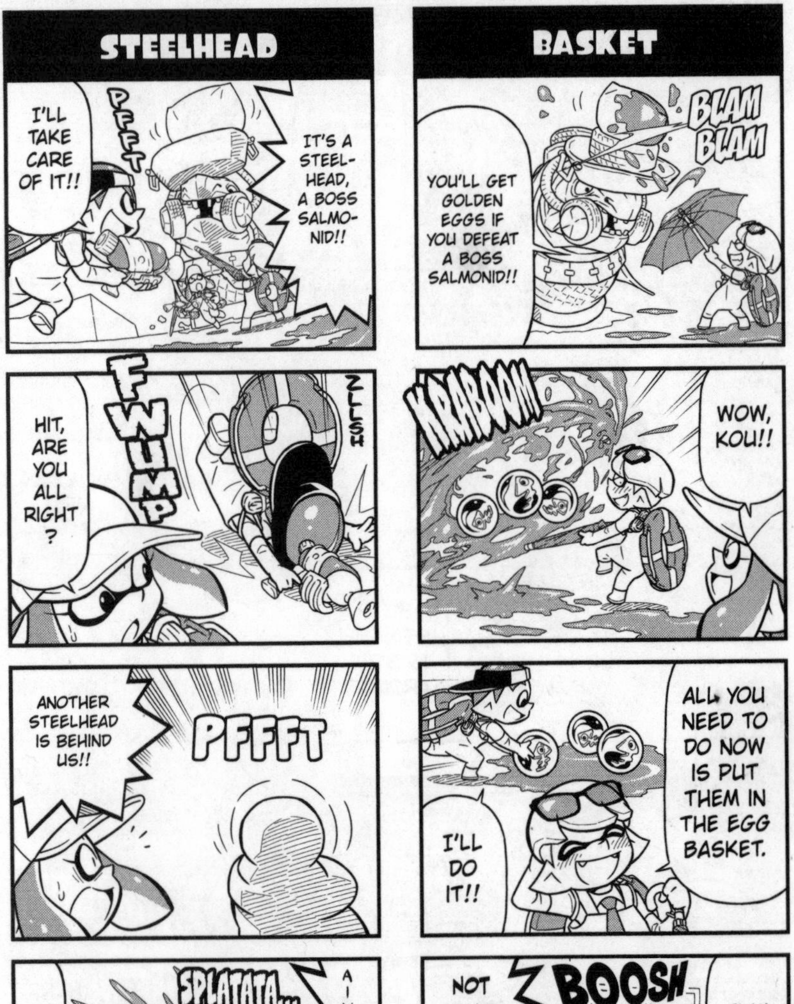
BASKET
BLAM BLAM
YOU'LL GET GOLDEN EGGS IF YOU DEFEAT A BOSS SALMONID!!
WOW, KOU!!
KRABOOM
ALL YOU NEED TO DO NOW IS PUT THEM IN THE EGG BASKET.
I'LL DO IT!!
SLAM DUUUNK!!
BOOSH
NOT THAT BASKET!!
STEELHEAD
IT'S A STEELHEAD, A BOSS SALMONID!!
PFFT
I'LL TAKE CARE OF IT!!
ZLLSH
FWUMP
HIT, ARE YOU ALL RIGHT?
PFFFT
ANOTHER STEELHEAD IS BEHIND US!!
AIYEEEE!!
SPLATATA...
IT'S ME...I BUMPED MY HEAD.

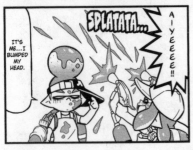

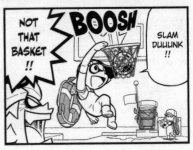

STINGER

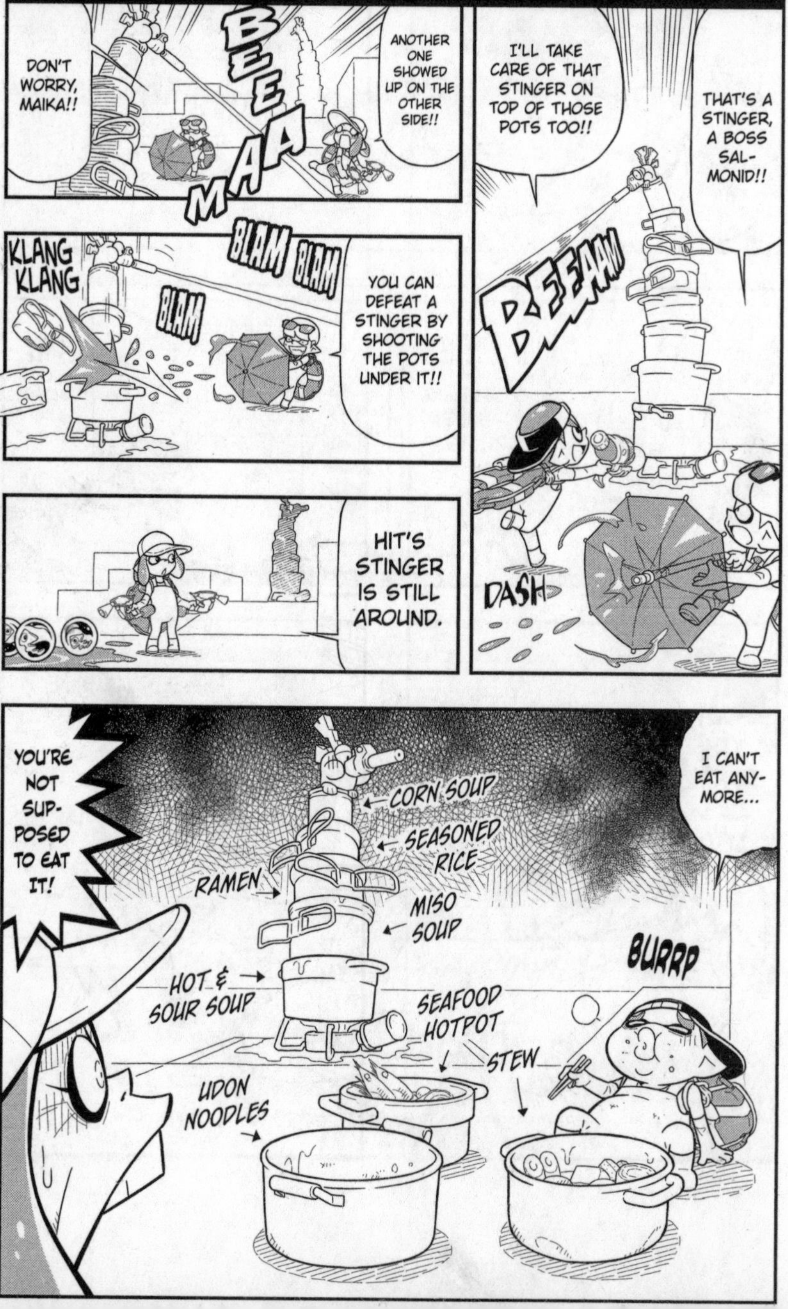
THAT'S A STINGER, A BOSS SAL-MONID!!
I'LL TAKE CARE OF THAT STINGER ON TOP OF THOSE POTS TOO!!
BEEAAM
DASH
ANOTHER ONE SHOWED UP ON THE OTHER SIDE!!
BEEMAA
DON'T WORRY, MAIKA!!
YOU CAN DEFEAT A STINGER BY SHOOTING THE POTS UNDER IT!!
BLAM BLAM
BLAM
KLANG KLANG
HIT'S STINGER IS STILL AROUND.
I CAN'T EAT ANY-MORE...
BURRP
YOU'RE NOT SUP-POSED TO EAT IT!
CORN SOUP
SEASONED RICE
RAMEN
MISO SOUP
HOT &
SOUR SOUP
SEAFOOD HOTPOT
STEW
UDON NOODLES

STEEL EEL

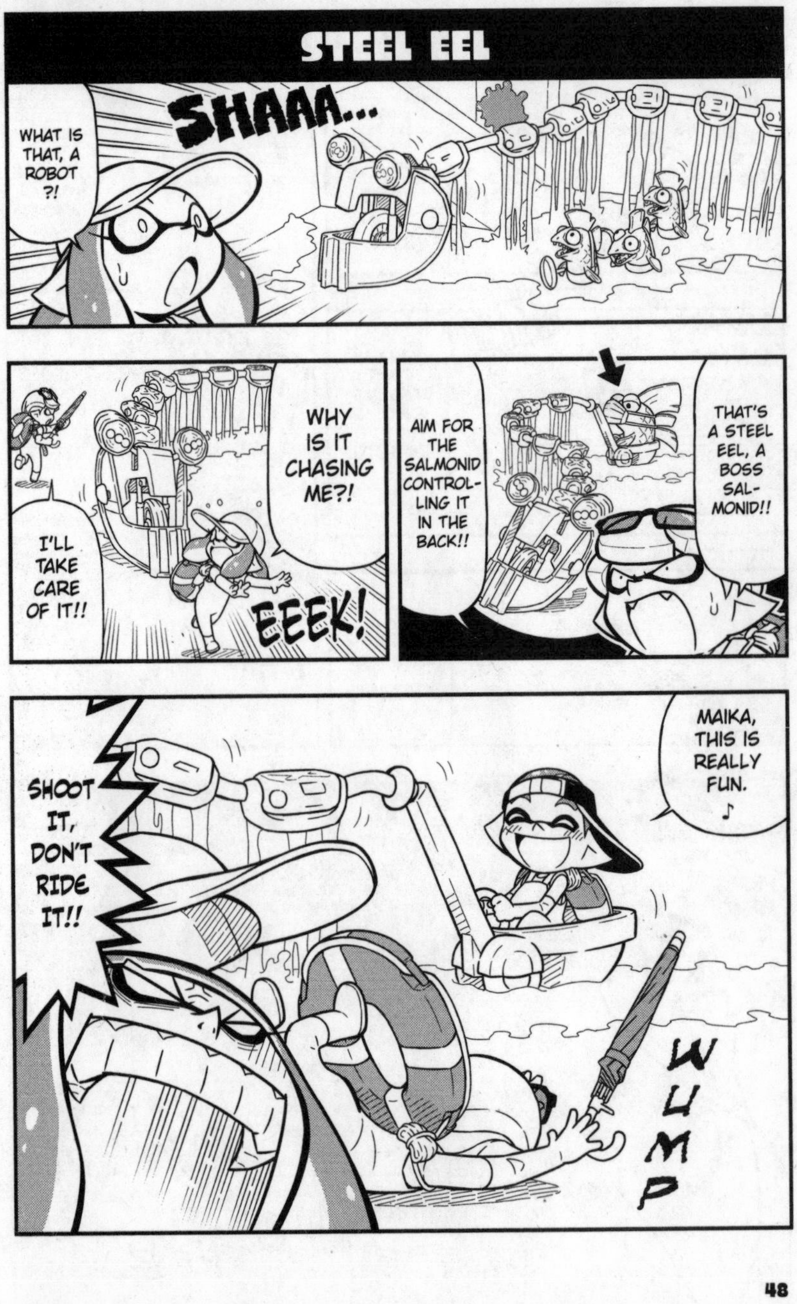
SHAAA...
WHAT IS THAT, A ROBOT?!
THAT'S A STEEL EEL, A BOSS SALMONID!!
AIM FOR THE SALMONID CONTROLLING IT IN THE BACK!!
WHY IS IT CHASING ME?!
EEEK!
I'LL TAKE CARE OF IT!!
MAIKA, THIS IS REALLY FUN. ♪
SHOOT IT, DON'T RIDE IT!!
WUMP

WHERE'S THE DRIVER?

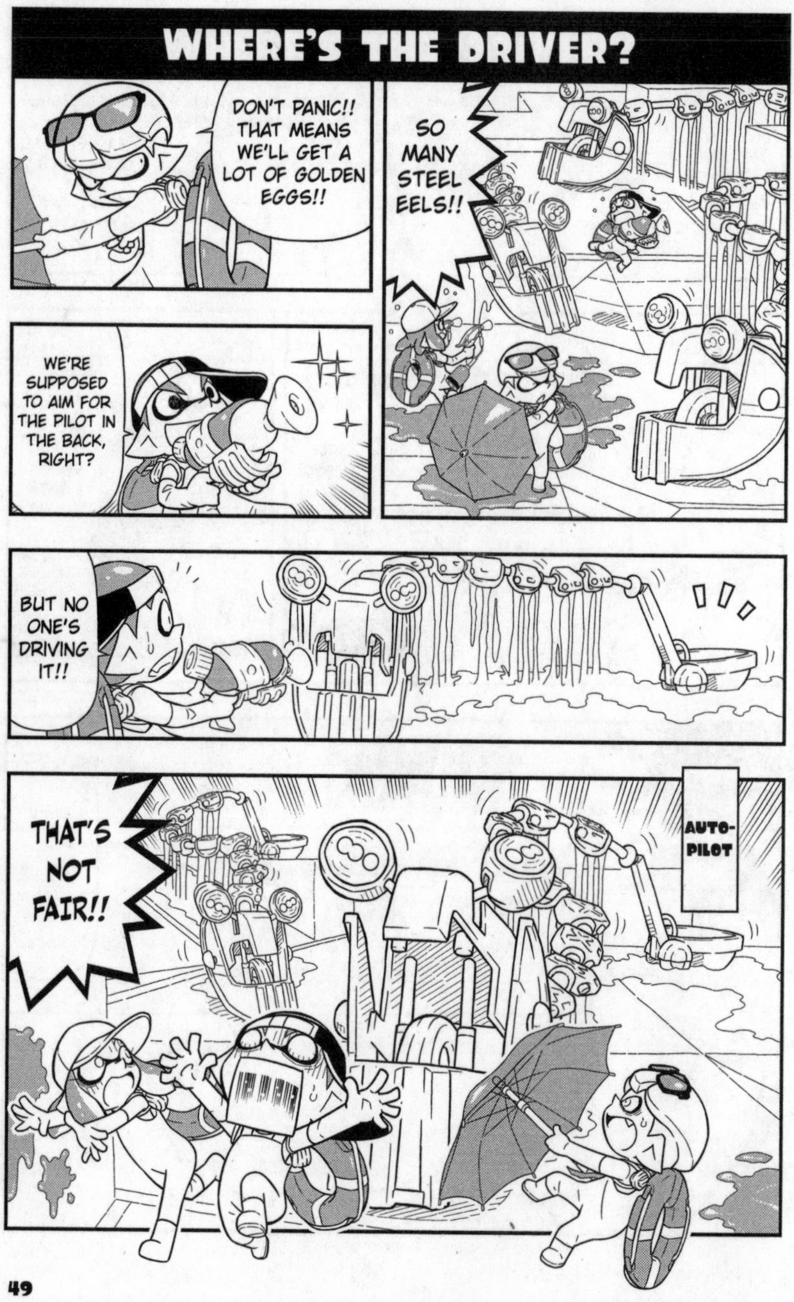
SO MANY STEEL EELS!!
DON'T PANIC!! THAT MEANS WE'LL GET A LOT OF GOLDEN EGGS!!
WE'RE SUPPOSED TO AIM FOR THE PILOT IN THE BACK, RIGHT?
BUT NO ONE'S DRIVING IT!!
AUTO-PILOT
THAT'S NOT FAIR!!

MULTIPURPOSE SPLAT CHARGER

THIS WEAPON HAS LONG RANGE. AND I CAN EVEN DEFEAT A STEELHEAD WITH ONE SHOT!!
BLAM
BOOYAH!! SPLAT CHARGER!!
BE CAREFUL, YOU'RE GOING TO GET EATEN FROM BELOW!!
KRRSHAA
THAT'S MAWS, A BOSS SALMONID!!
HIIIT!!
BOOYAH!! SPLAT CHARGER...
THUNGKT
DEFINITELY MULTIPURPOSE...

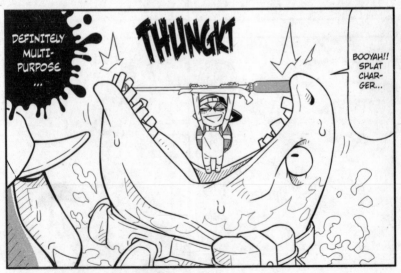

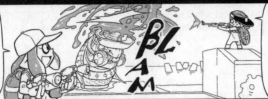

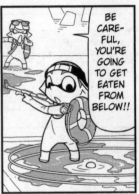

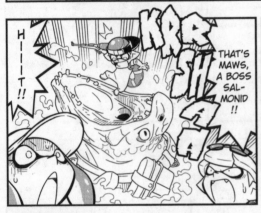

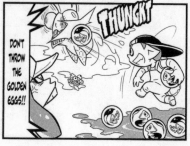

LIFESAVER

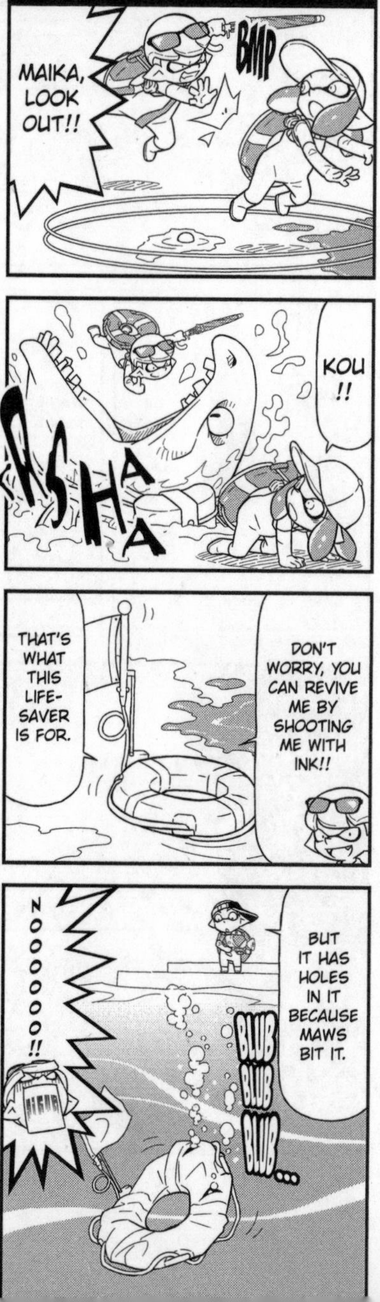
MAIKA, LOOK OUT!!
BMP
KOU !!
KRASHAA
DON'T WORRY, YOU CAN REVIVE ME BY SHOOTING ME WITH INK!!
THAT'S WHAT THIS LIFE-SAVER IS FOR.
BUT IT HAS HOLES IN IT BECAUSE MAWS BIT IT.
BLUB BLUB BLUB...
NOOOOOOO!!

IMPROVISE

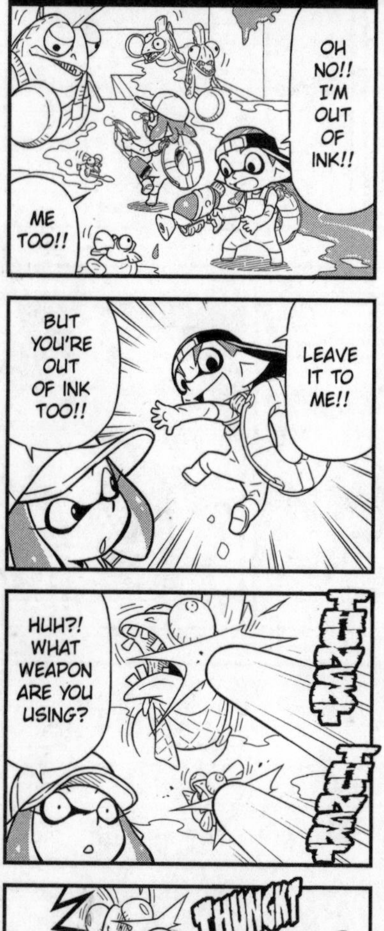
OH NO!! I'M OUT OF INK!!
ME TOO!!
LEAVE IT TO ME!!
BUT YOU'RE OUT OF INK TOO!!
THUNGKT
THUNGKT
HUH?! WHAT WEAPON ARE YOU USING?
THUNGKT
DON'T THROW THE GOLDEN EGGS!!

UNDERGROUND WORLD

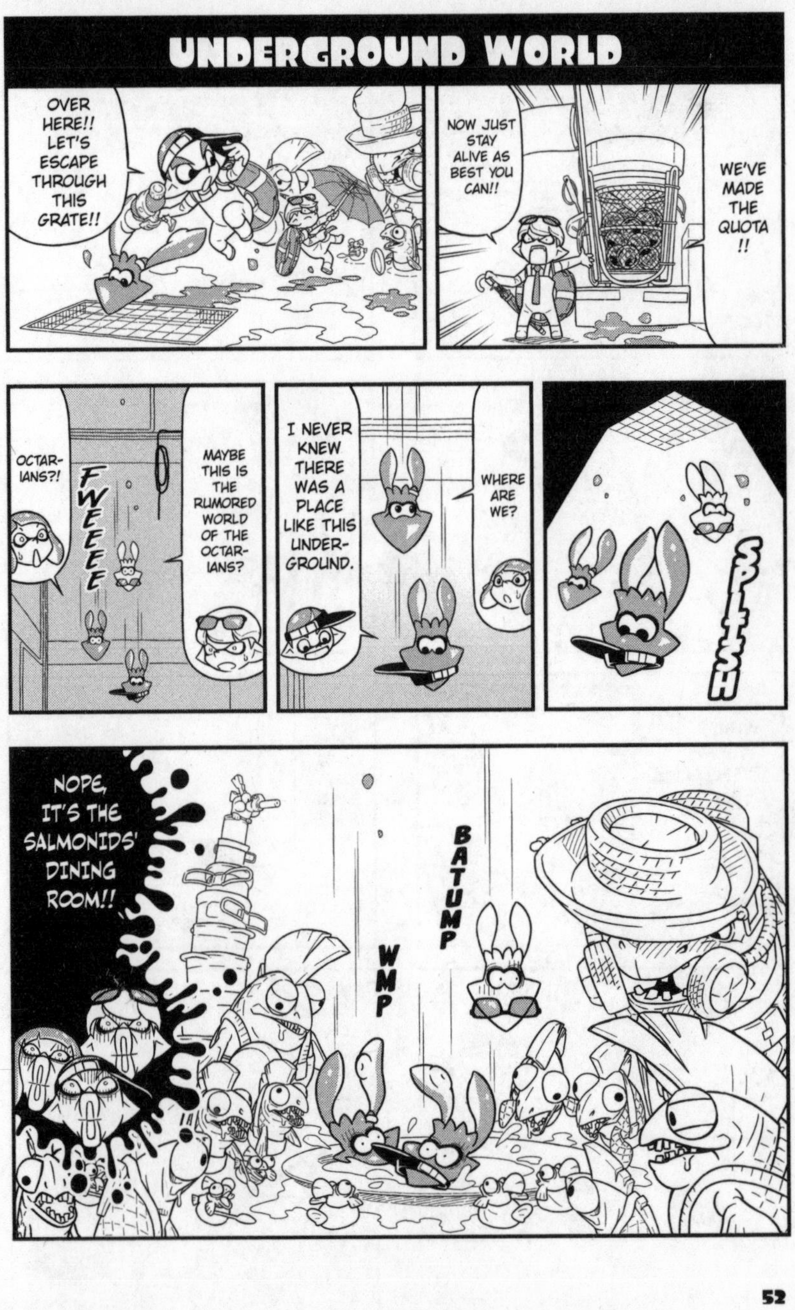
WE'VE MADE THE QUOTA !!
NOW JUST STAY ALIVE AS BEST YOU CAN!!
OVER HERE!! LET'S ESCAPE THROUGH THIS GRATE!!
SPLISH
WHERE ARE WE?
I NEVER KNEW THERE WAS A PLACE LIKE THIS UNDER-GROUND.
MAYBE THIS IS THE RUMORED WORLD OF THE OCTAR-IANS?
FWEEEE
OCTAR-IANS?!
BATUMP
WMP
NOPE, IT'S THE SALMONIDS' DINING ROOM!!

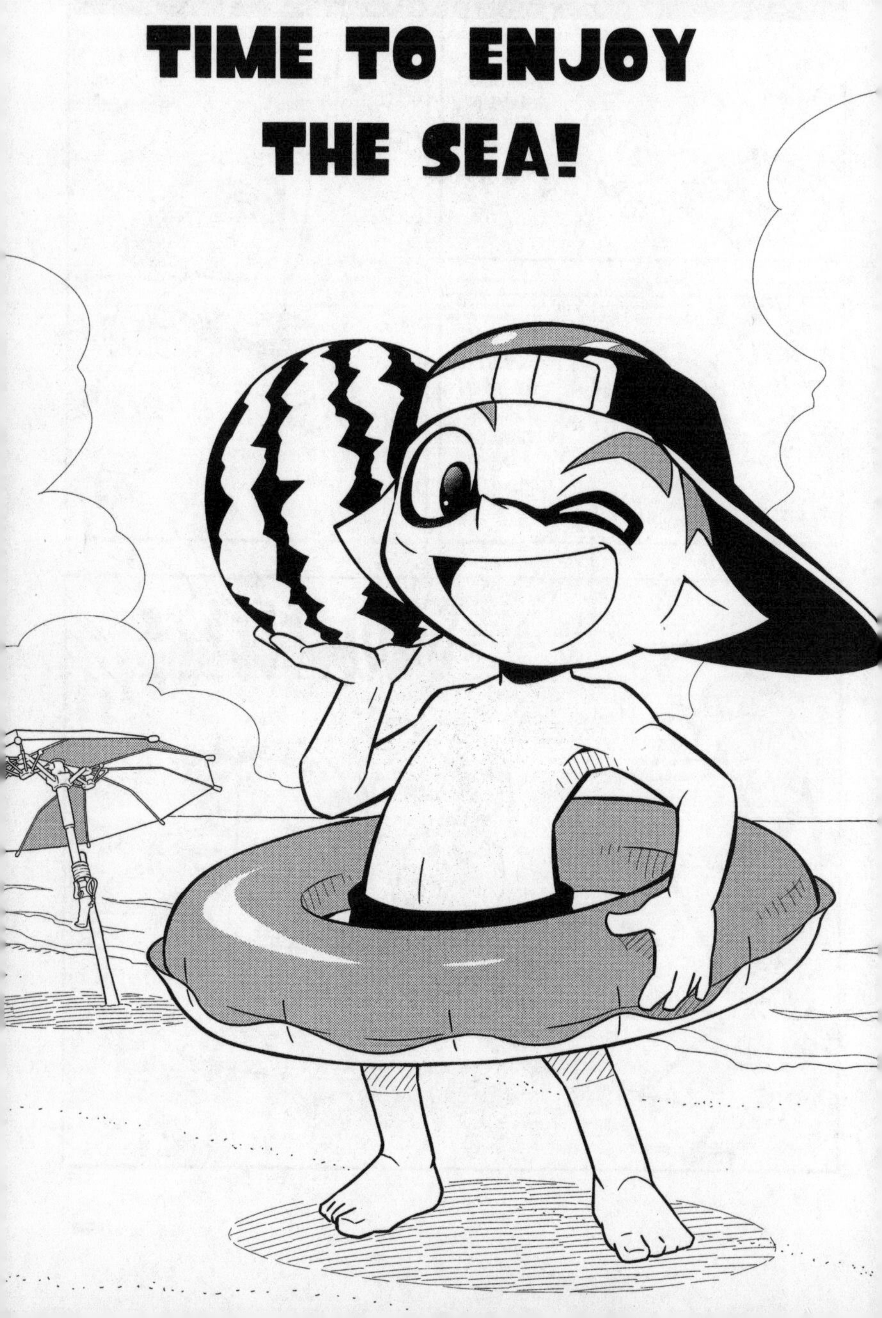
TIME TO ENJOY THE SEA!

SWIMMING

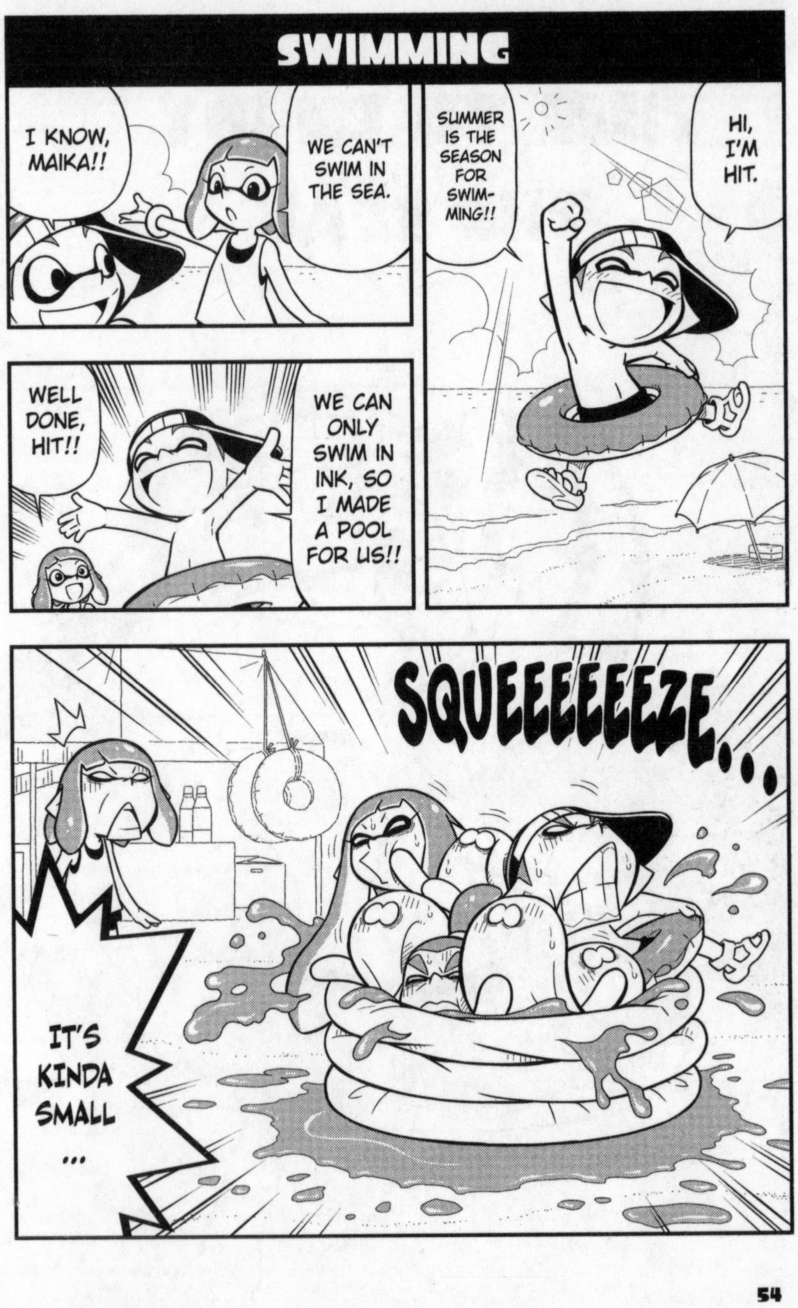
HI, I'M HIT.
SUMMER IS THE SEASON FOR SWIM-MING!!
WE CAN'T SWIM IN THE SEA.
I KNOW, MAIKA!!
WE CAN ONLY SWIM IN INK, SO I MADE A POOL FOR US!!
WELL DONE, HIT!!
SQUEEEEEEZE...
IT'S KINDA SMALL ...

HOMEMADE OCTOPUS DUMPLINGS

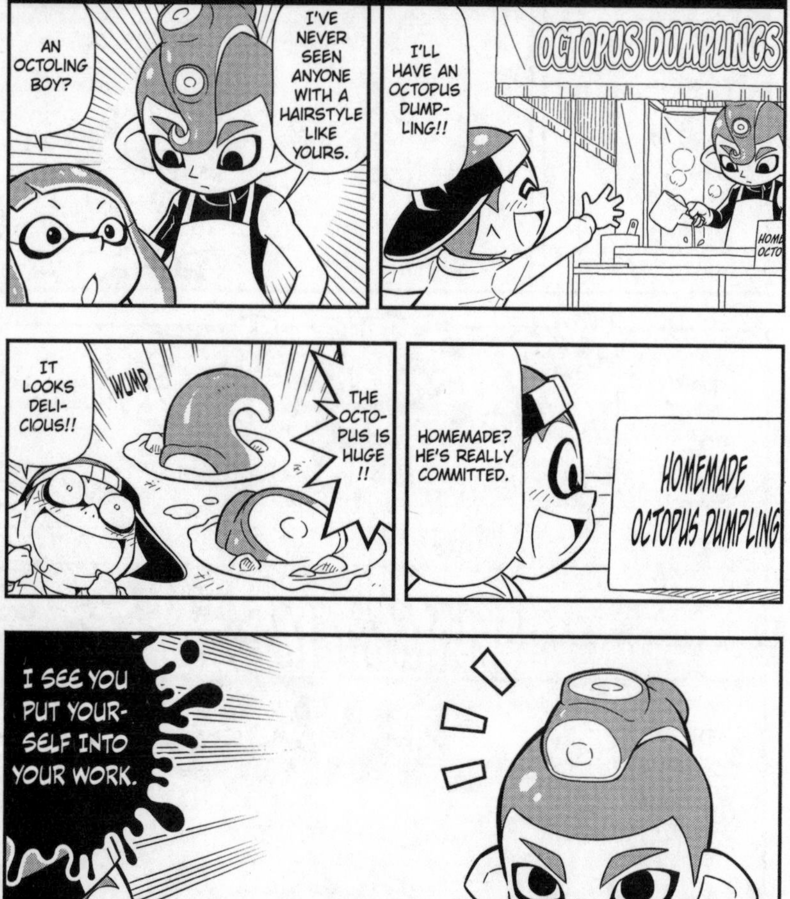
OCTOPUS DUMPLINGS
I'LL HAVE AN OCTOPUS DUMP-LING!!
I'VE NEVER SEEN ANYONE WITH A HAIRSTYLE LIKE YOURS.
AN OCTOLING BOY?
HOMEMADE OCTOPUS DUMPLING
HOMEMADE? HE'S REALLY COMMITTED.
THE OCTO-PUS IS HUGE !!
WUMP
IT LOOKS DELI-CIOUS!!
I SEE YOU PUT YOUR-SELF INTO YOUR WORK.

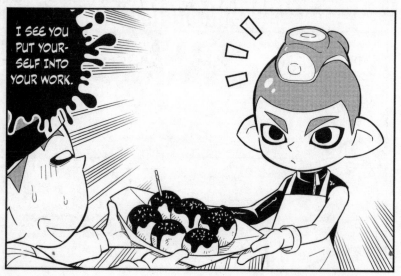

SPLAT ZONES

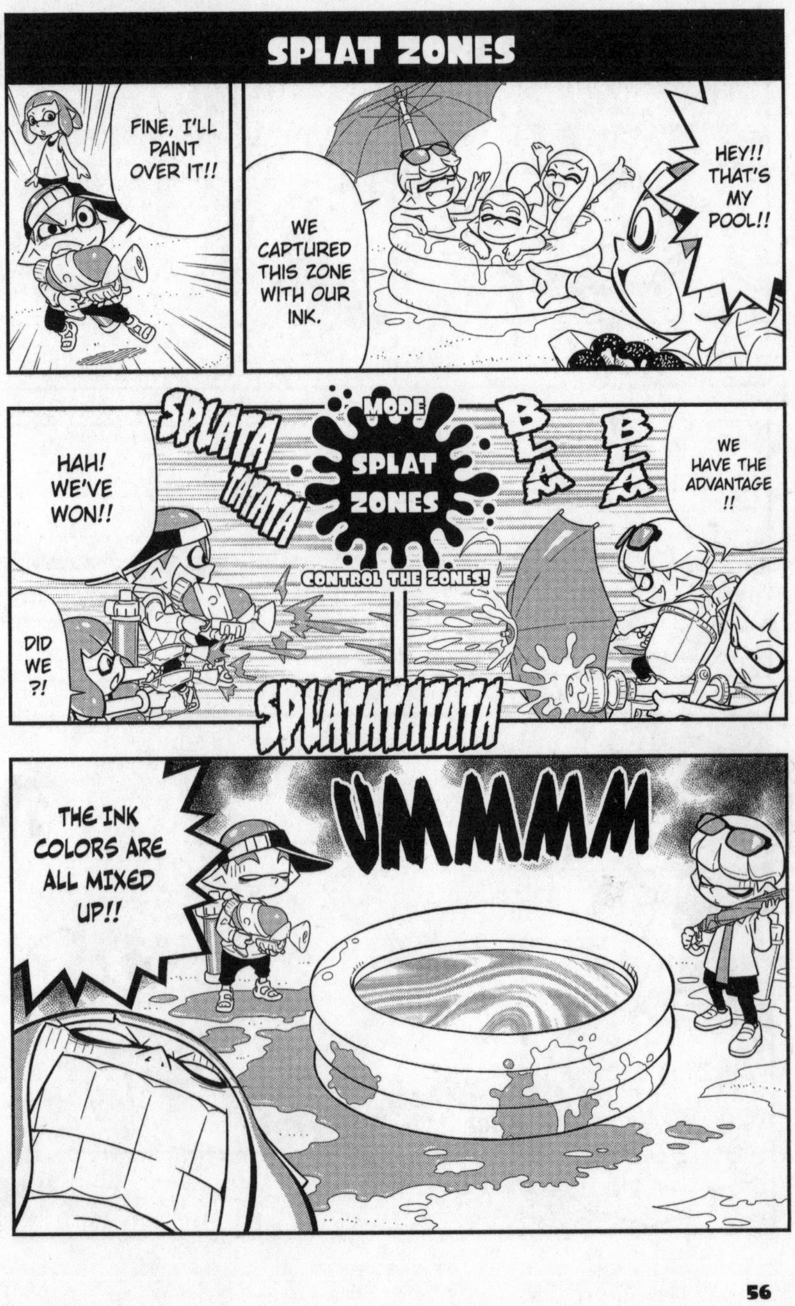

HEY!! THAT'S MY POOL!!
WE CAPTURED THIS ZONE WITH OUR INK.
FINE, I'LL PAINT OVER IT!!
BLAM
BLAM
WE HAVE THE ADVANTAGE!!
MODE
SPLAT ZONES
CONTROL THE ZONES!
SPLATA TATATA
HAH! WE'VE WON!!
DID WE?!
SPLATATATATA
UMMMM
THE INK COLORS ARE ALL MIXED UP!!

CAPTURING A ZONE

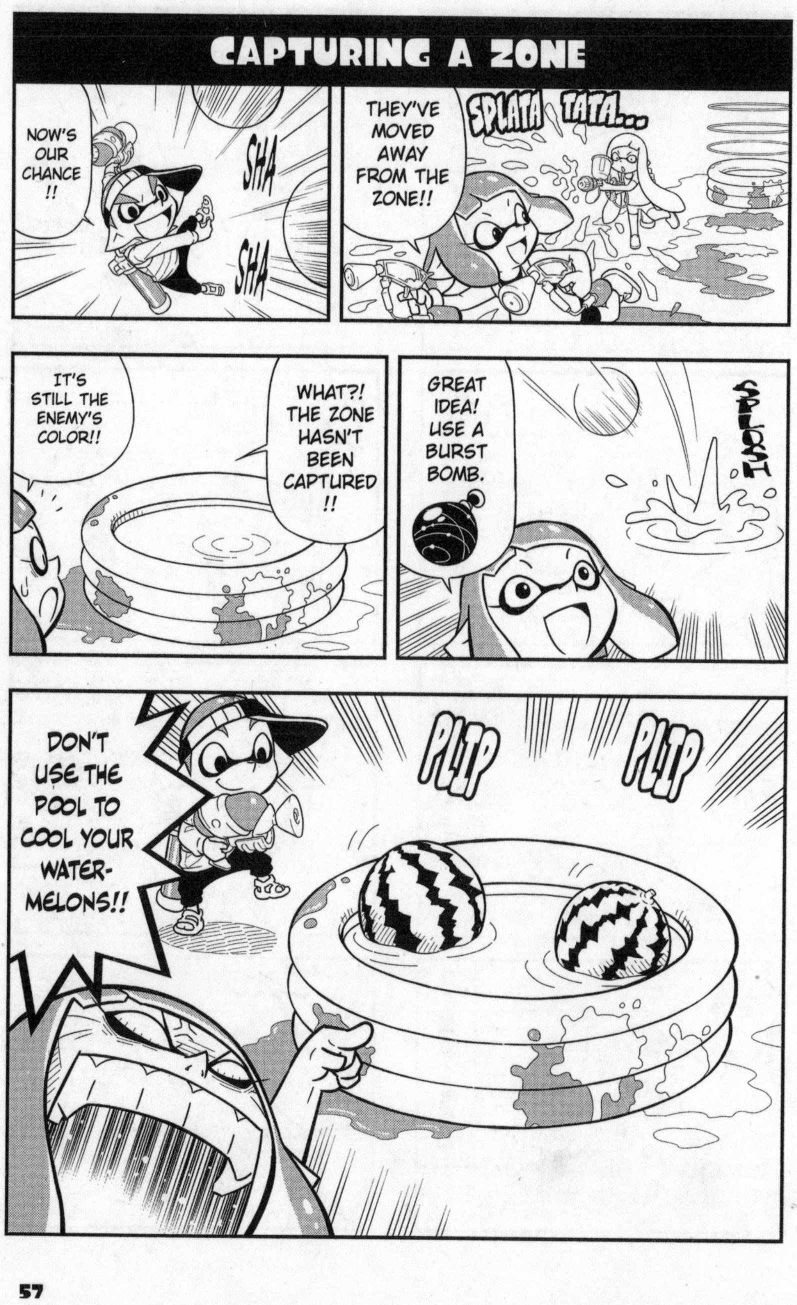

THEY'VE MOVED AWAY FROM THE ZONE!!
SPLATA TATA...
NOW'S OUR CHANCE!!
SHA
SHA
SPLOSH
GREAT IDEA! USE A BURST BOMB.
WHAT?! THE ZONE HASN'T BEEN CAPTURED!!
IT'S STILL THE ENEMY'S COLOR!!
PLIP
PLIP
DON'T USE THE POOL TO COOL YOUR WATER-MELONS!!

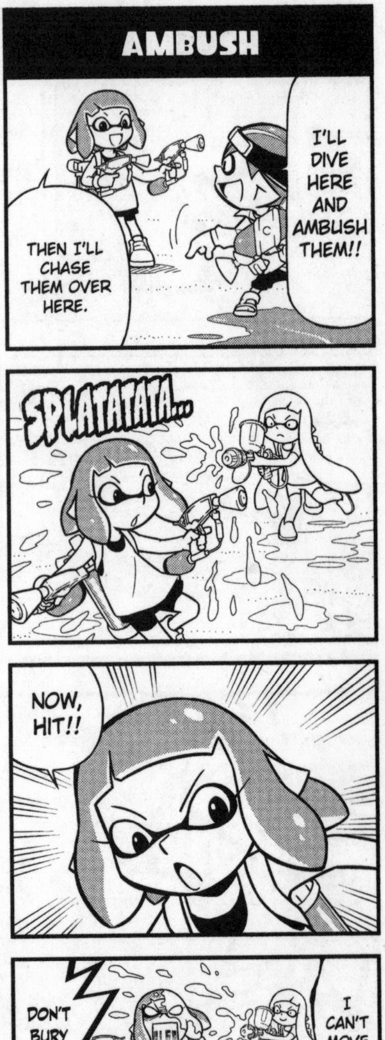
AMBUSH
I'LL DIVE HERE AND AMBUSH THEM!!
THEN I'LL CHASE THEM OVER HERE.
SPLATATATA...
NOW, HIT!!
I CAN'T MOVE ...
DON'T BURY YOUR-SELF IN THE SAND!!

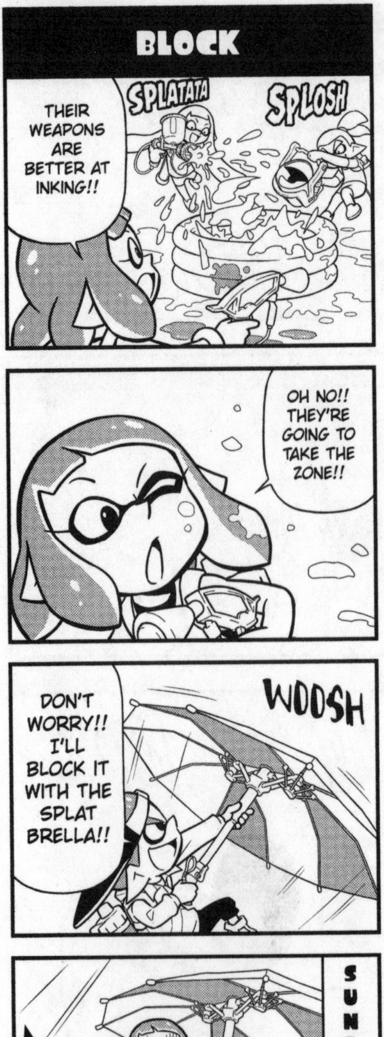
BLOCK
SPLOSH
SPLATATA
THEIR WEAPONS ARE BETTER AT INKING!!
OH NO!! THEY'RE GOING TO TAKE THE ZONE!!
WOOSH
DON'T WORRY!! I'LL BLOCK IT WITH THE SPLAT BRELLA!!
SUNBLOCK
WRONG KIND OF BLOCKING, HIT!!

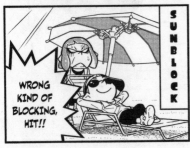

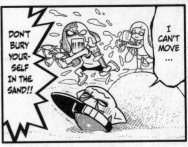

BOMB WAR

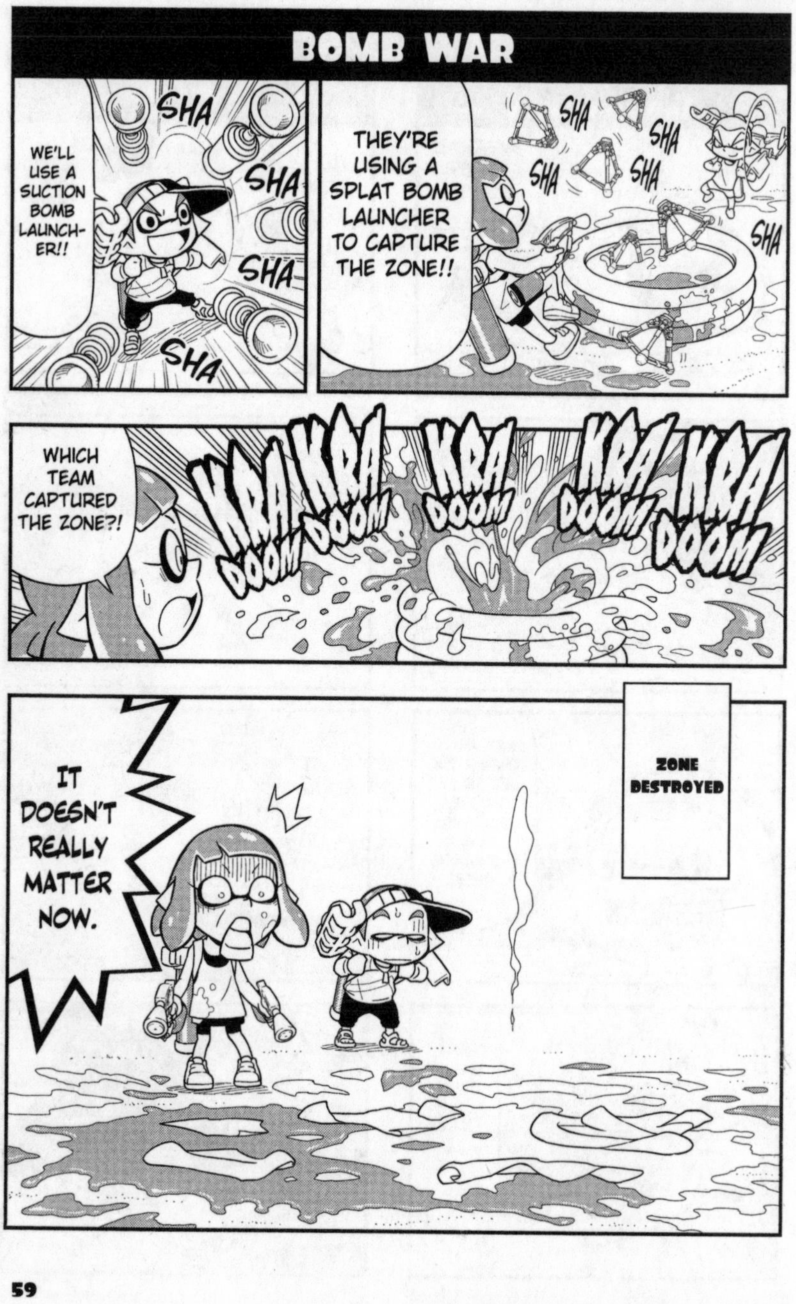
THEY'RE USING A SPLAT BOMB LAUNCHER TO CAPTURE THE ZONE!!
SHA
SHA
SHA
SHA
SHA
WE'LL USE A SUCTION BOMB LAUNCHER!!
SHA
SHA
SHA
SHA
KRA DOOM
KRA DOOM
KRA DOOM
KRA DOOM
KRA DOOM
WHICH TEAM CAPTURED THE ZONE?!
ZONE DESTROYED
IT DOESN'T REALLY MATTER NOW.

REWARD

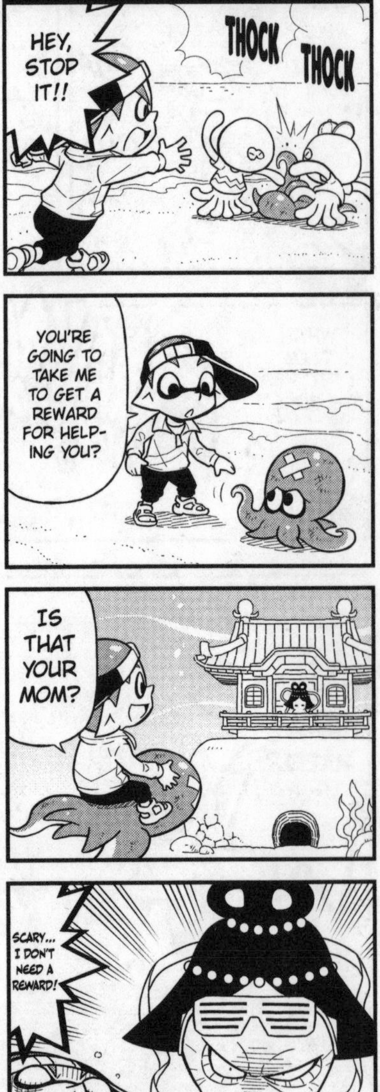
THOCK
THOCK
HEY, STOP IT!!
YOU'RE GOING TO TAKE ME TO GET A REWARD FOR HELP-ING YOU?
IS THAT YOUR MOM?
SCARY... I DON'T NEED A REWARD!

DANCE OF SEA BREAMS AND FLOUNDERS

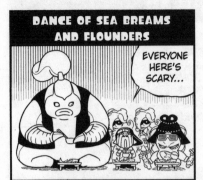

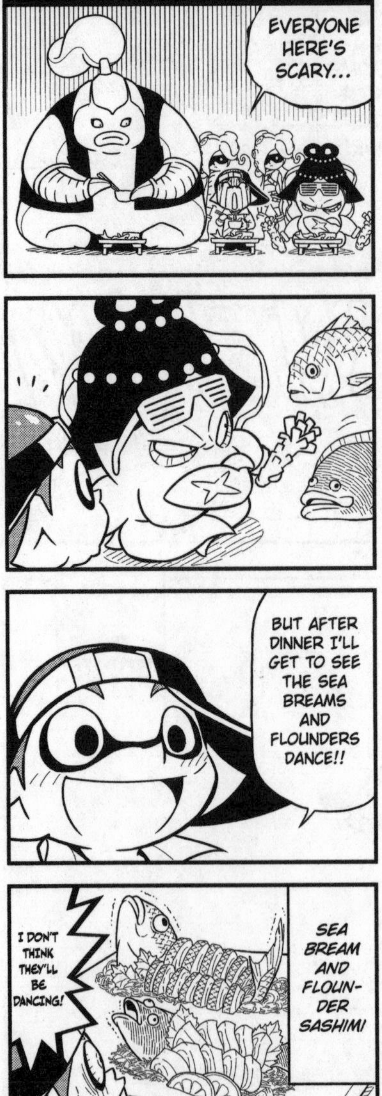
EVERYONE HERE'S SCARY...
BUT AFTER DINNER I'LL GET TO SEE THE SEA BREAMS AND FLOUNDERS DANCE!!
SEA BREAM AND FLOUN-DER SASHIMI
I DON'T THINK THEY'LL BE DANCING!

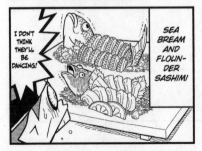

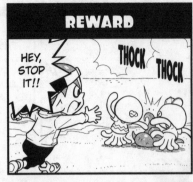

TREASURE BOX

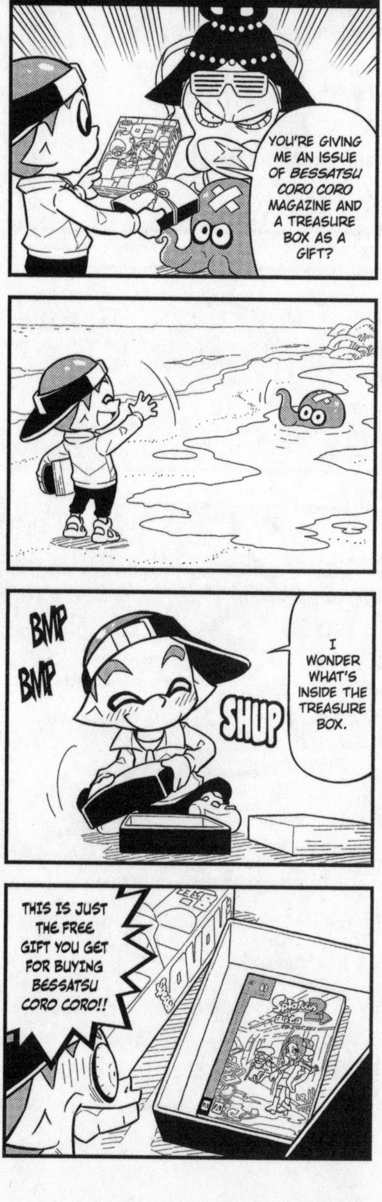
YOU'RE GIVING ME AN ISSUE OF BESSATSU CORO CORO MAGAZINE AND A TREASURE BOX AS A GIFT?
I WONDER WHAT'S INSIDE THE TREASURE BOX.
SHUP
BMP
BMP
THIS IS JUST THE FREE GIFT YOU GET FOR BUYING BESSATSU CORO CORO!!

OCTOPUS LEGS

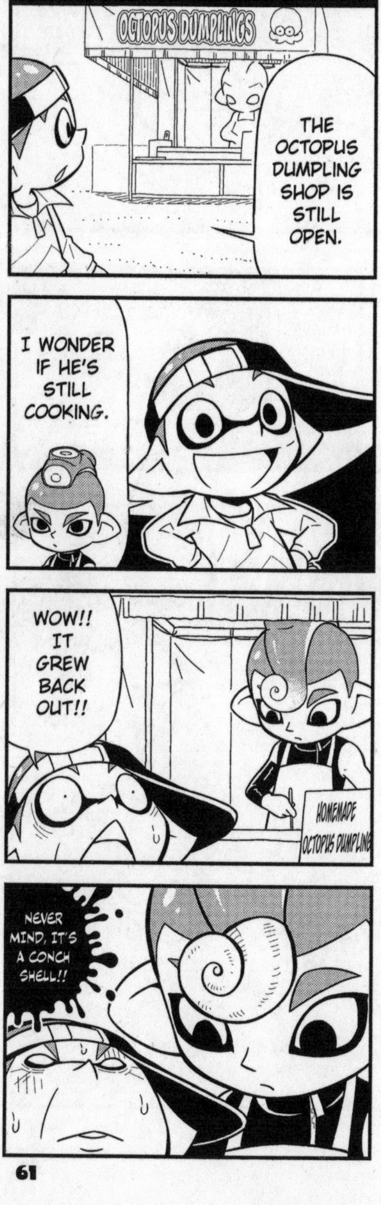
OCTOPUS DUMPLINGS
THE OCTOPUS DUMPLING SHOP IS STILL OPEN.
I WONDER IF HE'S STILL COOKING.
WOW!! IT GREW BACK OUT!!
HOMEMADE OCTOPUS DUMPLING
NEVER MIND, IT'S A CONCH SHELL!!

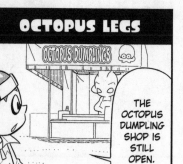

CRACK THE WATERMELON

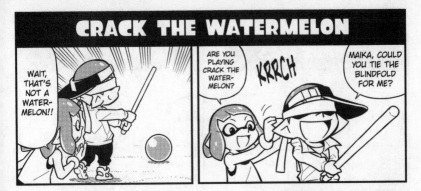

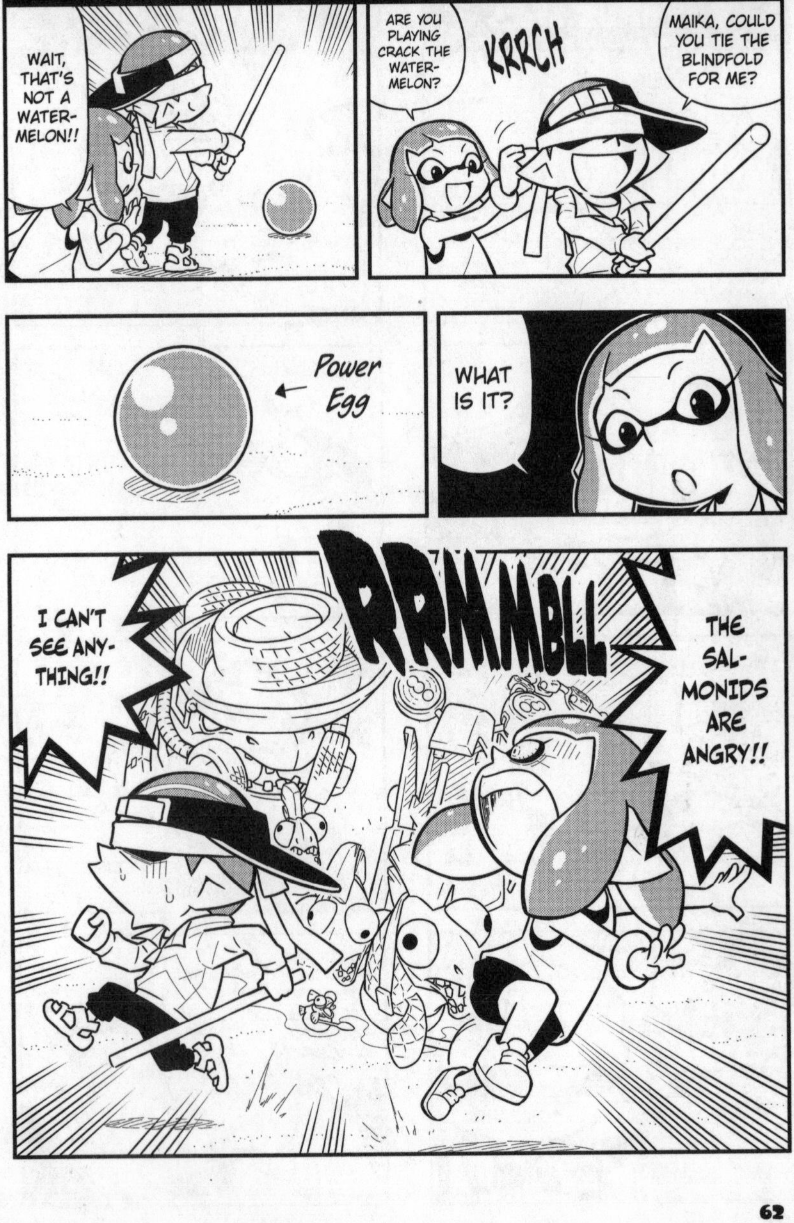
MAIKA, COULD YOU TIE THE BLINDFOLD FOR ME?
KRRCH
ARE YOU PLAYING CRACK THE WATER-MELON?
WAIT, THAT'S NOT A WATER-MELON!!
WHAT IS IT?
Power Egg
RRMMBLL
THE SAL-MONIDS ARE ANGRY!!
I CAN'T SEE ANY-THING!!

USE YOUR MELON

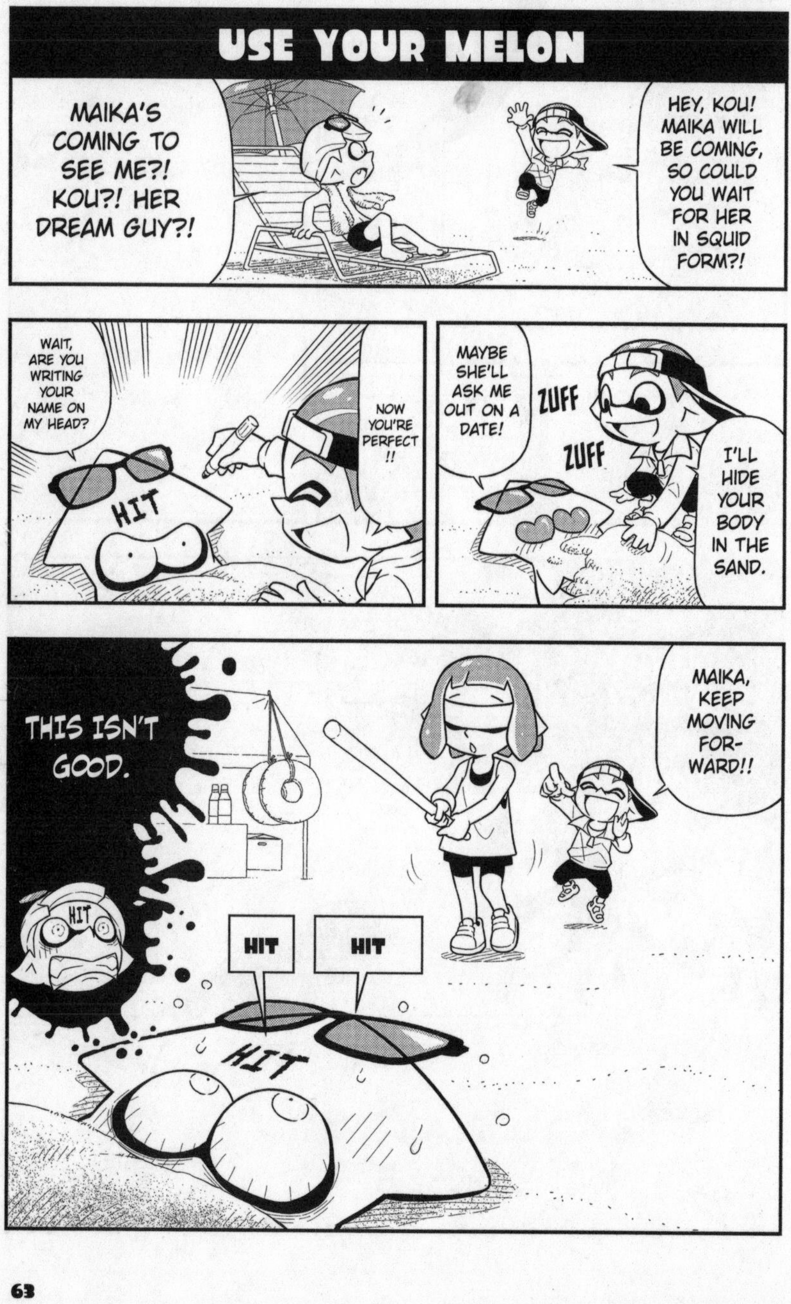
HEY, KOU! MAIKA WILL BE COMING, SO COULD YOU WAIT FOR HER IN SQUID FORM?!
MAIKA'S COMING TO SEE ME?! KOU?! HER DREAM GUY?!
I'LL HIDE YOUR BODY IN THE SAND.
ZUFF
ZUFF
MAYBE SHE'LL ASK ME OUT ON A DATE!
NOW YOU'RE PERFECT!!
WAIT, ARE YOU WRITING YOUR NAME ON MY HEAD?
HIT
MAIKA, KEEP MOVING FOR-WARD!!
HIT
HIT
HIT
THIS ISN'T GOOD.
HIT

HEATSTROKE

SHWAAA
I'M SOOO THIRSTY.
MY SKIN IS SO ROUGH.
THE SUMMER HEAT IS AWFUL. I'M TOO TIRED TO MOVE.
I'M TOO STIFF TO MOVE!!
ME TOO!! MAYBE WE HAVE HEAT-STROKE...
WE'RE SQUID JERKY!!

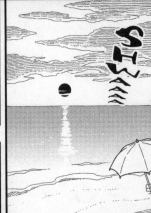

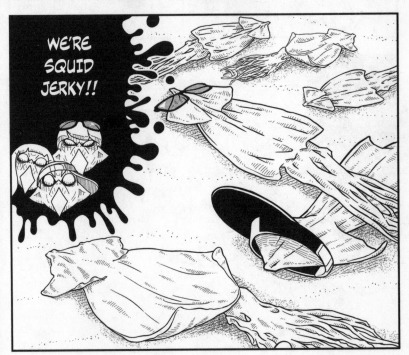

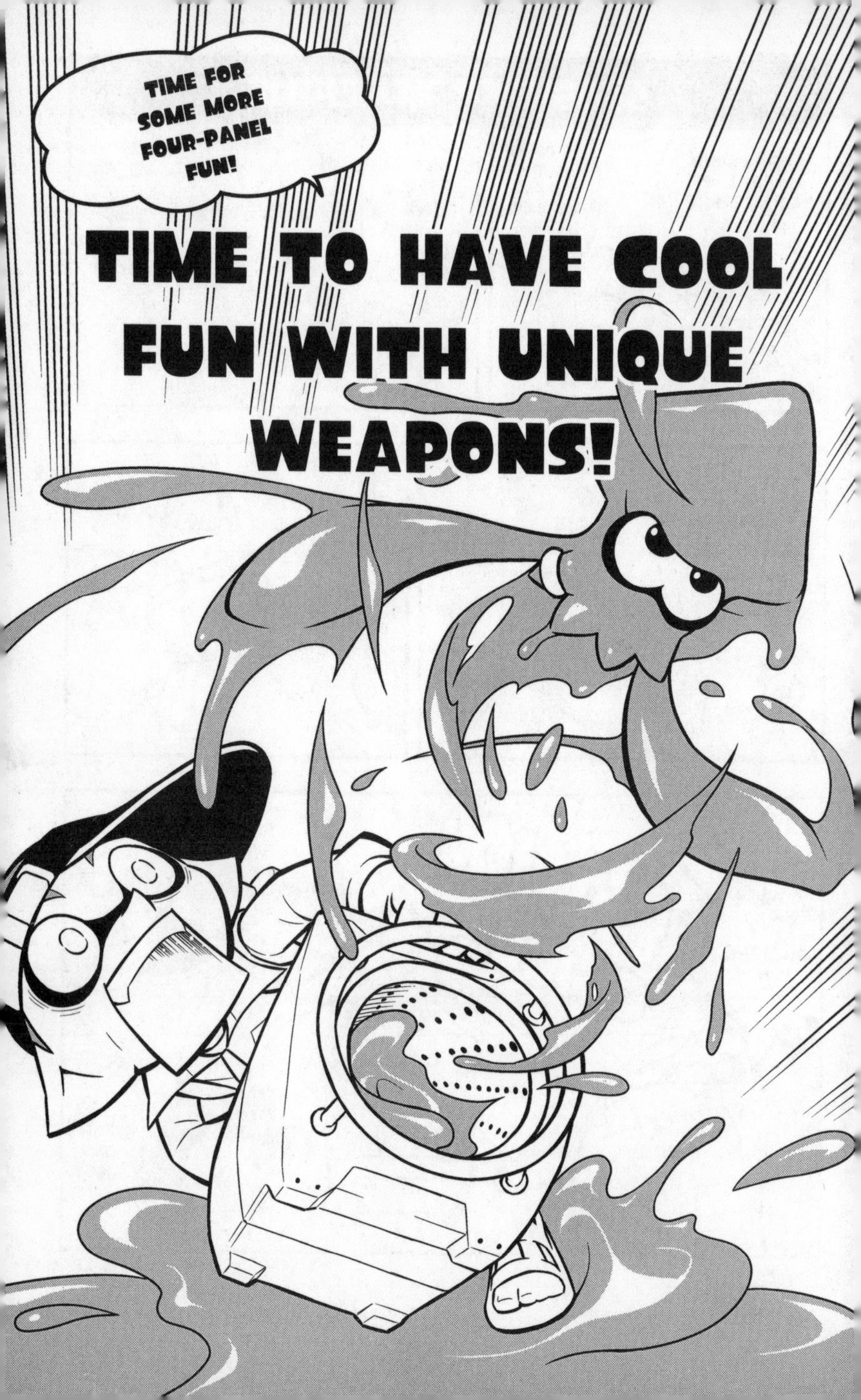
TIME FOR SOME MORE FOUR-PANEL FUN!
TIME TO HAVE COOL FUN WITH UNIQUE WEAPONS!

SLOSHING MACHINE

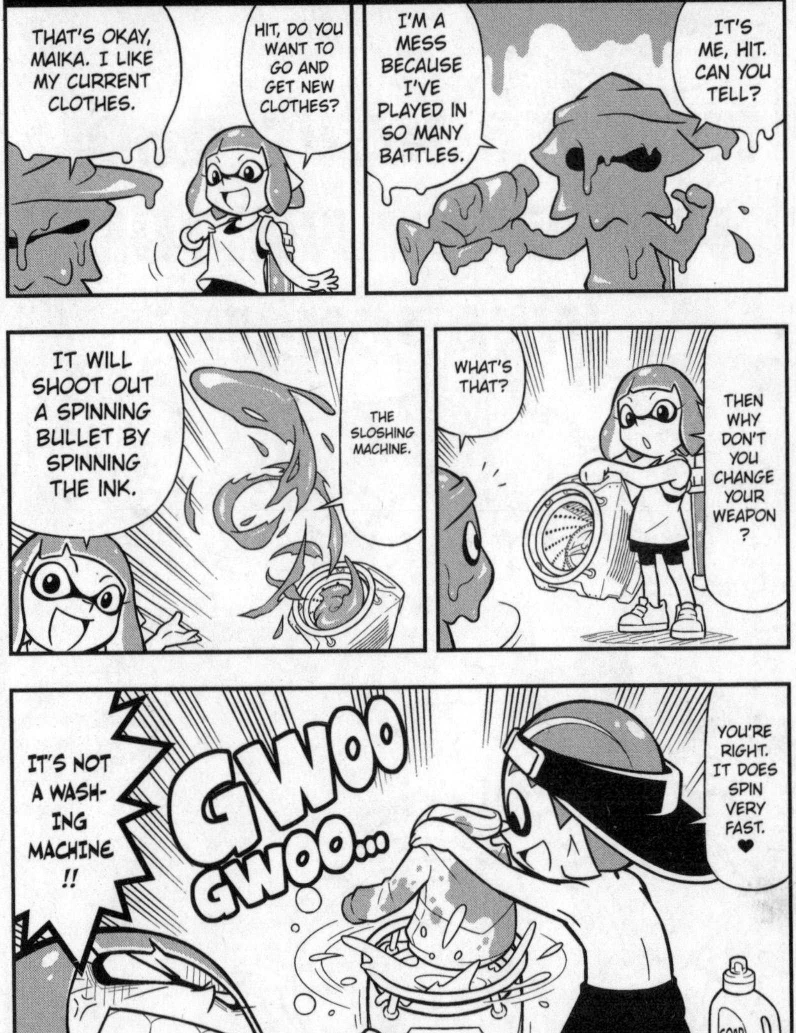

IT'S ME, HIT. CAN YOU TELL?
I'M A MESS BECAUSE I'VE PLAYED IN SO MANY BATTLES.
HIT, DO YOU WANT TO GO AND GET NEW CLOTHES?
THAT'S OKAY, MAIKA. I LIKE MY CURRENT CLOTHES.
THEN WHY DON'T YOU CHANGE YOUR WEAPON?
WHAT'S THAT?
THE SLOSHING MACHINE.
IT WILL SHOOT OUT A SPINNING BULLET BY SPINNING THE INK.
YOU'RE RIGHT. IT DOES SPIN VERY FAST. ❤
GWOO GWOO...
IT'S NOT A WASH-ING MACHINE!!
SOAP

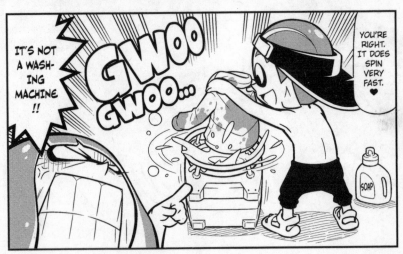

HIT 100%

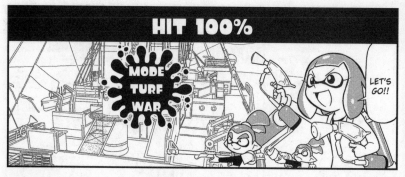

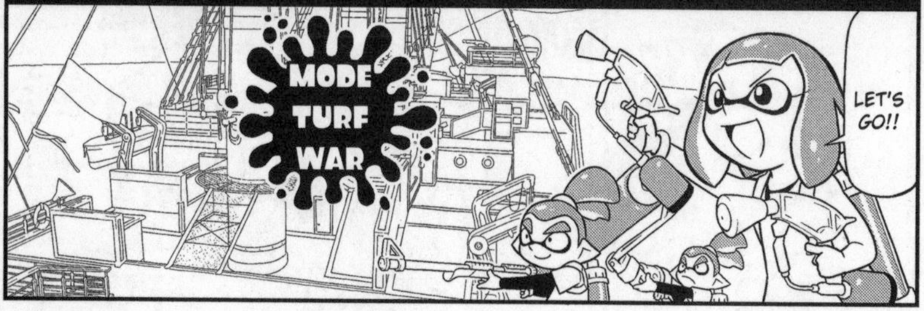
LET'S GO!!
MODE TURF WAR

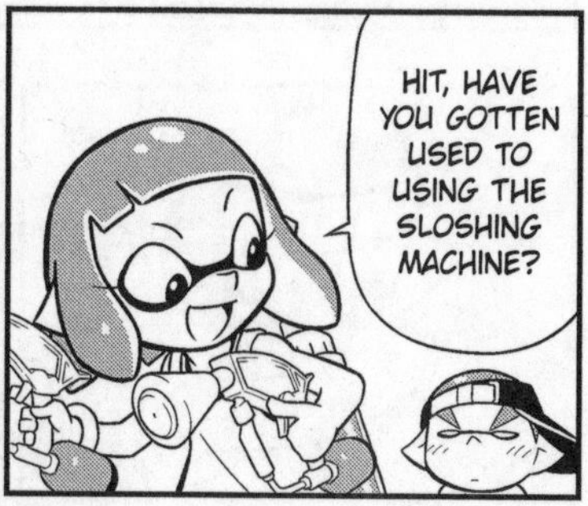
HIT, HAVE YOU GOTTEN USED TO USING THE SLOSHING MACHINE?

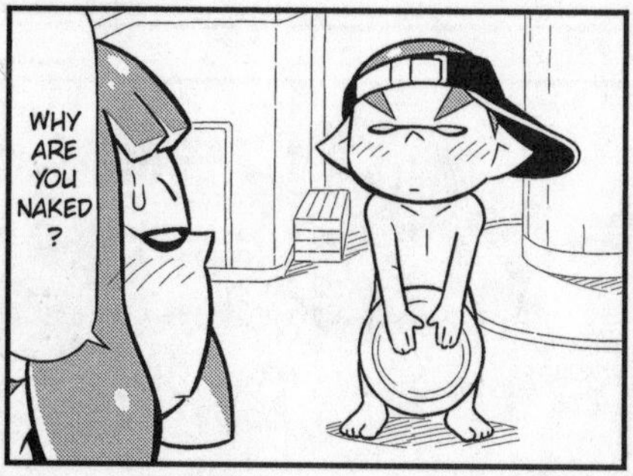
WHY ARE YOU NAKED?

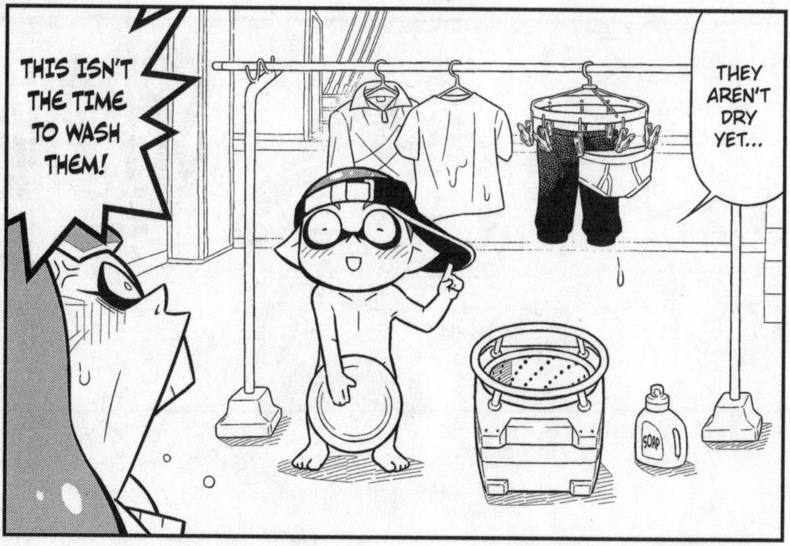
THEY AREN'T DRY YET...
THIS ISN'T THE TIME TO WASH THEM!
SOAP

HOME ELECTRONICS

SPLATA
TA
TA
TA TA
WE'RE GOING TO ATTACK THE ENEMY'S TERRI-TORY!!
GRRP
GRRRRP...
WHAT'S WRONG, HIT?!
I CAN'T... MOVE...
SPRIIING
THAT'S A WASHING MACHINE!!
Hnngh...
POWER CORD

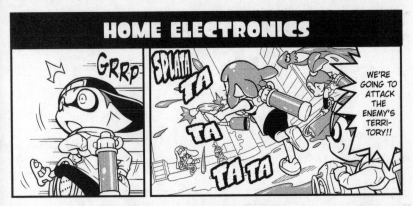

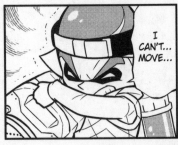

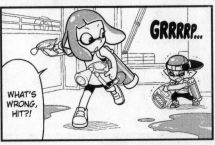

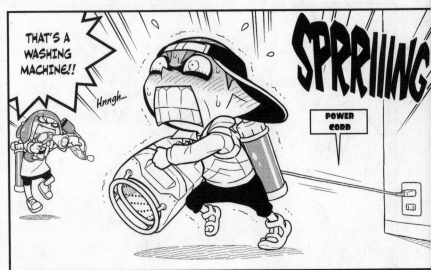

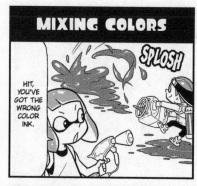

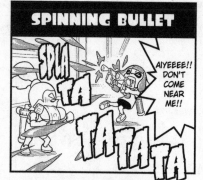

SPINNING BULLET

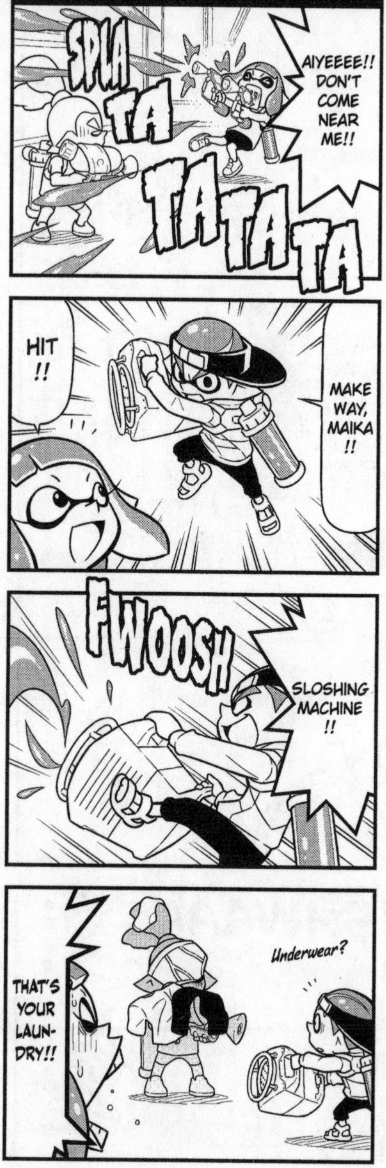
AIYEEEE!! DON'T COME NEAR ME!!
SPLA
TA
TA TA TA TA
MAKE WAY, MAIKA!!
HIT!!
FWOOSH
SLOSHING MACHINE!!
Underwear?
THAT'S YOUR LAUN-DRY!!

MIXING COLORS

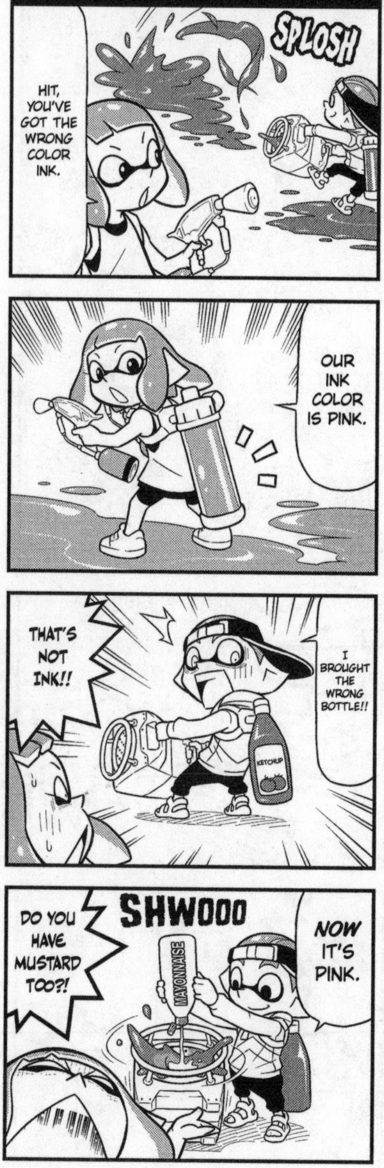
SPLOSH
HIT, YOU'VE GOT THE WRONG COLOR INK.
OUR INK COLOR IS PINK.
I BROUGHT THE WRONG BOTTLE!!
KETCHUP
THAT'S NOT INK!!
NOW IT'S PINK.
SHWOOO
MAYONNAISE
DO YOU HAVE MUSTARD TOO?!

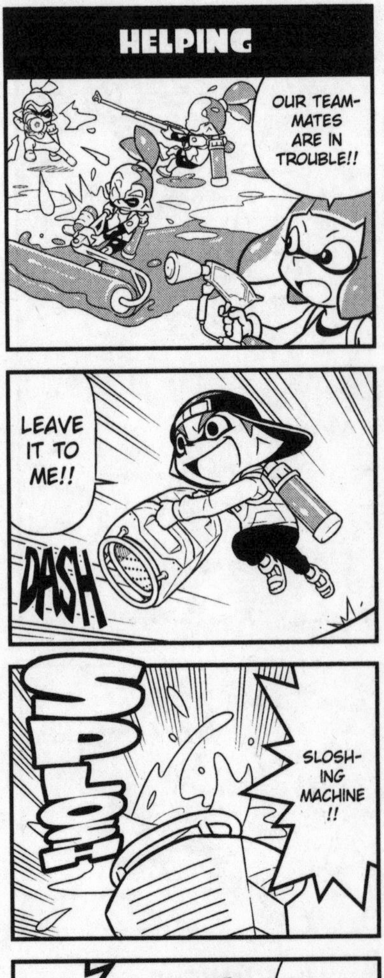
HELPING
OUR TEAM-MATES ARE IN TROUBLE!!
LEAVE IT TO ME!!
DASH
SLOSHING MACHINE!!
SPLOOSH!
THEY'LL BE CLEAN IN NO TIME.
GWOOSH
MORE LAUNDRY?!

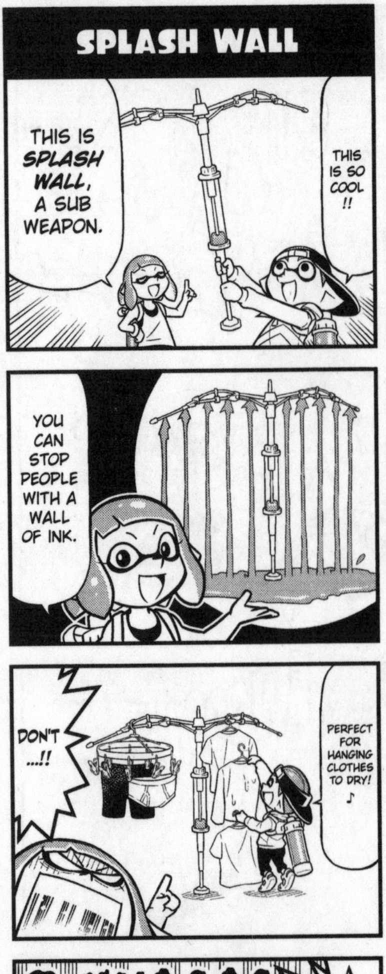
SPLASH WALL
THIS IS SO COOL!!
THIS IS SPLASH WALL, A SUB WEAPON.
YOU CAN STOP PEOPLE WITH A WALL OF INK.
PERFECT FOR HANGING CLOTHES TO DRY! ♪
DON'T ...!!
ARRRRGH!!
SHWAAAA

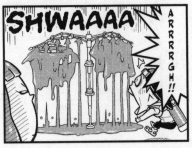

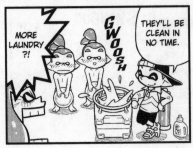

WALL?

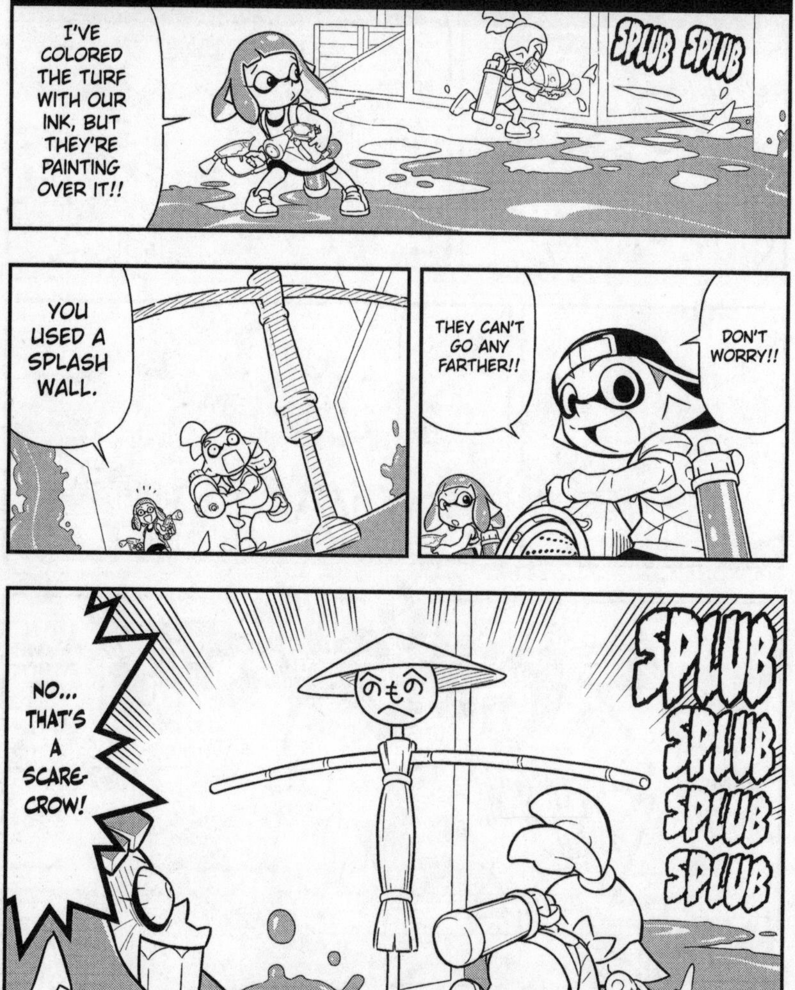
SPLUB SPLUB
I'VE COLORED THE TURF WITH OUR INK, BUT THEY'RE PAINTING OVER IT!!
DON'T WORRY!!
THEY CAN'T GO ANY FARTHER!!
YOU USED A SPLASH WALL.
SPLUB SPLUB SPLUB SPLUB
NO... THAT'S A SCARE-CROW!

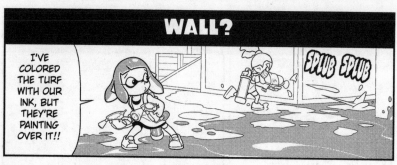

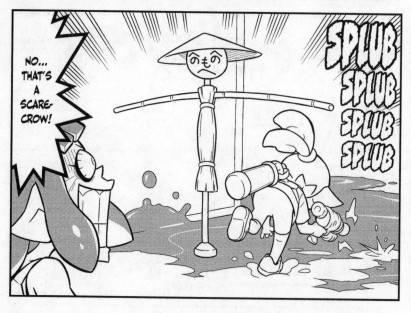

INK ARMOR

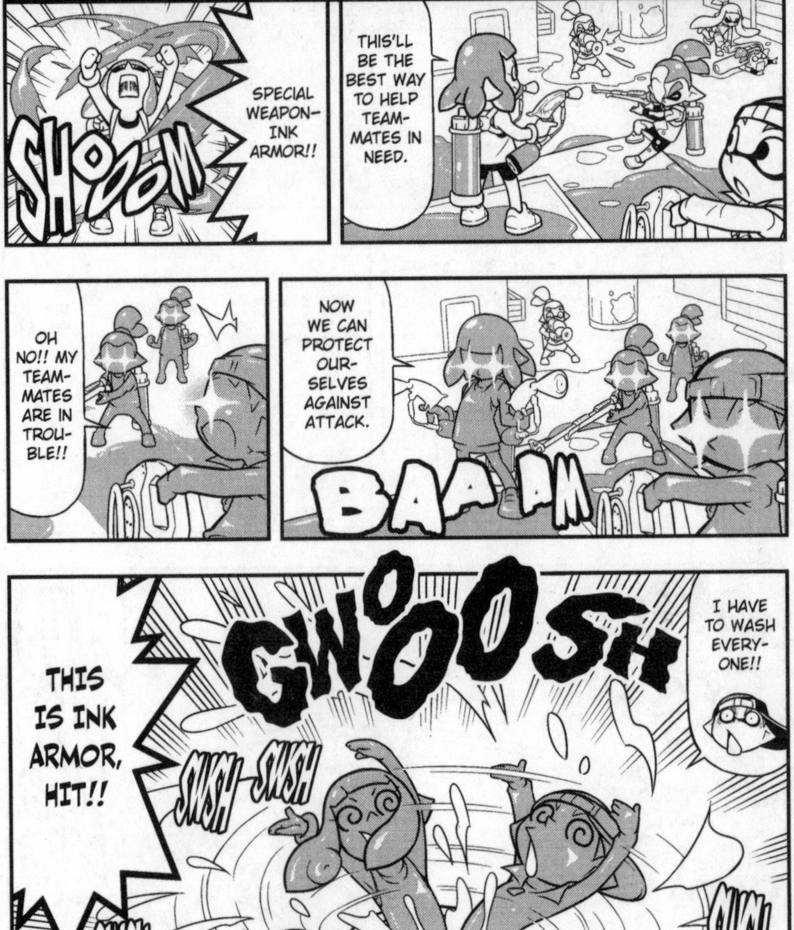
THIS'LL BE THE BEST WAY TO HELP TEAM-MATES IN NEED.
SPECIAL WEAPON—INK ARMOR!!
SHOOOM
NOW WE CAN PROTECT OUR-SELVES AGAINST ATTACK.
BAAAM
OH NO!! MY TEAM-MATES ARE IN TROU-BLE!!
I HAVE TO WASH EVERY-ONE!!
GWOOOSH
THIS IS INK ARMOR, HIT!!
SWSH SWSH
SWSH
SWSH
SWSH
SWSH
SLOSHING MACHINE
SOAP

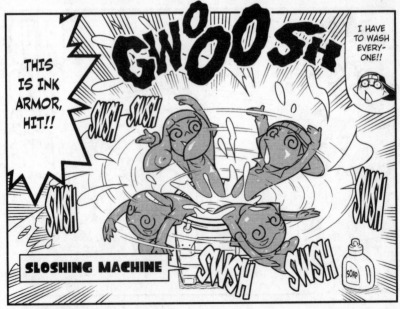

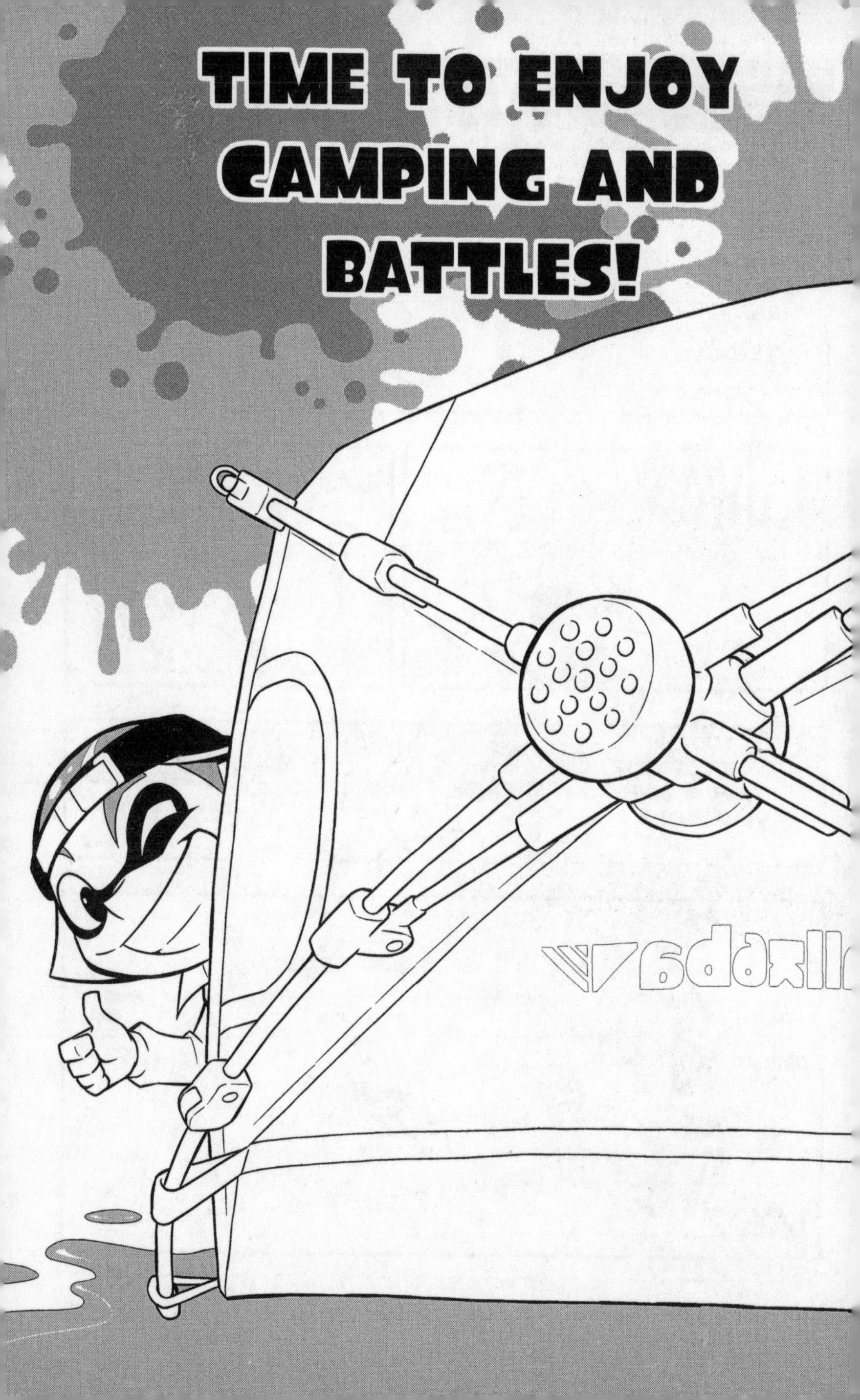
TIME TO ENJOY CAMPING AND BATTLES!

TENTA BRELLA

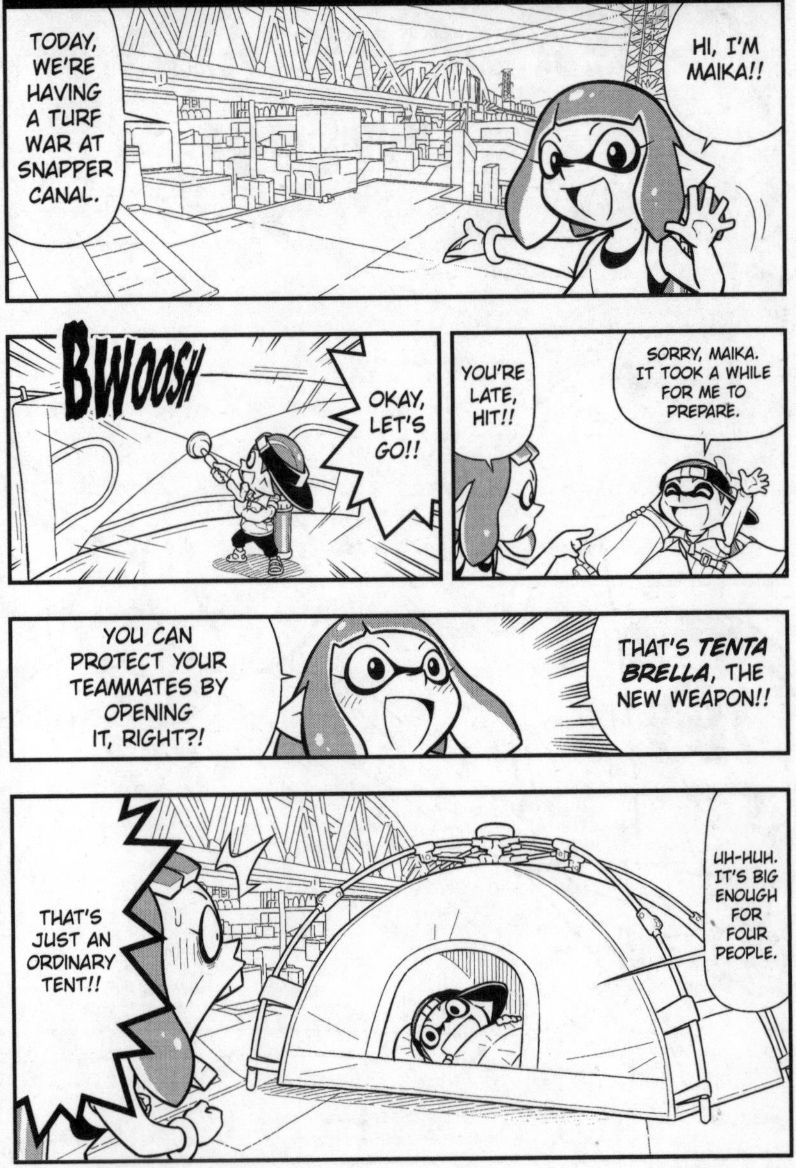

HI, I'M MAIKA!!
TODAY, WE'RE HAVING A TURF WAR AT SNAPPER CANAL.
YOU'RE LATE, HIT!!
SORRY, MAIKA. IT TOOK A WHILE FOR ME TO PREPARE.
BWOOSH
OKAY, LET'S GO!!
THAT'S *TENTA BRELLA*, THE NEW WEAPON!!
YOU CAN PROTECT YOUR TEAMMATES BY OPENING IT, RIGHT?!
UH-HUH. IT'S BIG ENOUGH FOR FOUR PEOPLE.
THAT'S JUST AN ORDINARY TENT!!

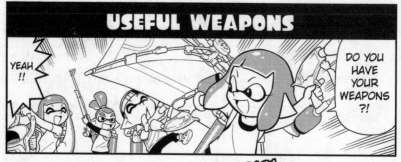

USEFUL WEAPONS

DO YOU HAVE YOUR WEAPONS ?!
YEAH !!
SPLATATA
LET'S GO!!
TATA...
OH?! WHERE ARE THE OTHERS ?
TENTA BRELLA
SPLAT CHARGER
WE'RE NOT HERE TO CAMP!!
SLOSHER

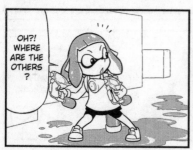

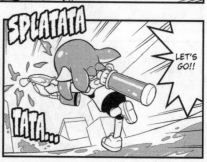

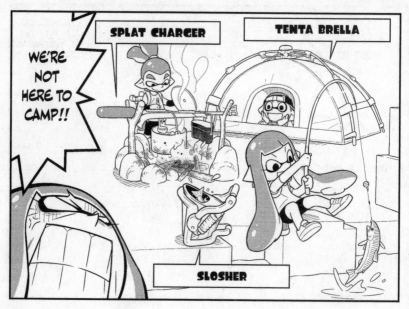

IT LOOKS LIKE A BURST BOMB

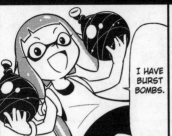

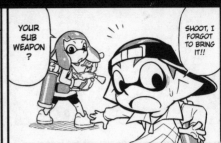

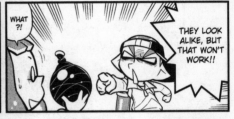

SHOOT, I FORGOT TO BRING IT!!
YOUR SUB WEAPON?
I HAVE BURST BOMBS.
THEY LOOK ALIKE, BUT THAT WON'T WORK!!
WHAT?!
IS THERE SOME OTHER SUB WEAPON THAT LOOKS LIKE A BURST BOMB?
I'LL GO BUY THE ONIONS I FORGOT!!
KA-KLAK KLAK KA-KLAK KLAK
WE DON'T NEED TO MAKE CURRY!!

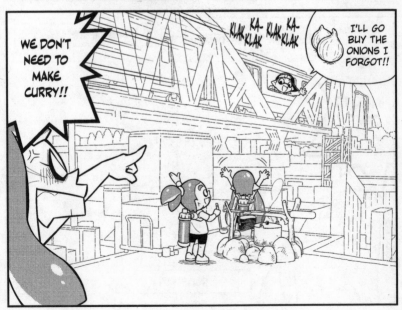

BRELLAS FOR EXPERIENCED INKLINGS

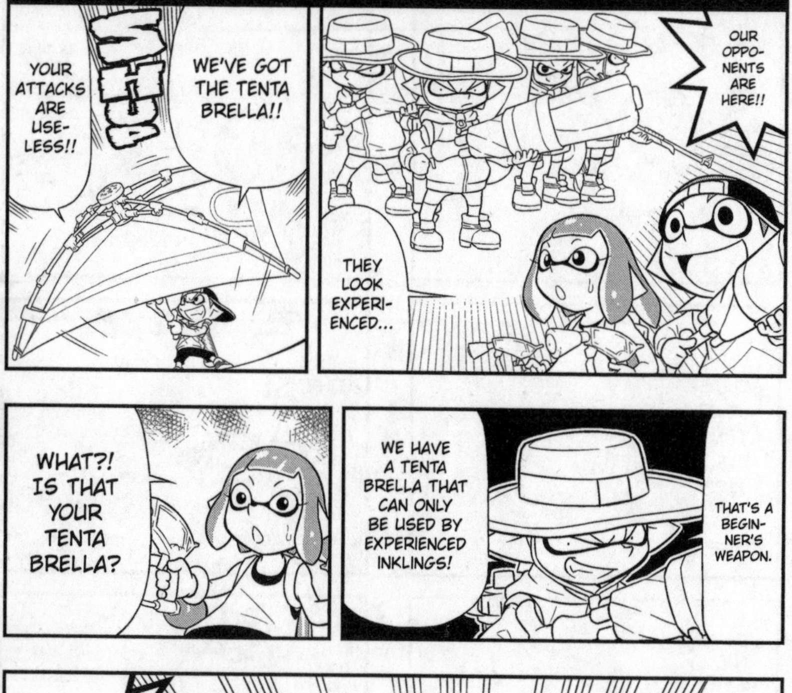

OUR OPPONENTS ARE HERE!!
THEY LOOK EXPERIENCED...
WE'VE GOT THE TENTA BRELLA!!
SHUA
YOUR ATTACKS ARE USELESS!!
THAT'S A BEGINNER'S WEAPON.
WE HAVE A TENTA BRELLA THAT CAN ONLY BE USED BY EXPERIENCED INKLINGS!
WHAT?! IS THAT YOUR TENTA BRELLA?
COOL, IT'S SO RETRO. ♪
KLAK KLAK
IT'S JUST AN OLD TENT!!

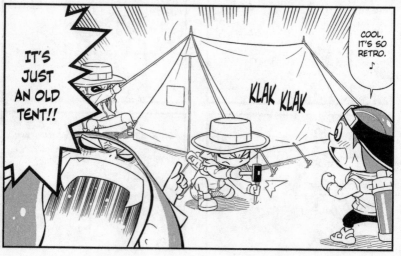

OPEN BRELLA

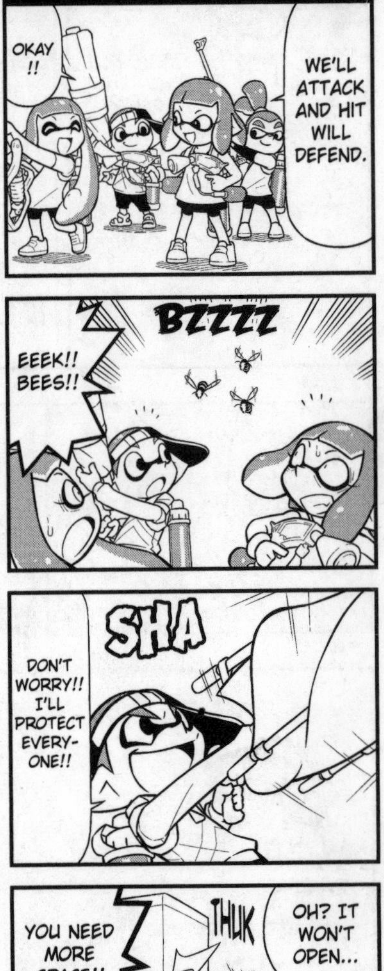
WE'LL ATTACK AND HIT WILL DEFEND.
OKAY!!
BZZZZ
EEEK!! BEES!!
SHA
DON'T WORRY!! I'LL PROTECT EVERY-ONE!!
OH? IT WON'T OPEN...
THUK
THUK
YOU NEED MORE SPACE!!

TINY SPACE

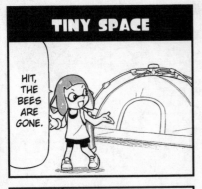

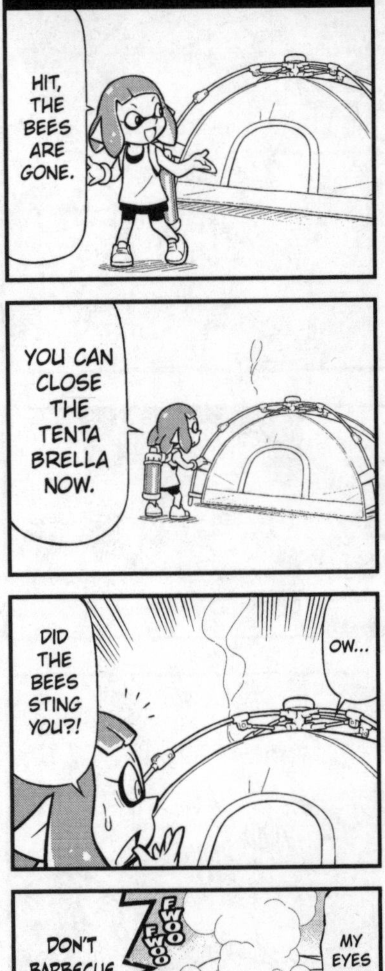
HIT, THE BEES ARE GONE.
YOU CAN CLOSE THE TENTA BRELLA NOW.
OW...
DID THE BEES STING YOU?!
MY EYES HURT ...
FWOO FWOO
DON'T BARBECUE IN THERE!!
KOFF KOFF...

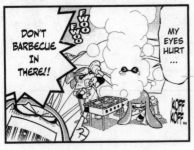

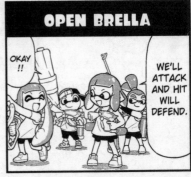

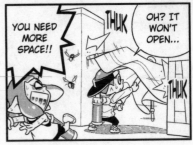

YELLOW INK

THEY'RE ATTACK-ING!!
BLAM BLAM
NOW!! SLOSHER !!
SPLOSH
WHAT?! IT'S NOT WORK-ING?!
THE INK COLOR IS DIFFERENT !!
Yellow?
IT'S CURRY !!

OBSERVATION WINDOW

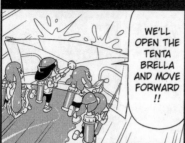

WE'LL OPEN THE TENTA BRELLA AND MOVE FORWARD !!
BUT WE CAN'T ATTACK THE ENEMIES LIKE THIS.
ZIIIIIP
IF WE OPEN THE WINDOW, WE CAN SHOOT THROUGH IT!!
SHUP...
SO CAN THEY !!

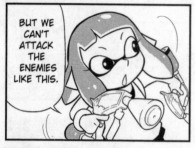

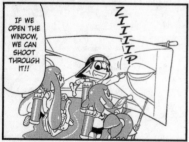

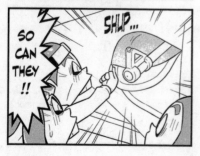

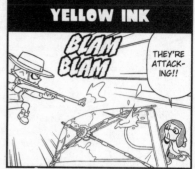

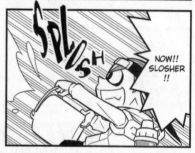

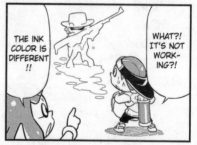

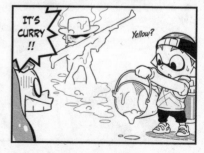

RESTING

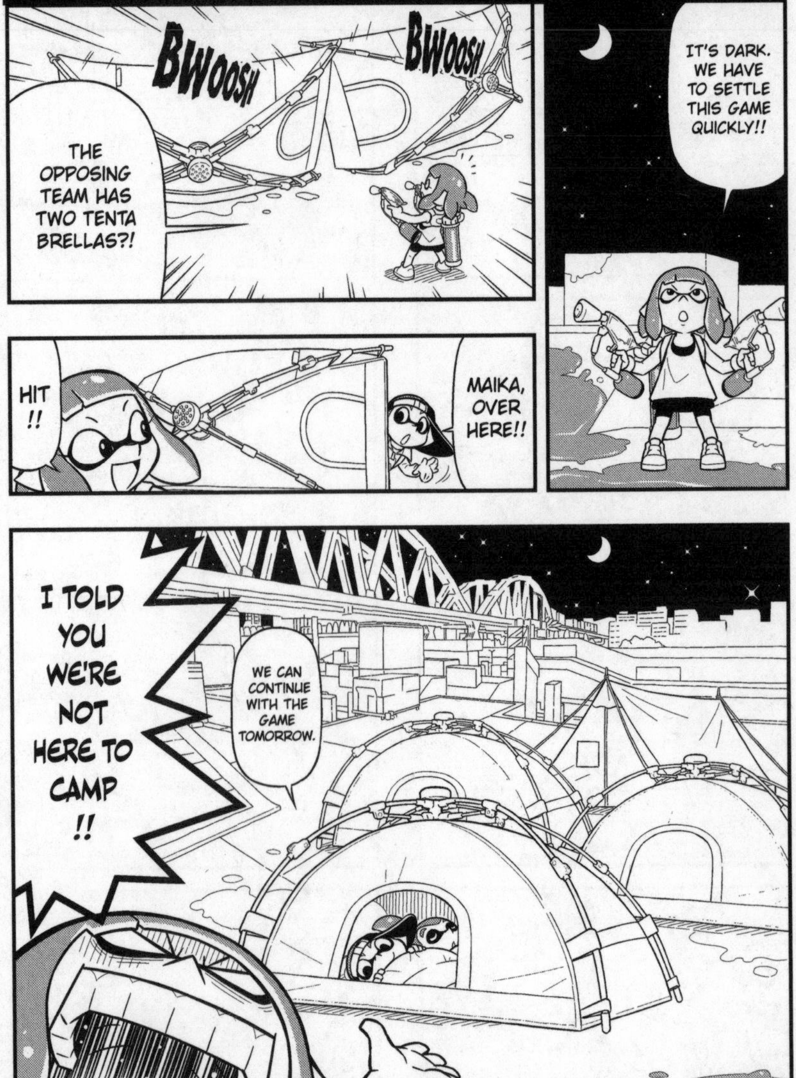

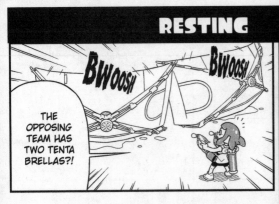

IT'S DARK. WE HAVE TO SETTLE THIS GAME QUICKLY!!
BWOOSH
BWOOSH
THE OPPOSING TEAM HAS TWO TENTA BRELLAS?!
MAIKA, OVER HERE!!
HIT !!
WE CAN CONTINUE WITH THE GAME TOMORROW.
I TOLD YOU WE'RE NOT HERE TO CAMP !!

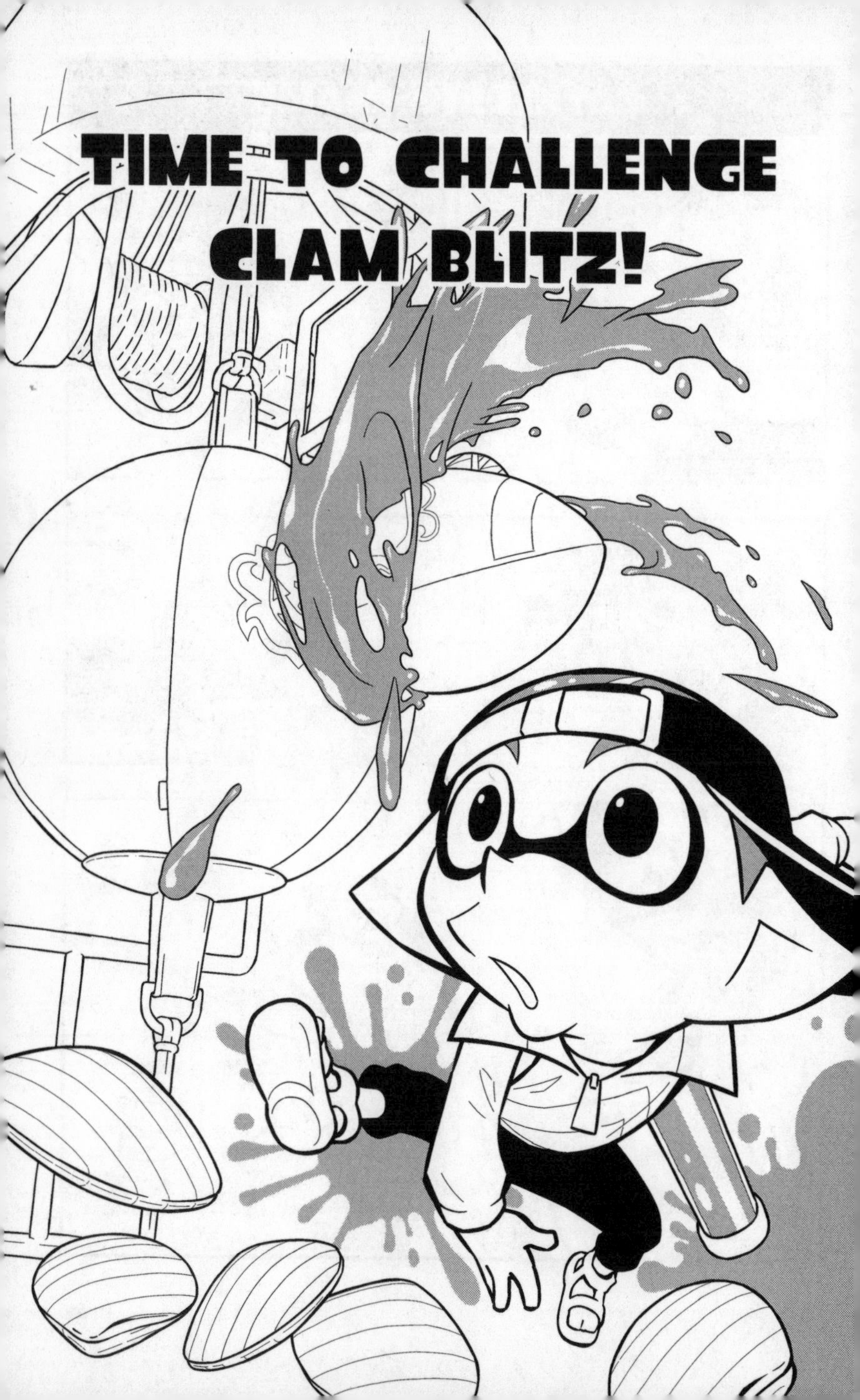
TIME TO CHALLENGE
CLAM BLITZ!

GATHERING CLAMS

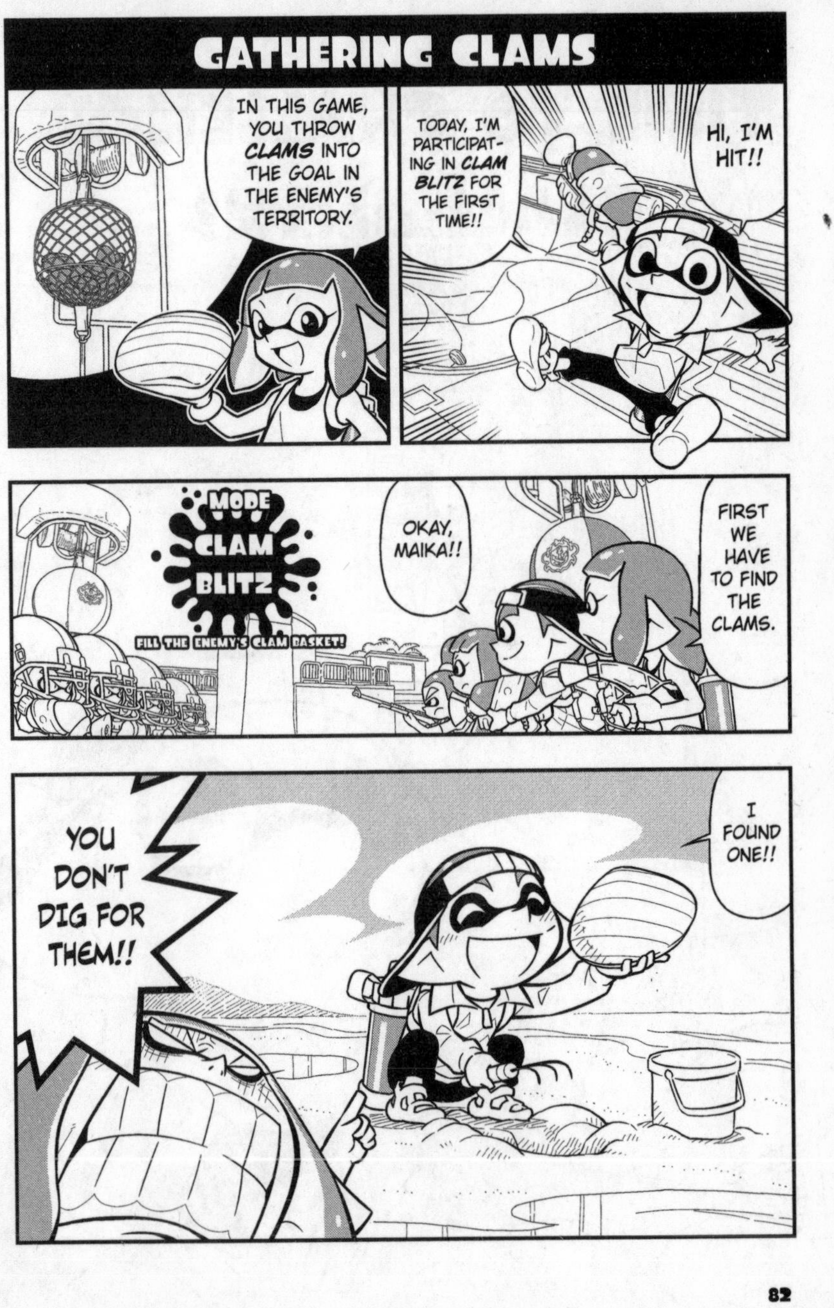
HI, I'M HIT!!
TODAY, I'M PARTICIPATING IN CLAM BLITZ FOR THE FIRST TIME!!
IN THIS GAME, YOU THROW CLAMS INTO THE GOAL IN THE ENEMY'S TERRITORY.
FIRST WE HAVE TO FIND THE CLAMS.
OKAY, MAIKA!!
MODE
CLAM BLITZ
FILL THE ENEMY'S CLAM BASKET!
I FOUND ONE!!
YOU DON'T DIG FOR THEM!!

GATHER TEN TO TRANSFORM

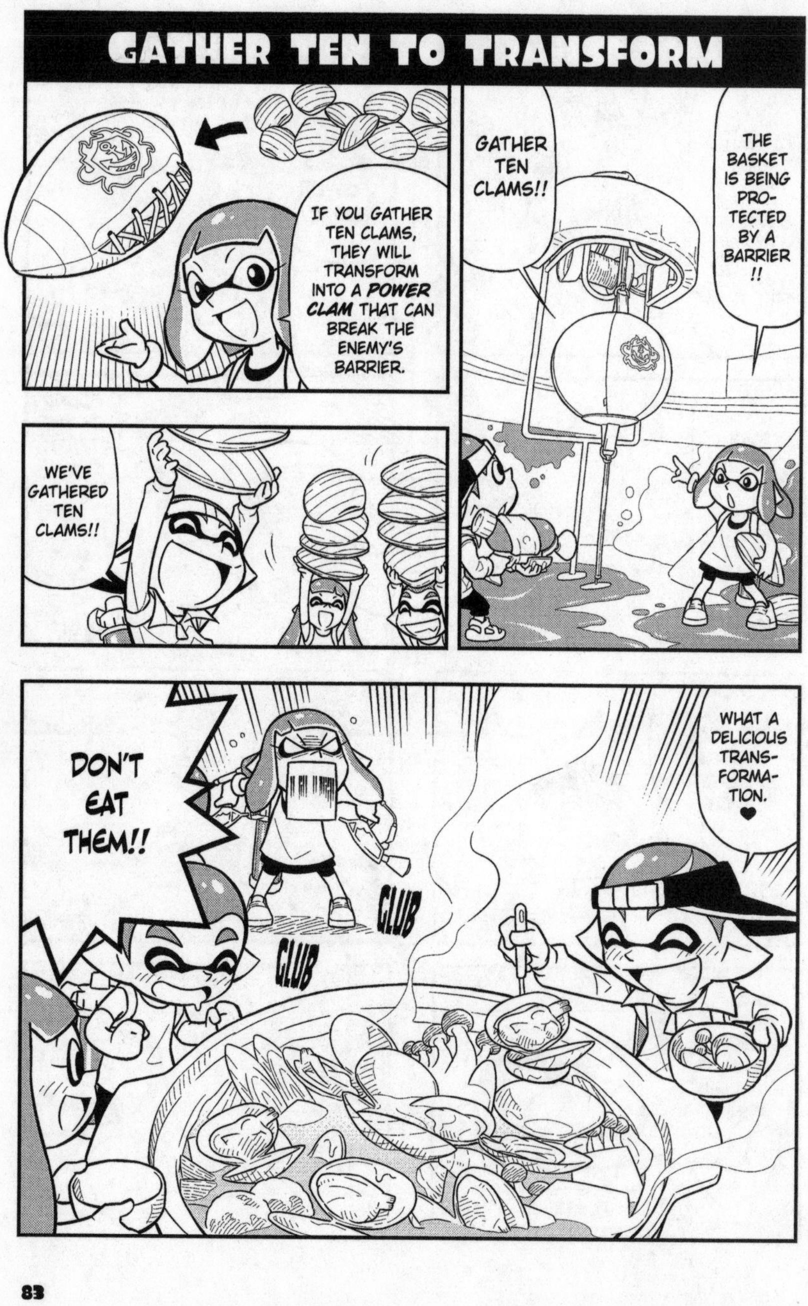
THE BASKET IS BEING PRO-TECTED BY A BARRIER!!
GATHER TEN CLAMS!!
IF YOU GATHER TEN CLAMS, THEY WILL TRANSFORM INTO A *POWER CLAM* THAT CAN BREAK THE ENEMY'S BARRIER.
WE'VE GATHERED TEN CLAMS!!
WHAT A DELICIOUS TRANS-FORMA-TION. ♥
DON'T EAT THEM!!
CLUB
CLUB

NONTRANSFORMING CLAMS

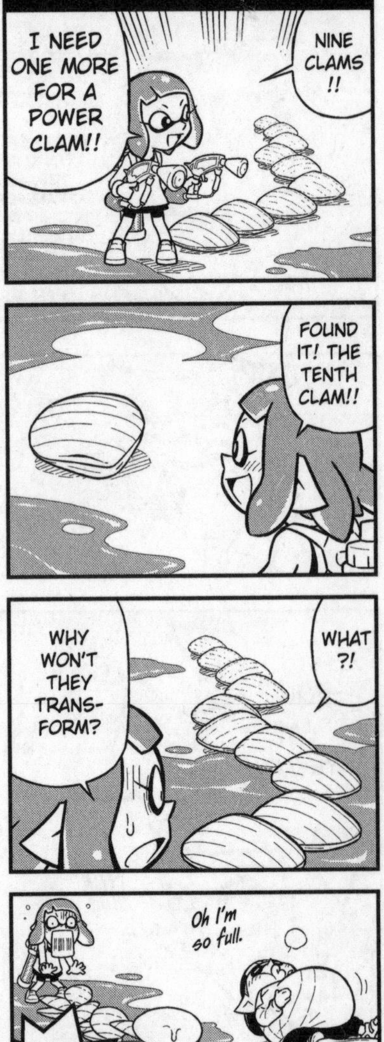
NINE CLAMS !!
I NEED ONE MORE FOR A POWER CLAM!!
FOUND IT! THE TENTH CLAM!!
WHAT ?!
WHY WON'T THEY TRANS-FORM?
Oh I'm so full.
THEY'RE JUST SHELLS!!

SPLAT BRELLA

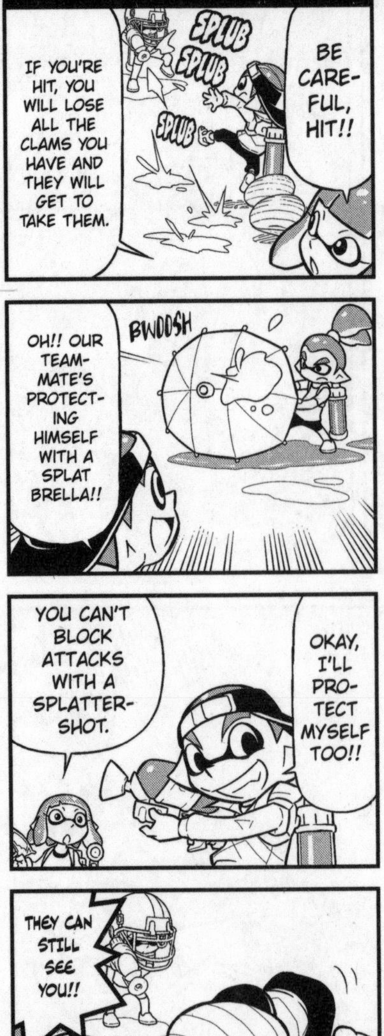
BE CARE-FUL, HIT!!
SPLUB
SPLUB
SPLUB
IF YOU'RE HIT, YOU WILL LOSE ALL THE CLAMS YOU HAVE AND THEY WILL GET TO TAKE THEM.
BWOOSH
OH!! OUR TEAM-MATE'S PROTECT-ING HIMSELF WITH A SPLAT BRELLA!!
OKAY, I'LL PRO-TECT MYSELF TOO!!
YOU CAN'T BLOCK ATTACKS WITH A SPLATTER-SHOT.
THEY CAN STILL SEE YOU!!
CLAM

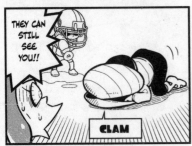

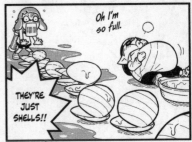

LOTS OF CLAMS

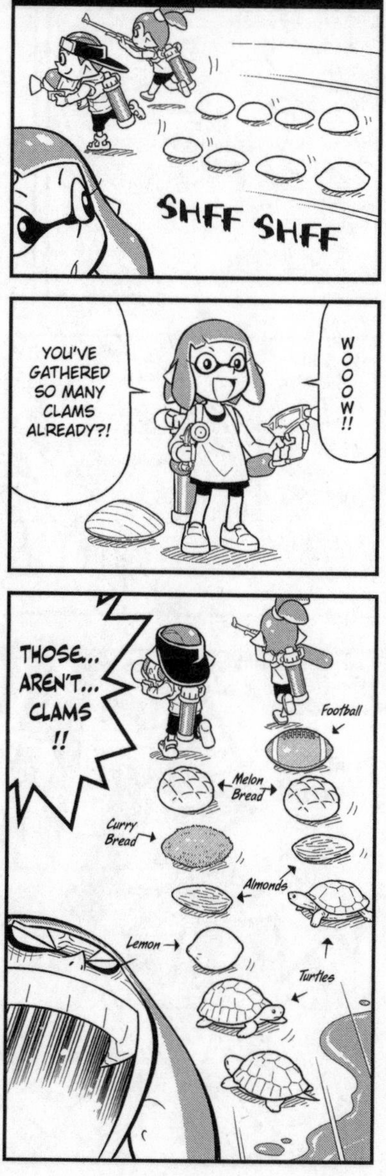
SHFF SHFF
WOOOOW!!
YOU'VE GATHERED SO MANY CLAMS ALREADY?!
THOSE... AREN'T... CLAMS!!
Football
Melon Bread
Curry Bread
Almonds
Lemon
Turtles

HIDING

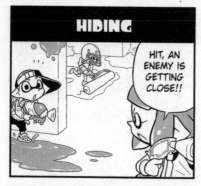

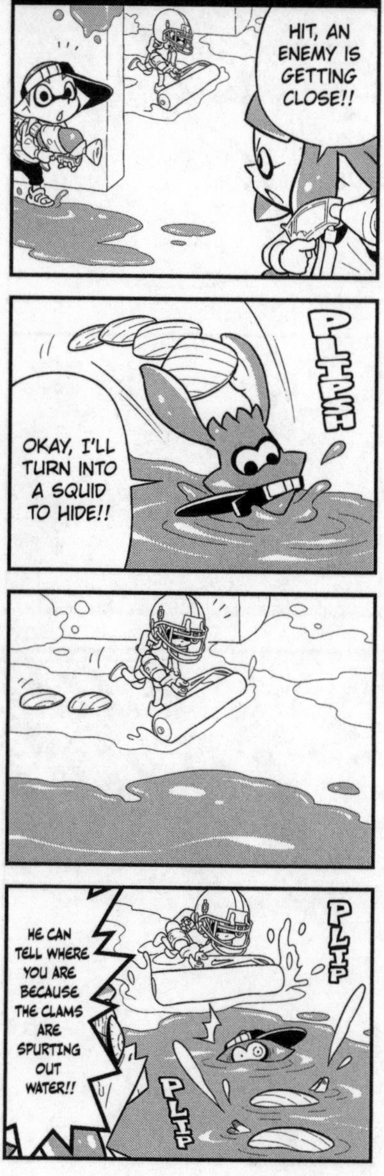
HIT, AN ENEMY IS GETTING CLOSE!!
PLIPSH
OKAY, I'LL TURN INTO A SQUID TO HIDE!!
PLIP
PLIP
HE CAN TELL WHERE YOU ARE BECAUSE THE CLAMS ARE SPURTING OUT WATER!!

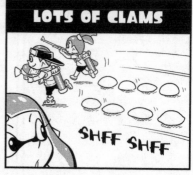

POWER CLAM

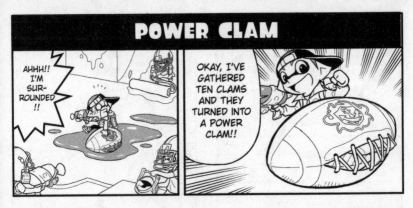

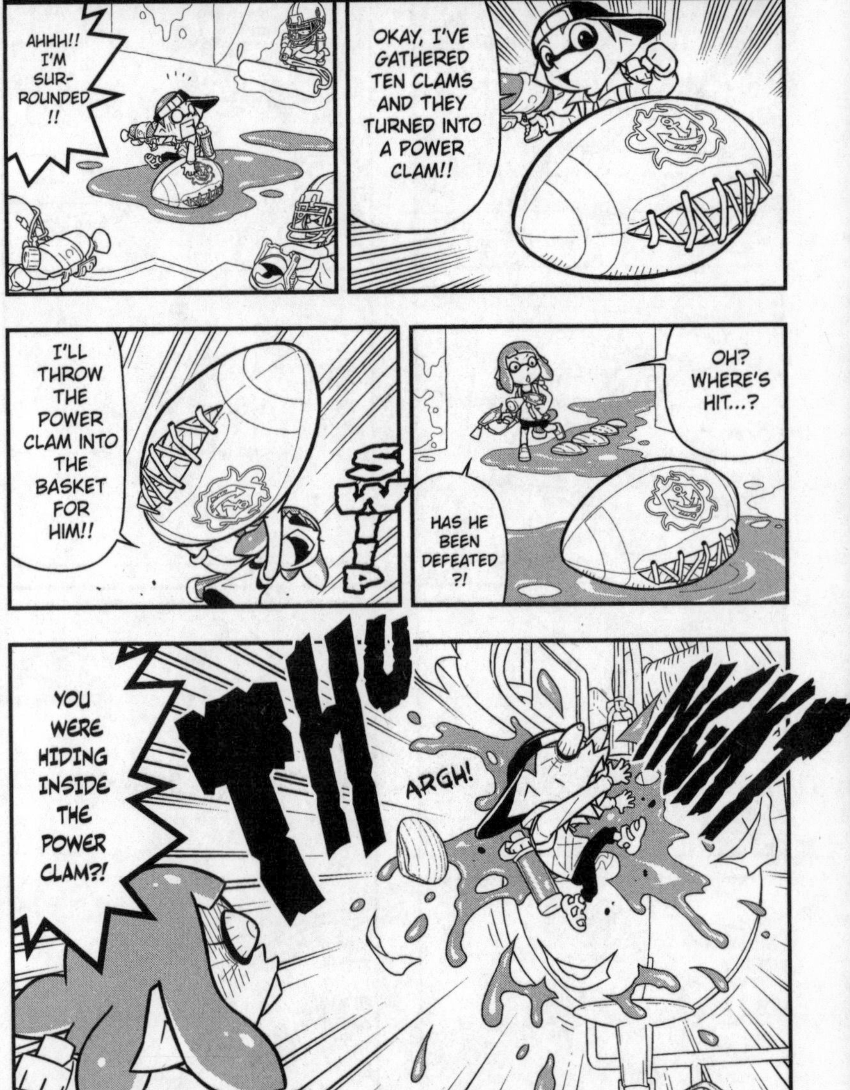
OKAY, I'VE GATHERED TEN CLAMS AND THEY TURNED INTO A POWER CLAM!!
AHHH!! I'M SUR-ROUNDED!!
OH? WHERE'S HIT...?
HAS HE BEEN DEFEATED?!
SWIP
I'LL THROW THE POWER CLAM INTO THE BASKET FOR HIM!!
THU
ARGH!
YOU WERE HIDING INSIDE THE POWER CLAM?!

PASS THE CLAM

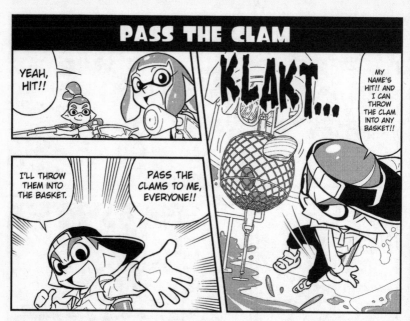

KLAKT...
MY NAME'S HIT!! AND I CAN THROW THE CLAM INTO ANY BASKET!!
YEAH, HIT!!
PASS THE CLAMS TO ME, EVERYONE!!
I'LL THROW THEM INTO THE BASKET.
THK THK THK THK
ONE AT A TIME! ONE AT A TIME!
THK

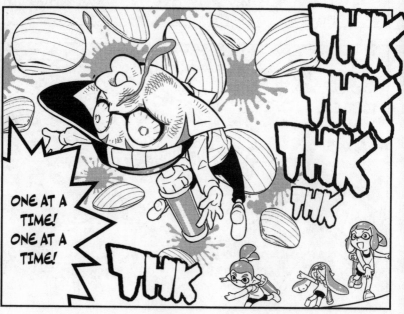

NUMBER OF CLAMS

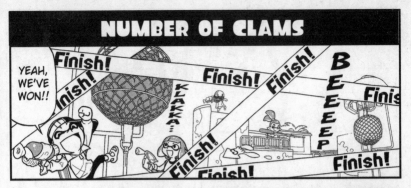

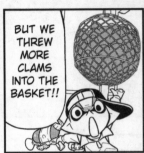

BEEEEEP
Finish!
Finish!
Finish!
KLAKKA...
YEAH, WE'VE WON!!
Finish!
Finish!
Finish!
LOSE...
WHAAAT? WE LOST? WHY?!
BAAAAAM
BAD GUYS
45 COUNT
225p
BUT WE THREW MORE CLAMS INTO THE BASKET!!
KLAKT...
OH... TURTLES... NOT CLAMS!

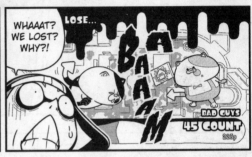

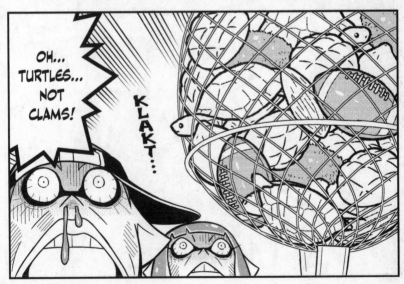

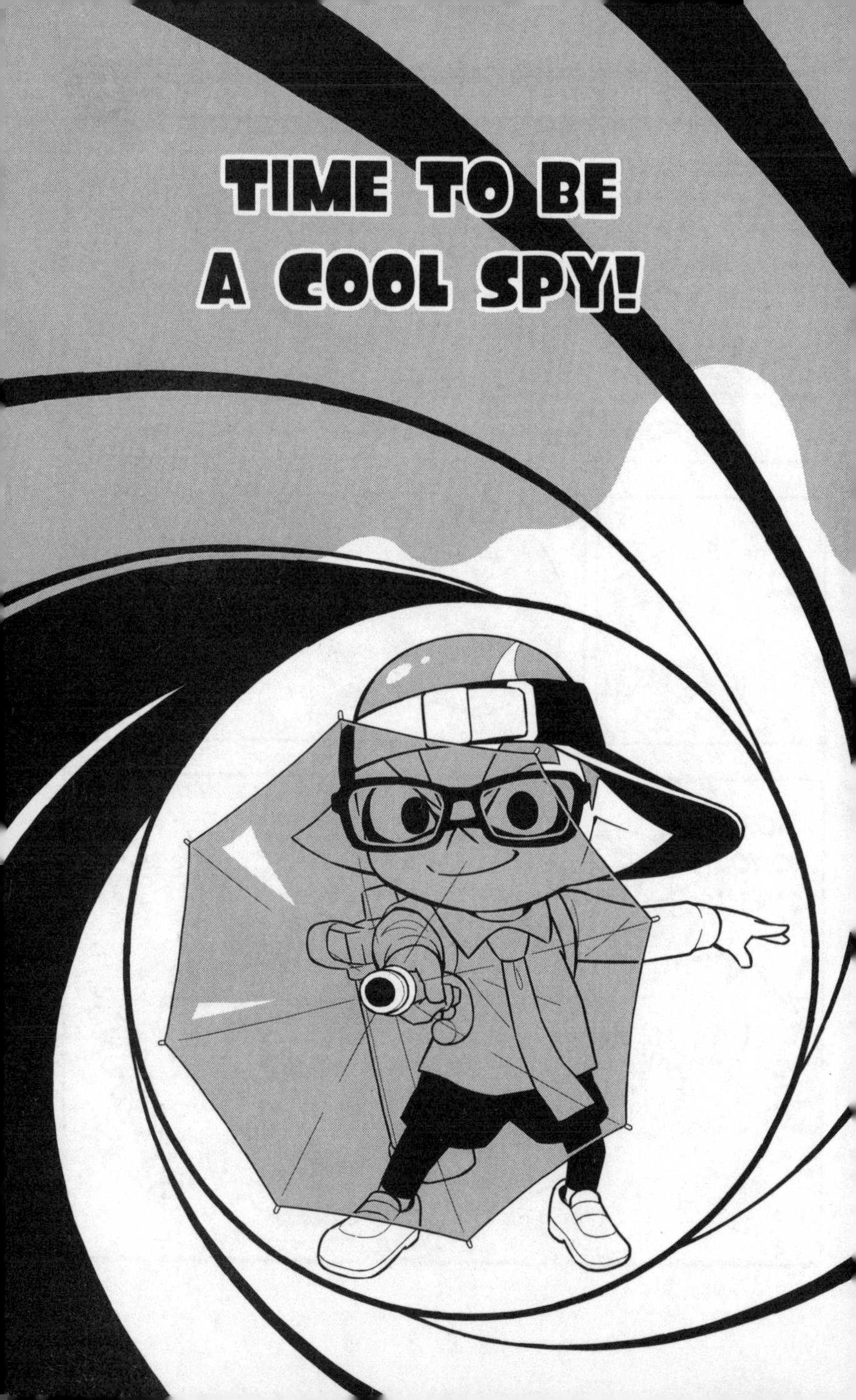
TIME TO BE
A COOL SPY!

BLACK UNDERCOVER BRELLA

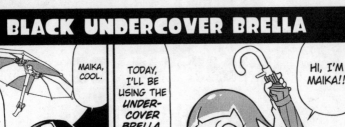

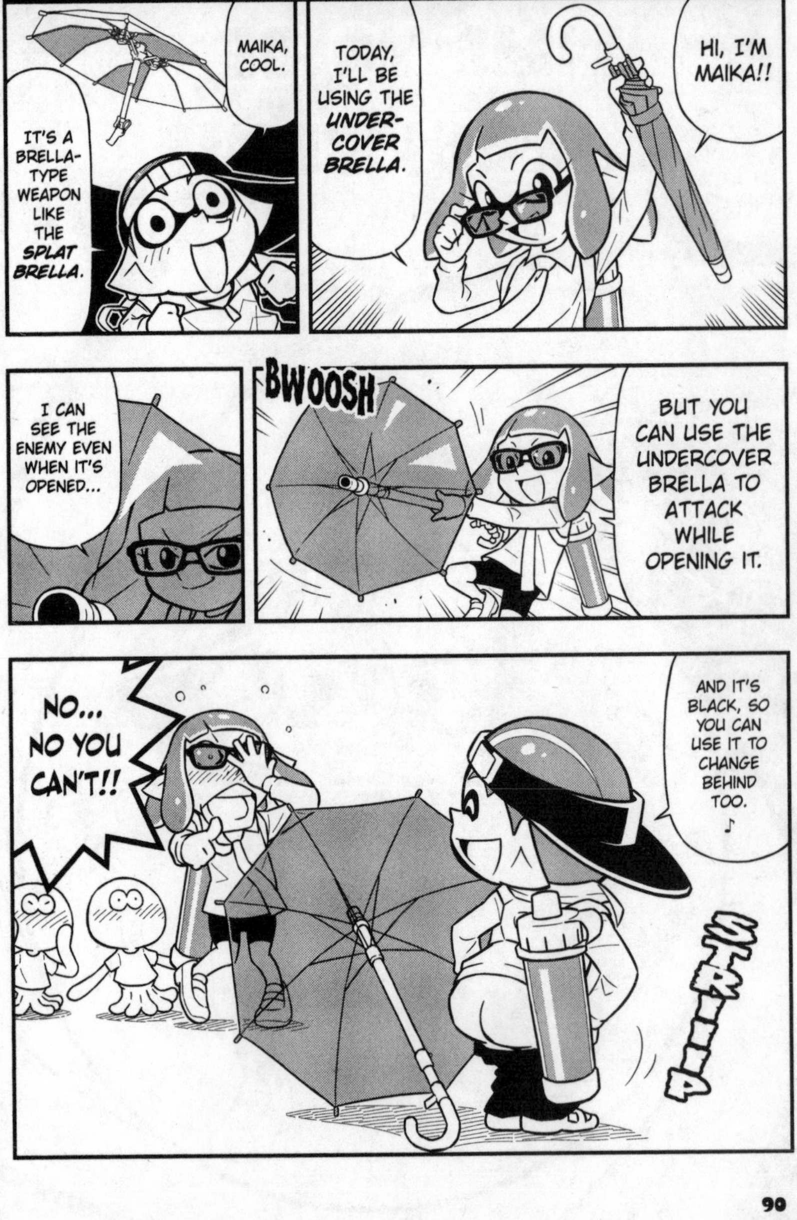
HI, I'M MAIKA!!
TODAY, I'LL BE USING THE *UNDERCOVER BRELLA*.
MAIKA, COOL.
IT'S A BRELLA-TYPE WEAPON LIKE THE *SPLAT BRELLA*.
BWOOSH
BUT YOU CAN USE THE UNDERCOVER BRELLA TO ATTACK WHILE OPENING IT.
I CAN SEE THE ENEMY EVEN WHEN IT'S OPENED...
AND IT'S BLACK, SO YOU CAN USE IT TO CHANGE BEHIND TOO. ♪
STRIIIP
NO... NO YOU CAN'T!!

SPY

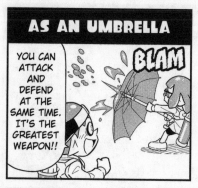

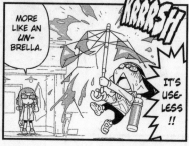

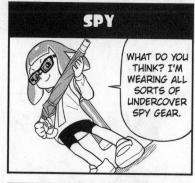

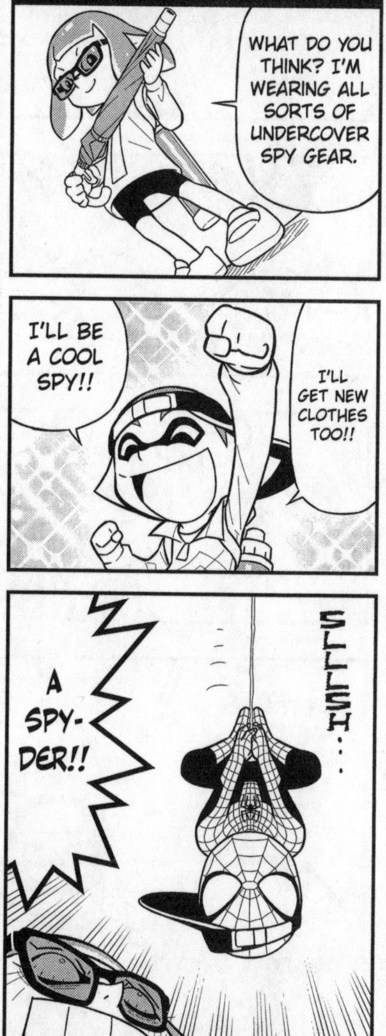
WHAT DO YOU THINK? I'M WEARING ALL SORTS OF UNDERCOVER SPY GEAR.
I'LL GET NEW CLOTHES TOO!!
I'LL BE A COOL SPY!!
SLLLSH...
A SPY-DER!!

AS AN UMBRELLA

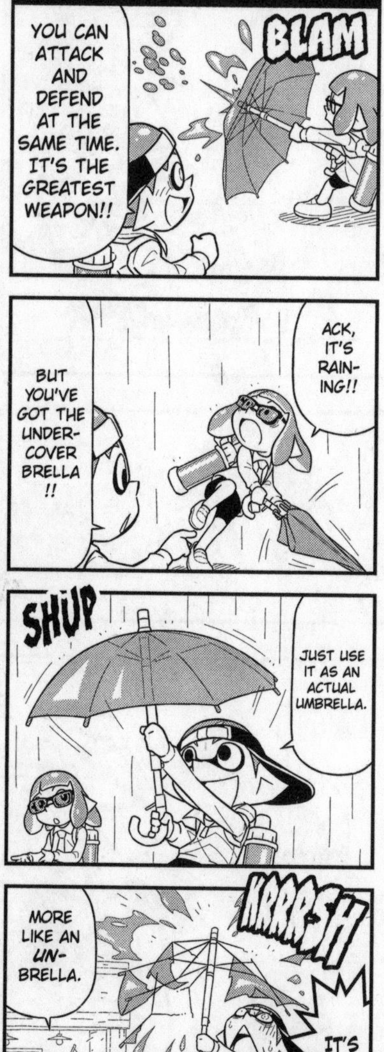
BLAM
YOU CAN ATTACK AND DEFEND AT THE SAME TIME. IT'S THE GREATEST WEAPON!!
ACK, IT'S RAIN-ING!!
BUT YOU'VE GOT THE UNDER-COVER BRELLA!!
JUST USE IT AS AN ACTUAL UMBRELLA.
SHÜP
KRRRSH
IT'S USE-LESS!!
MORE LIKE AN UN-BRELLA.

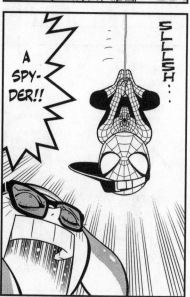

ALL SPIES

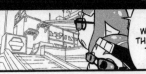

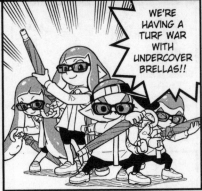

WE'RE HAVING A TURF WAR WITH UNDERCOVER BRELLAS!!
OH?! WHERE'S THE OTHER TEAM?
BLAM
BLAM
EEEK !!
WHOA !!
WAIT, AREN'T YOU...
...ON OUR SIDE?!
SHUP
THEY'RE GOOD ...
VINEGAR
LEMON
YEAH, IT'S HARD TO DISGUISE THOSE FLAVORS.

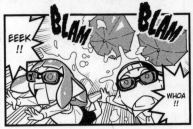

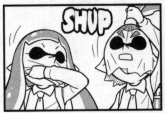

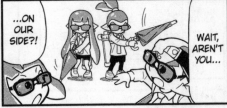

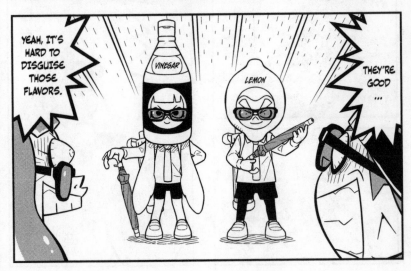

RADIOS

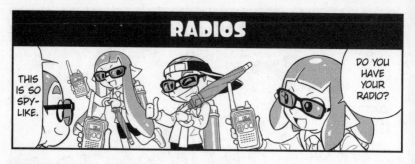

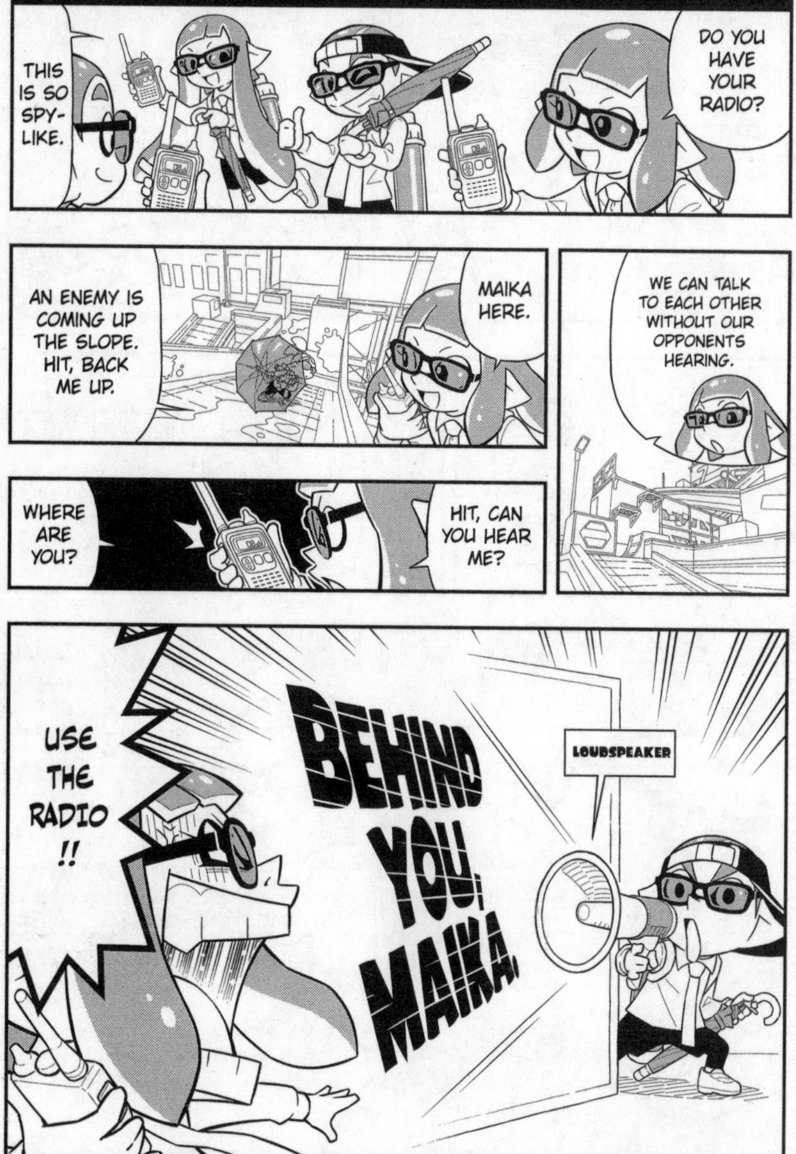
DO YOU HAVE YOUR RADIO?
THIS IS SO SPY-LIKE.
WE CAN TALK TO EACH OTHER WITHOUT OUR OPPONENTS HEARING.
MAIKA HERE.
AN ENEMY IS COMING UP THE SLOPE. HIT, BACK ME UP.
HIT, CAN YOU HEAR ME?
WHERE ARE YOU?
LOUDSPEAKER
BEHIND YOU, MAIKA!
USE THE RADIO!!

SPARE UNDERCOVER BRELLAS

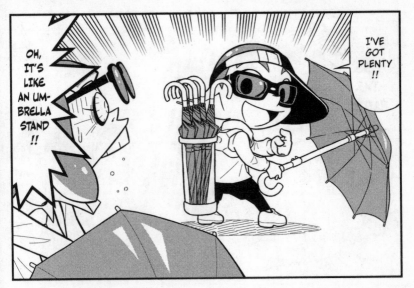

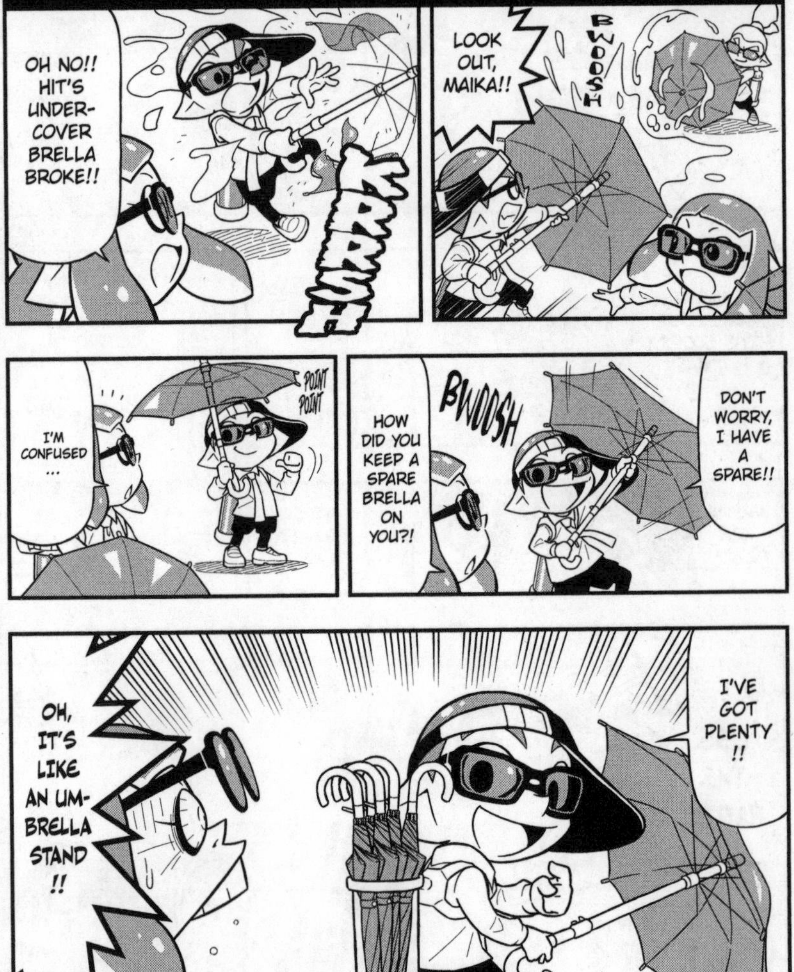
BWOOSH
LOOK OUT, MAIKA!!
OH NO!! HIT'S UNDER-COVER BRELLA BROKE!!
KRRSH
DON'T WORRY, I HAVE A SPARE!!
BWOOSH
HOW DID YOU KEEP A SPARE BRELLA ON YOU?!
POINT POINT
I'M CONFUSED ...
I'VE GOT PLENTY !!
OH, IT'S LIKE AN UM-BRELLA STAND !!

SUPER SLOW

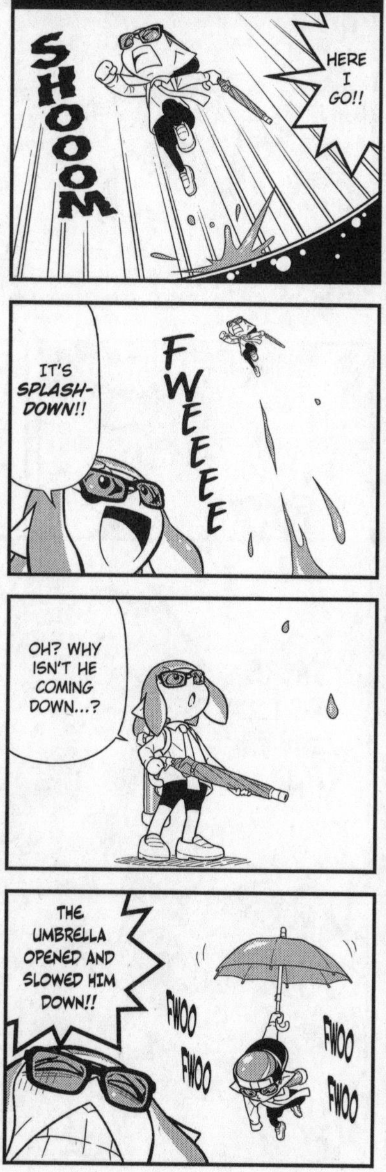
HERE I GO!!
SHOOOM
FWEEEE
IT'S *SPLASH-DOWN!!*
OH? WHY ISN'T HE COMING DOWN...?
THE UMBRELLA OPENED AND SLOWED HIM DOWN!!
FWOO FWOO
FWOO FWOO

INK MINE

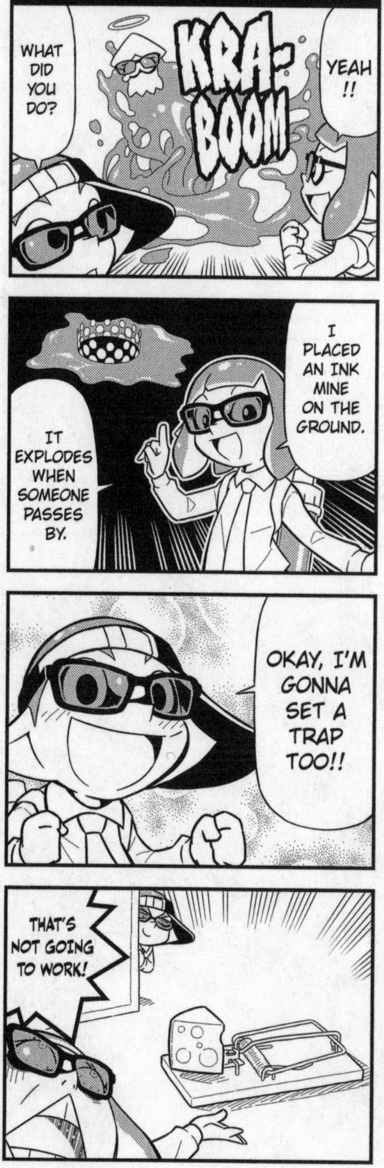
YEAH!!
KRA-BOOM
WHAT DID YOU DO?
I PLACED AN INK MINE ON THE GROUND.
IT EXPLODES WHEN SOMEONE PASSES BY.
OKAY, I'M GONNA SET A TRAP TOO!!
THAT'S NOT GOING TO WORK!

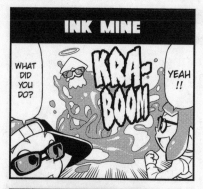

INK MINES GALORE

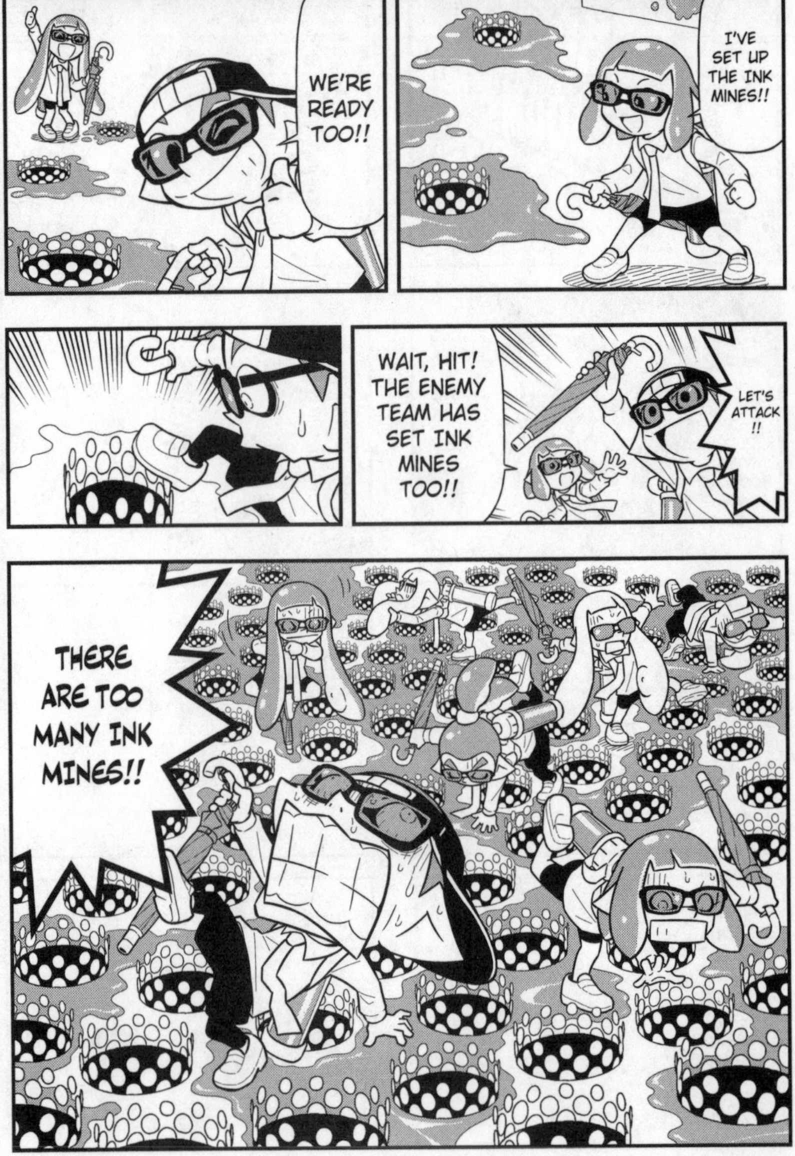

I'VE SET UP THE INK MINES!!
WE'RE READY TOO!!
LET'S ATTACK!!
WAIT, HIT! THE ENEMY TEAM HAS SET INK MINES TOO!!
THERE ARE TOO MANY INK MINES!!

TIME TO PLAY AT THE SUPERMARKET!

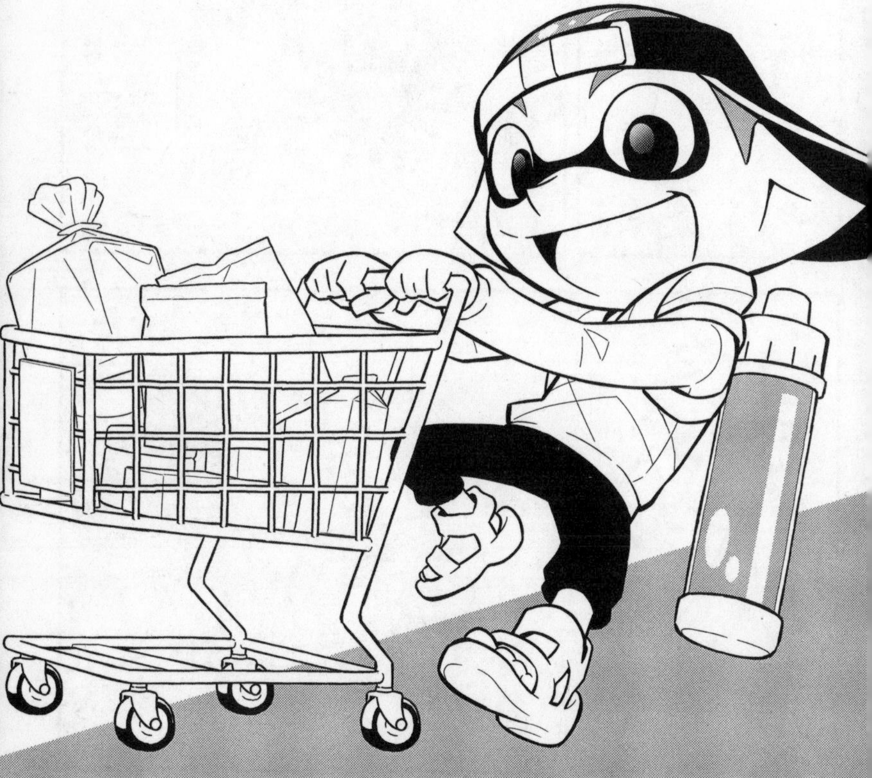

MAKOMART

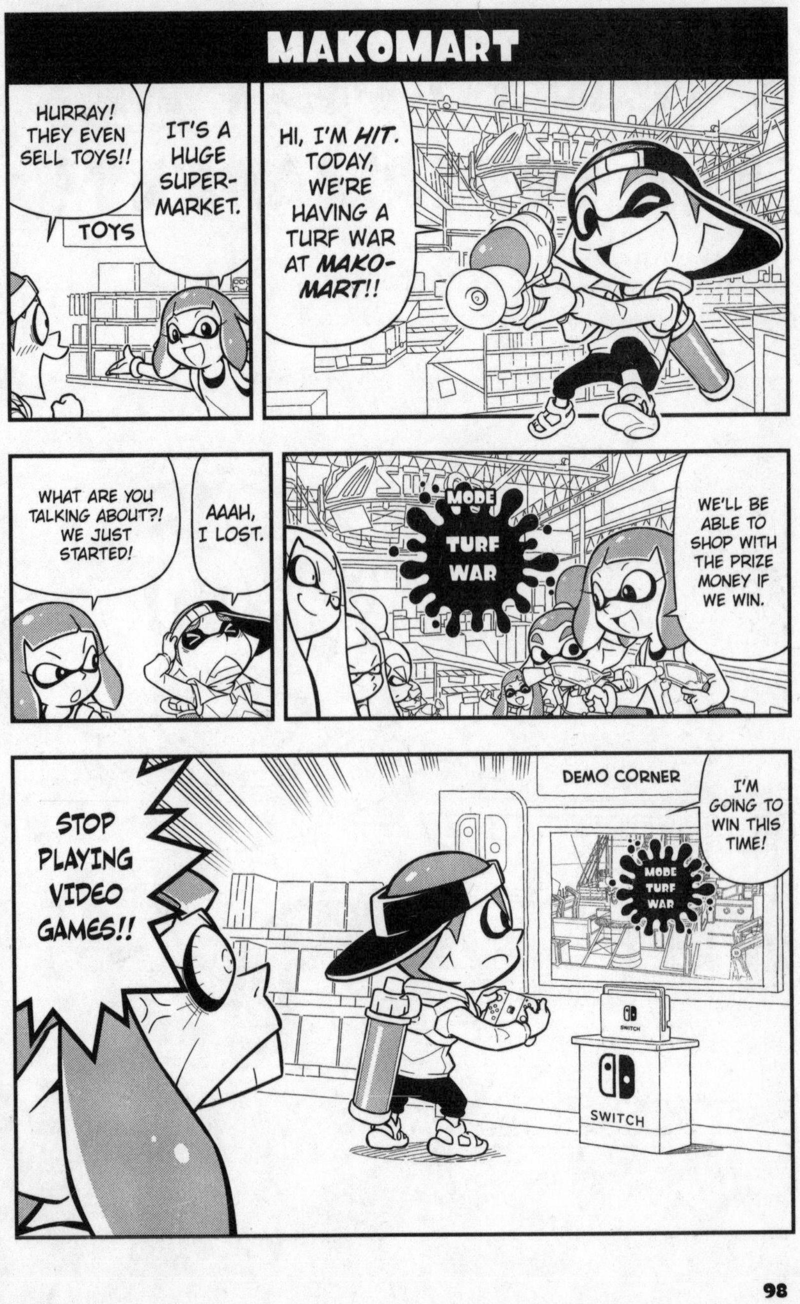
HI, I'M HIT. TODAY, WE'RE HAVING A TURF WAR AT MAKOMART!!
IT'S A HUGE SUPERMARKET.
HURRAY! THEY EVEN SELL TOYS!!
TOYS
WE'LL BE ABLE TO SHOP WITH THE PRIZE MONEY IF WE WIN.
MODE
TURF WAR
AAAH, I LOST.
WHAT ARE YOU TALKING ABOUT?! WE JUST STARTED!
I'M GOING TO WIN THIS TIME!
DEMO CORNER
MODE
TURF WAR
SWITCH
SWITCH
STOP PLAYING VIDEO GAMES!!

WORKING

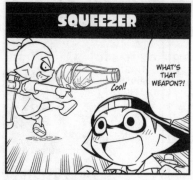

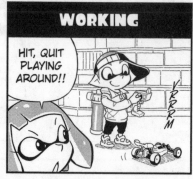

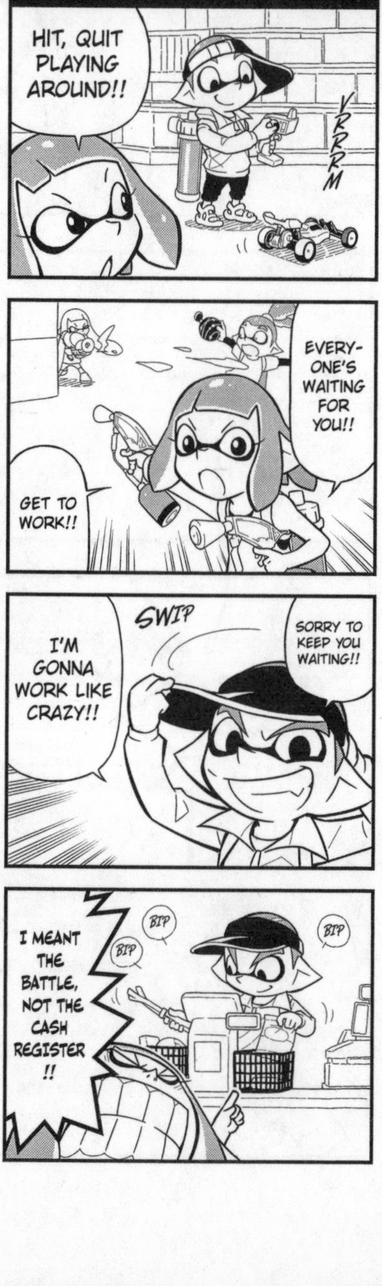
HIT, QUIT PLAYING AROUND!!
VRRRM
EVERY-ONE'S WAITING FOR YOU!!
GET TO WORK!!
SORRY TO KEEP YOU WAITING!!
SWIP
I'M GONNA WORK LIKE CRAZY!!
BIP
BIP
BIP
I MEANT THE BATTLE, NOT THE CASH REGISTER!!

SQUEEZER

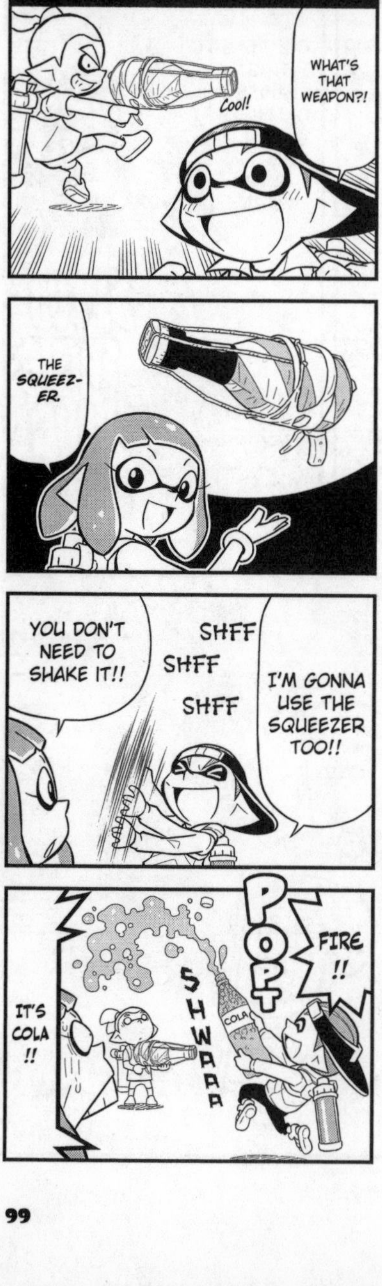
WHAT'S THAT WEAPON?!
Cool!
THE SQUEEZ-ER.
I'M GONNA USE THE SQUEEZER TOO!!
SHFF
SHFF
SHFF
YOU DON'T NEED TO SHAKE IT!!
FIRE!!
POP
SHWAAA
COLA
IT'S COLA!!

DISAPPEARING INK

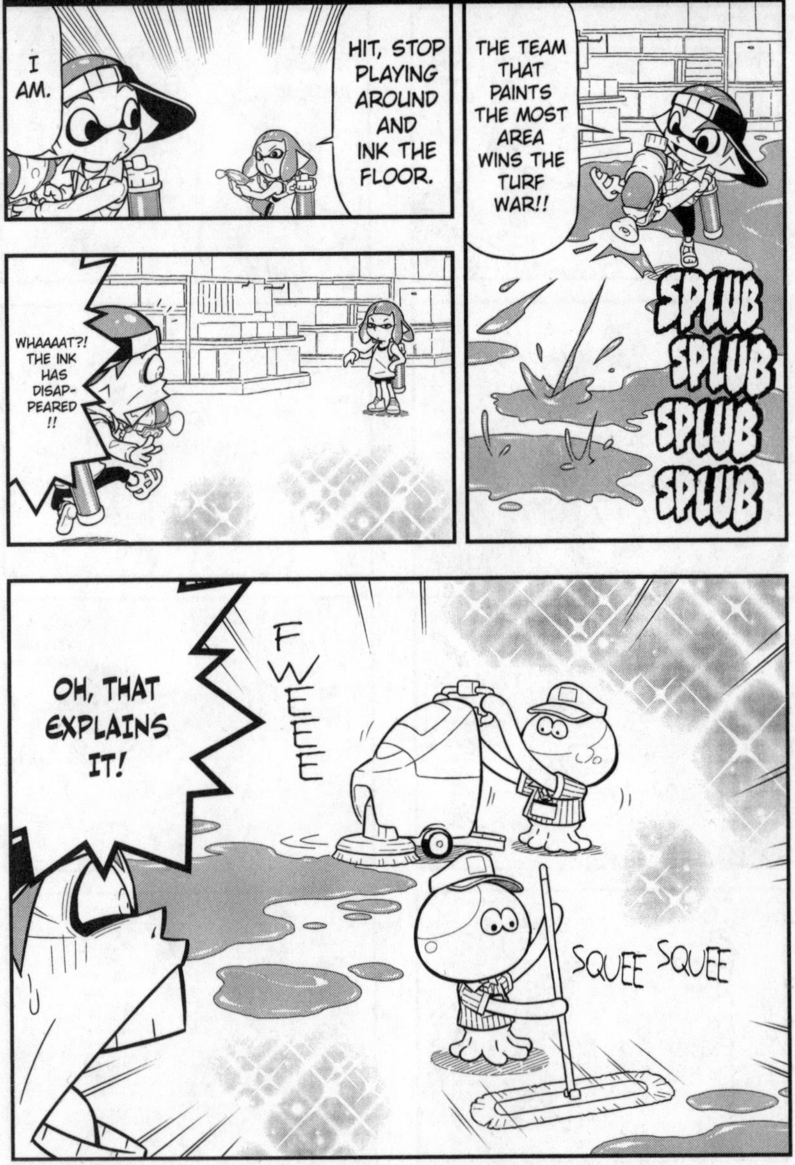
HIT, STOP PLAYING AROUND AND INK THE FLOOR.
I AM.
THE TEAM THAT PAINTS THE MOST AREA WINS THE TURF WAR!!
SPLUB SPLUB SPLUB SPLUB
WHAAAAT?! THE INK HAS DISAP-PEARED !!
OH, THAT EXPLAINS IT!
FWEEE
SQUEE SQUEE

GET THERE FAST

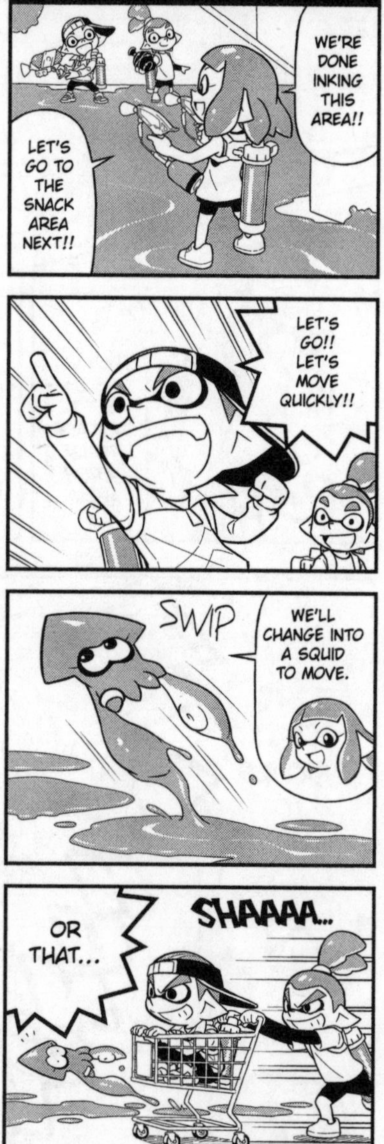
WE'RE DONE INKING THIS AREA!!
LET'S GO TO THE SNACK AREA NEXT!!
LET'S GO!! LET'S MOVE QUICKLY!!
WE'LL CHANGE INTO A SQUID TO MOVE.
SWIP
SHAAAA...
OR THAT...

REFILL

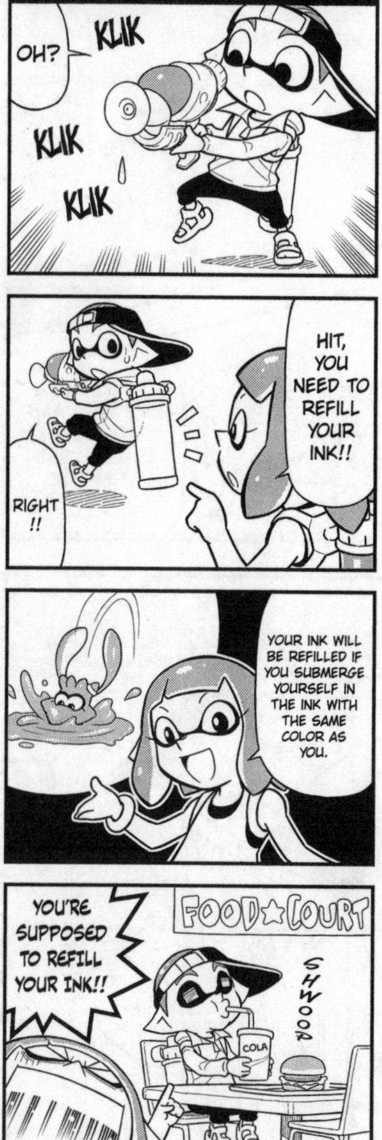
KLIK
OH?
KLIK
KLIK
HIT, YOU NEED TO REFILL YOUR INK!!
RIGHT!!
YOUR INK WILL BE REFILLED IF YOU SUBMERGE YOURSELF IN THE INK WITH THE SAME COLOR AS YOU.
FOOD★COURT
SHWOOR
YOU'RE SUPPOSED TO REFILL YOUR INK!!
COLA

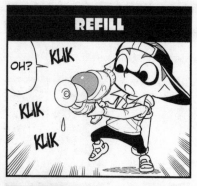

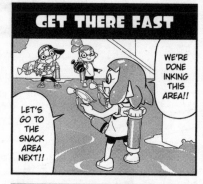

ATTACK FROM ABOVE

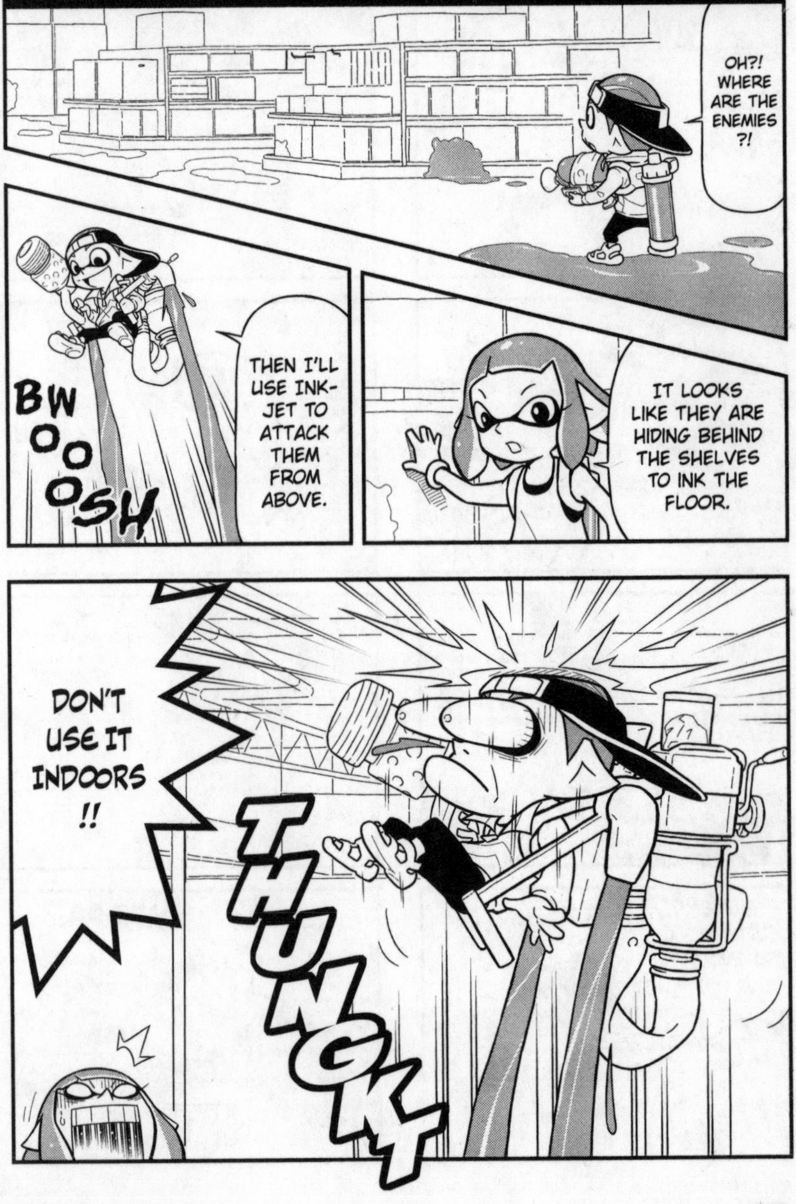
OH?! WHERE ARE THE ENEMIES ?!
IT LOOKS LIKE THEY ARE HIDING BEHIND THE SHELVES TO INK THE FLOOR.
THEN I'LL USE INK-JET TO ATTACK THEM FROM ABOVE.
BWOOOOSH
THUNK
DON'T USE IT INDOORS !!

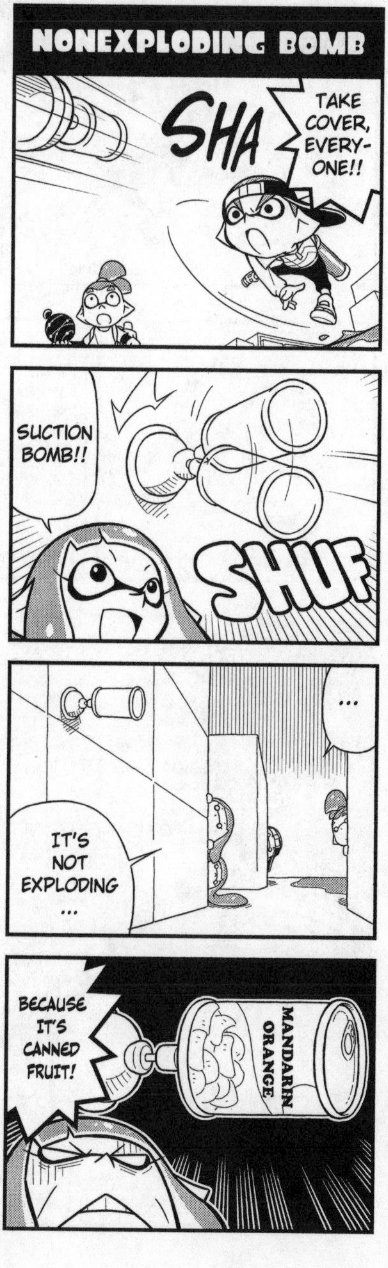
NONEXPLODING BOMB
TAKE COVER, EVERY-ONE!!
SHA
SUCTION BOMB!!
SHUF
...
IT'S NOT EXPLODING ...
MANDARIN ORANGE
BECAUSE IT'S CANNED FRUIT!

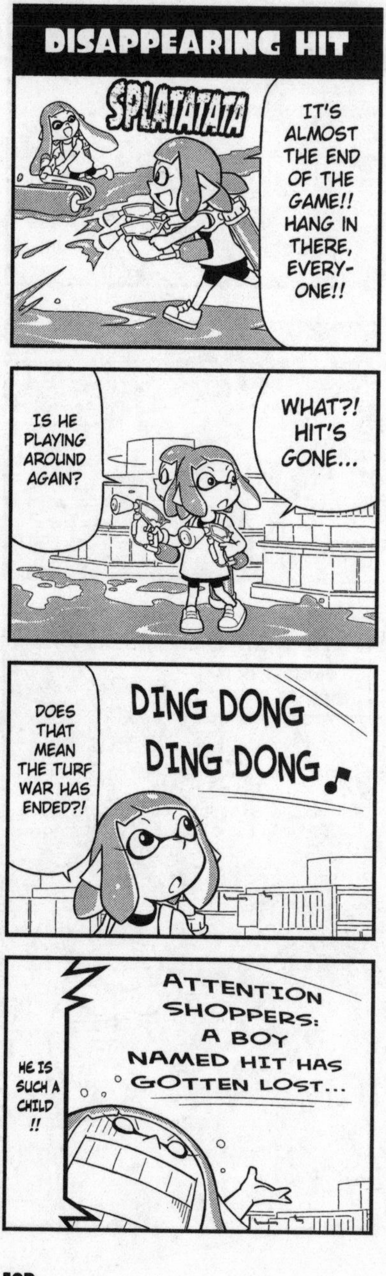
DISAPPEARING HIT
IT'S ALMOST THE END OF THE GAME!! HANG IN THERE, EVERY-ONE!!
SPLATATATA
WHAT?! HIT'S GONE...
IS HE PLAYING AROUND AGAIN?
DING DONG DING DONG
DOES THAT MEAN THE TURF WAR HAS ENDED?!
ATTENTION SHOPPERS: A BOY NAMED HIT HAS GOTTEN LOST...
HE IS SUCH A CHILD !!

AFTER THE MATCH

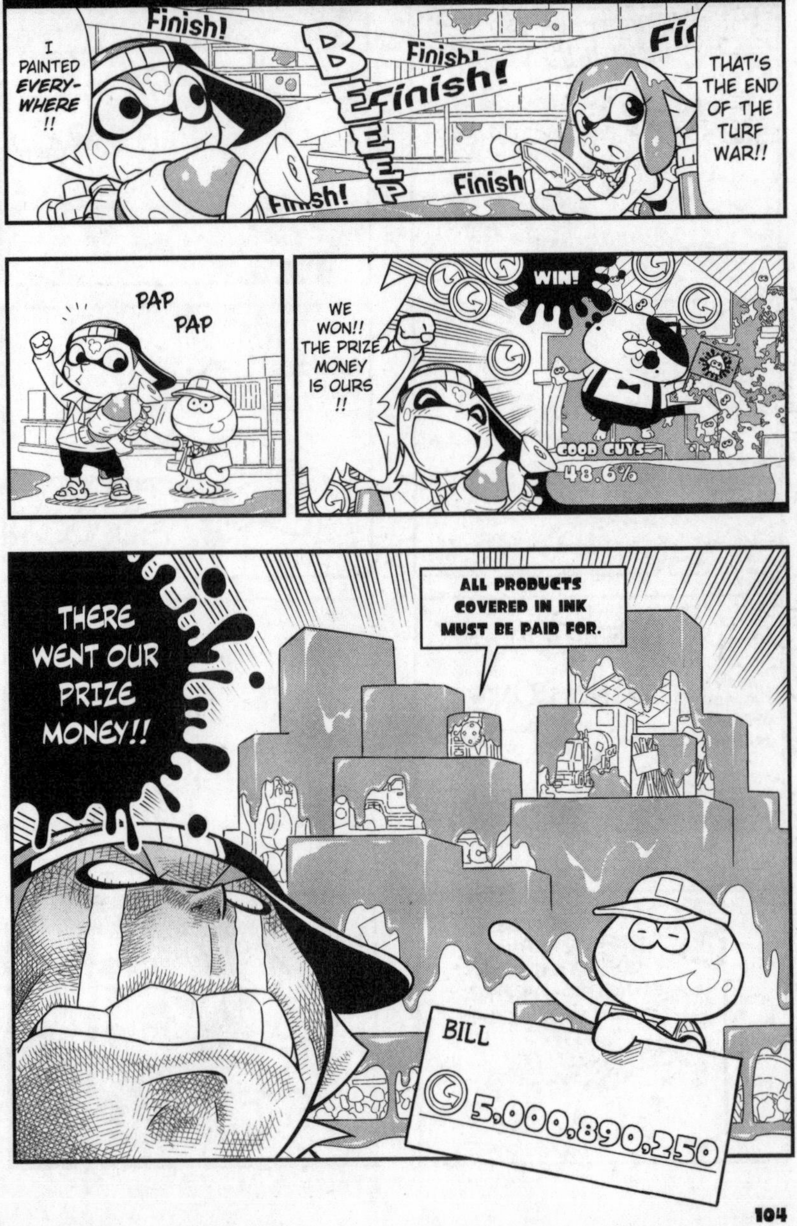
THAT'S THE END OF THE TURF WAR!!
Finish!
BEEEEP
I PAINTED EVERYWHERE!!
WIN!
WE WON!! THE PRIZE MONEY IS OURS!!
GOOD GUYS
48.6%
PAP PAP
ALL PRODUCTS COVERED IN INK MUST BE PAID FOR.
THERE WENT OUR PRIZE MONEY!!
BILL
5,000,890,250

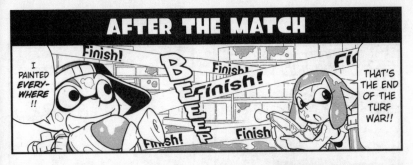

TIME TO PLAY SOME BASKETBALL FOR A CHANGE!

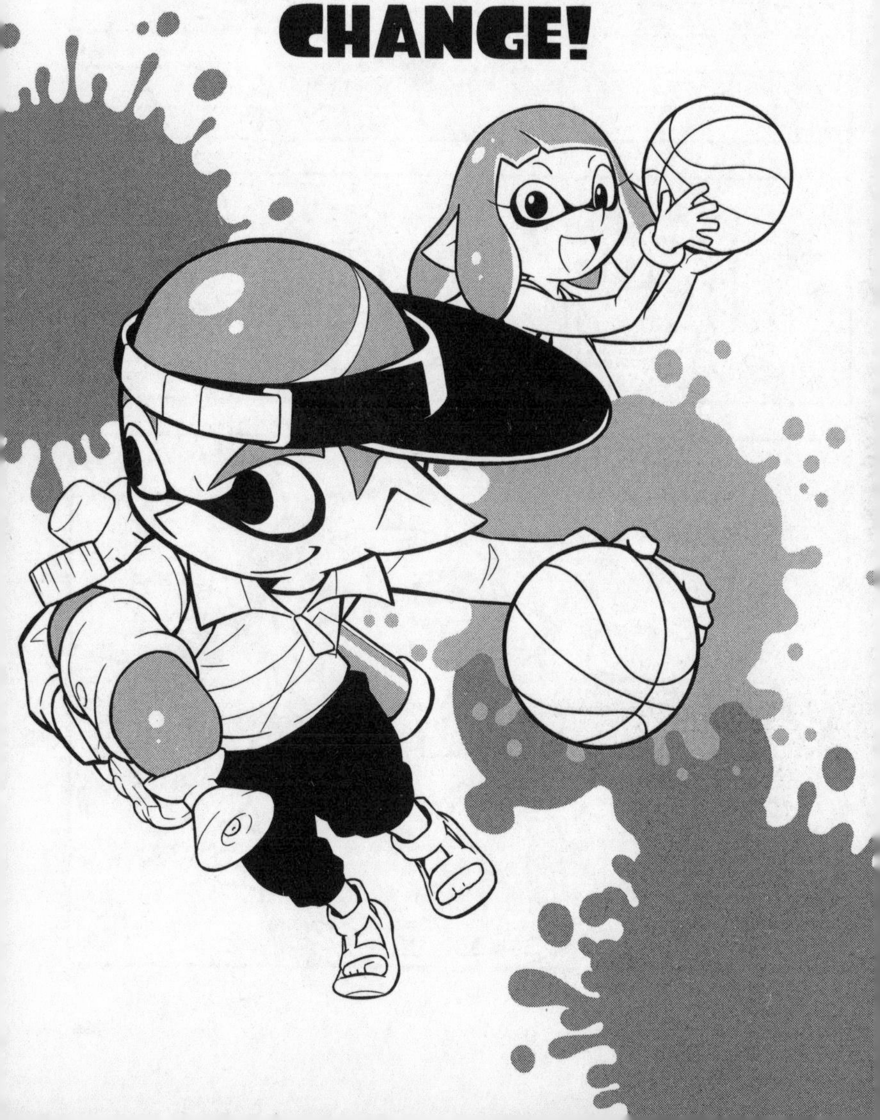

GOBY STADIUM

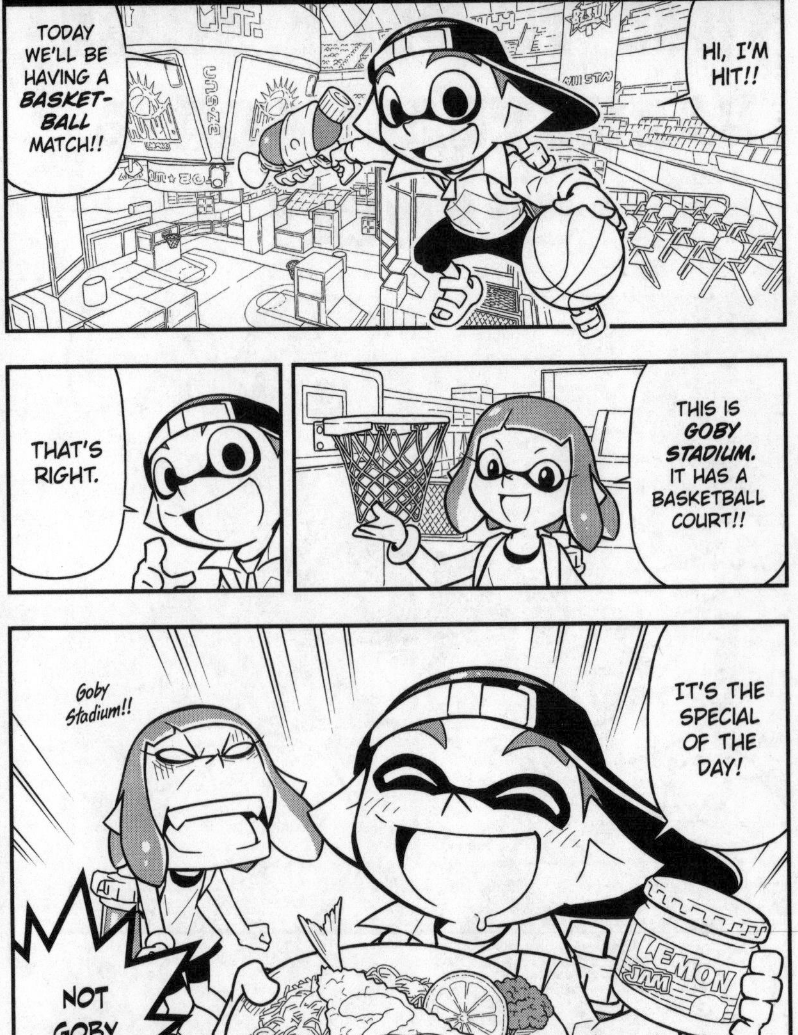
HI, I'M HIT!!
TODAY WE'LL BE HAVING A *BASKETBALL* MATCH!!
THIS IS *GOBY STADIUM.* IT HAS A BASKETBALL COURT!!
THAT'S RIGHT.
IT'S THE SPECIAL OF THE DAY!
Goby Stadium!!
LEMON JAM
NOT GOBY AND JAM!!

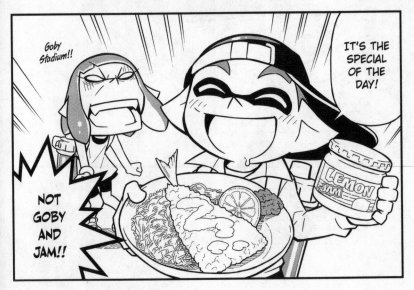

DRIBBLE

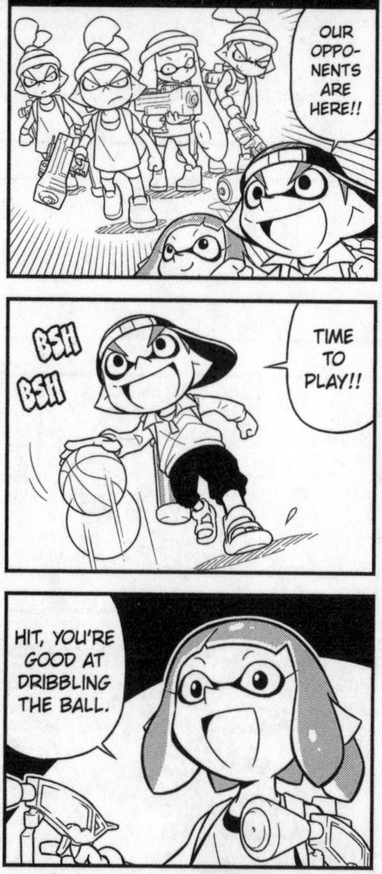
OUR OPPONENTS ARE HERE!!
TIME TO PLAY!!
BSH
BSH
HIT, YOU'RE GOOD AT DRIBBLING THE BALL.
IT'S A BURST BOMB YOYO!!
BSH
BSH

IMPENETRABLE NET

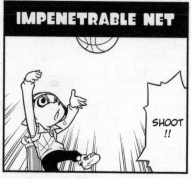

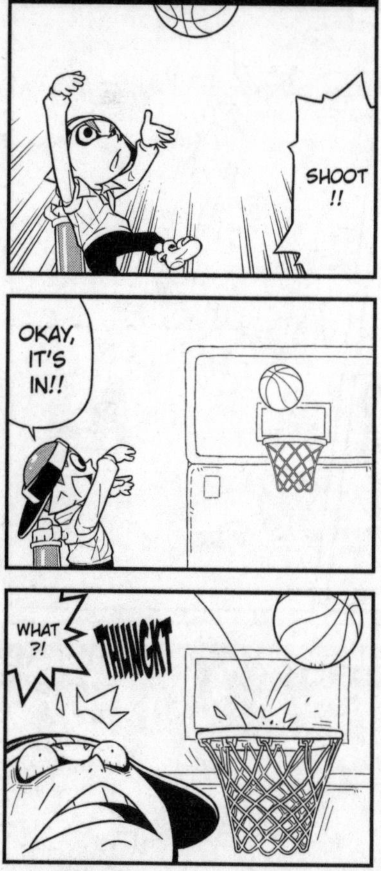
SHOOT!!
OKAY, IT'S IN!!
WHAT?!
THUNGKT
A STRAINER?!
Why?!

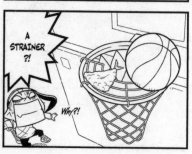

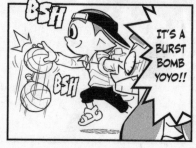

PASS

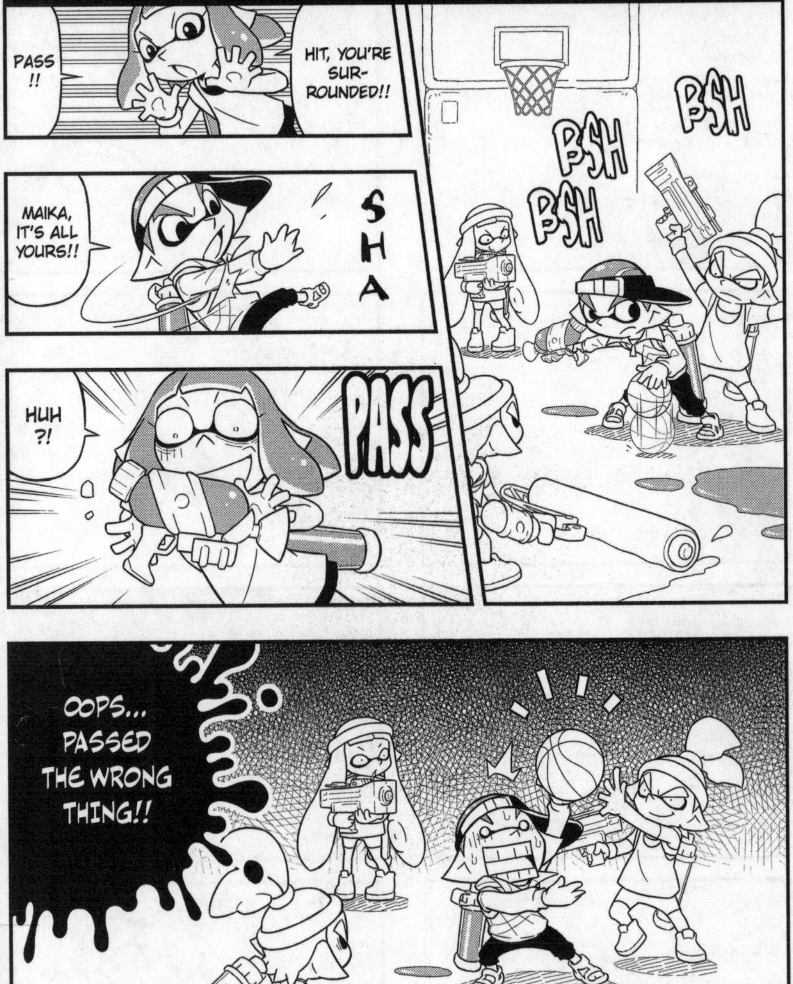
BSH
BSH
BSH
HIT, YOU'RE SUR-ROUNDED!!
PASS !!
SHA
MAIKA, IT'S ALL YOURS!!
PASS
HUH ?!
OOPS... PASSED THE WRONG THING!!

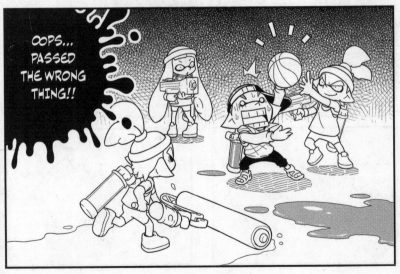

PASS CUT

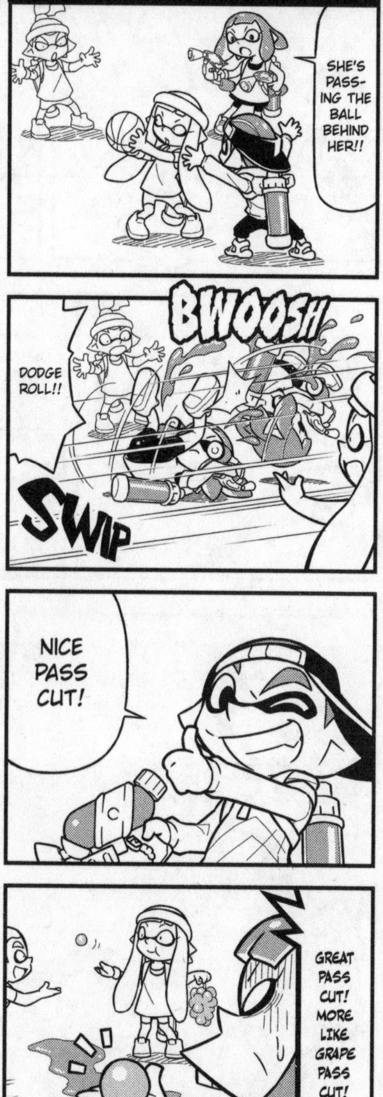

SHE'S PASSING THE BALL BEHIND HER!!
BWOOSH
DODGE ROLL!!
SWIP
NICE PASS CUT!
GREAT PASS CUT! MORE LIKE GRAPE PASS CUT!

SUCTION BOMB GUARD

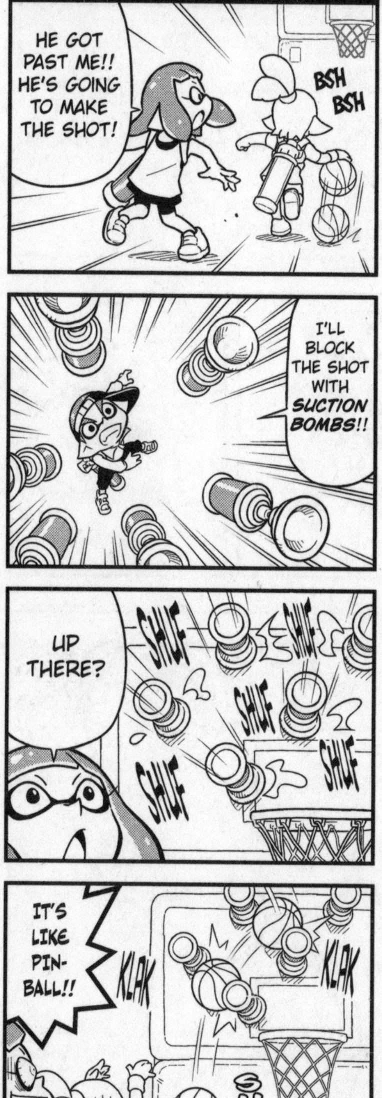

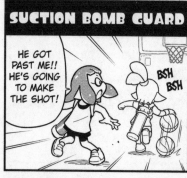

HE GOT PAST ME!! HE'S GOING TO MAKE THE SHOT!
BSH BSH
I'LL BLOCK THE SHOT WITH *SUCTION BOMBS*!!
SHUF
SHUF
SHUF
SHUF
SHUF
UP THERE?
KLAK
KLAK
IT'S LIKE PIN-BALL!!
SHUP

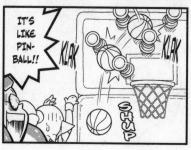

THE NET

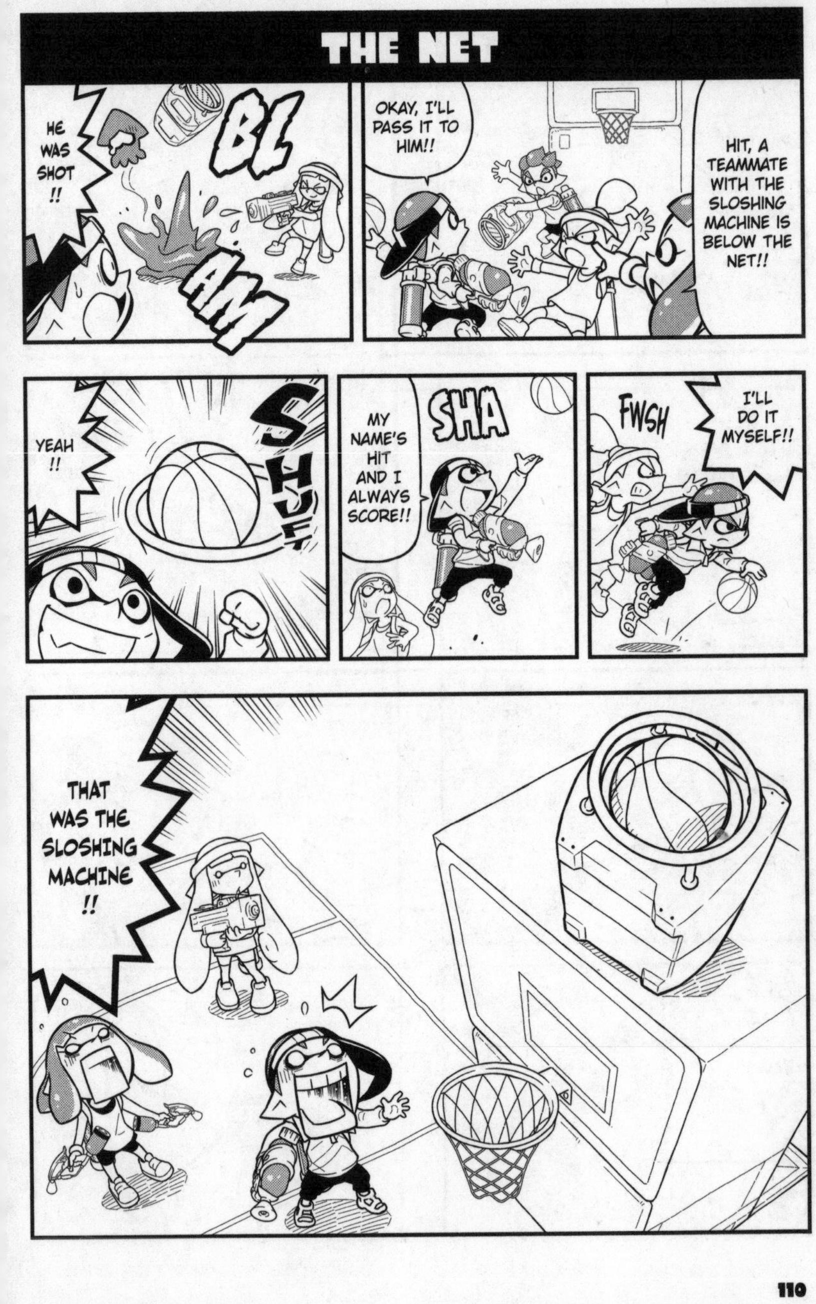

HIT, A TEAMMATE WITH THE SLOSHING MACHINE IS BELOW THE NET!!
OKAY, I'LL PASS IT TO HIM!!
BL
AM
HE WAS SHOT!!
I'LL DO IT MYSELF!!
FWSH
SHA
MY NAME'S HIT AND I ALWAYS SCORE!!
SHUF
YEAH!!
THAT WAS THE SLOSHING MACHINE!!

AUDIENCE

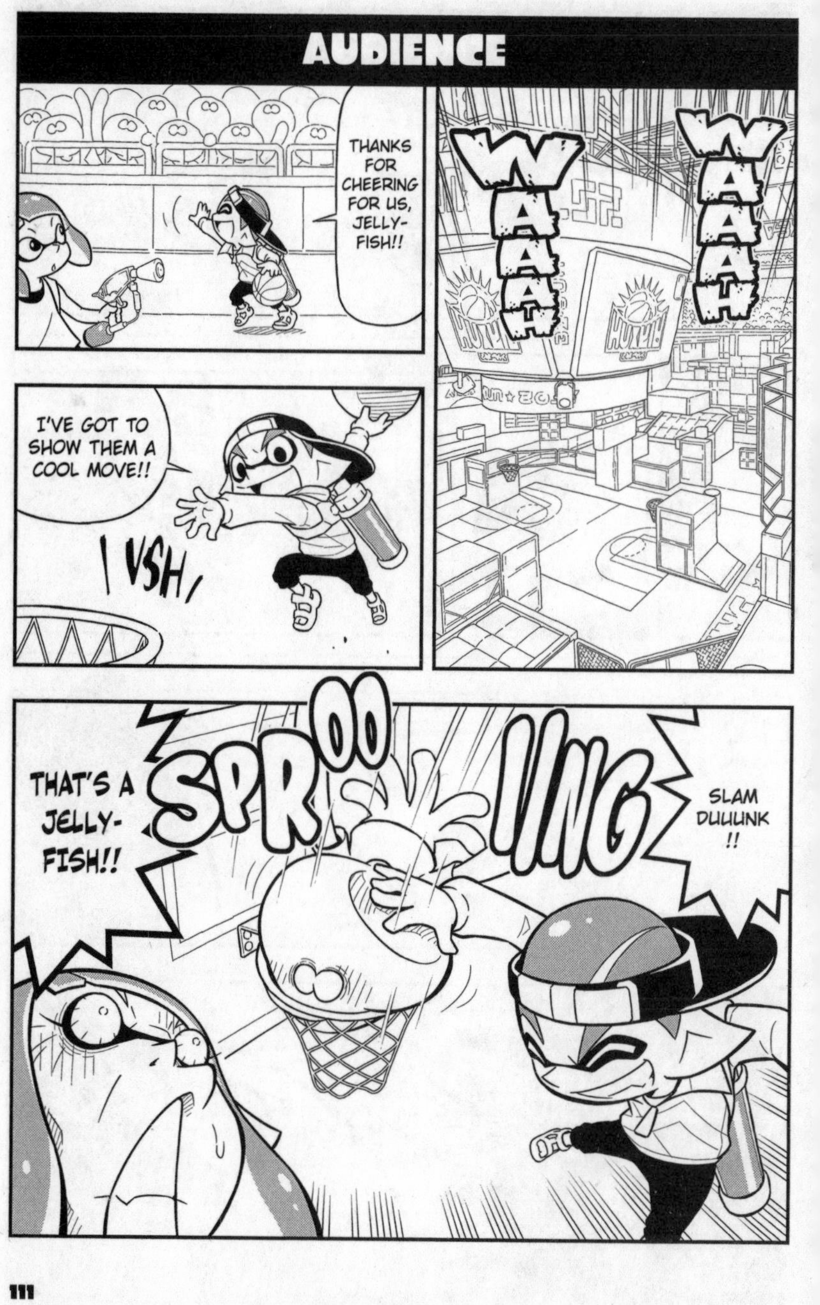
WAAAH
WAAAH
THANKS FOR CHEERING FOR US, JELLY-FISH!!
I'VE GOT TO SHOW THEM A COOL MOVE!!
VSH
SLAM DUUUNK !!
SPROOOING
THAT'S A JELLY-FISH!!

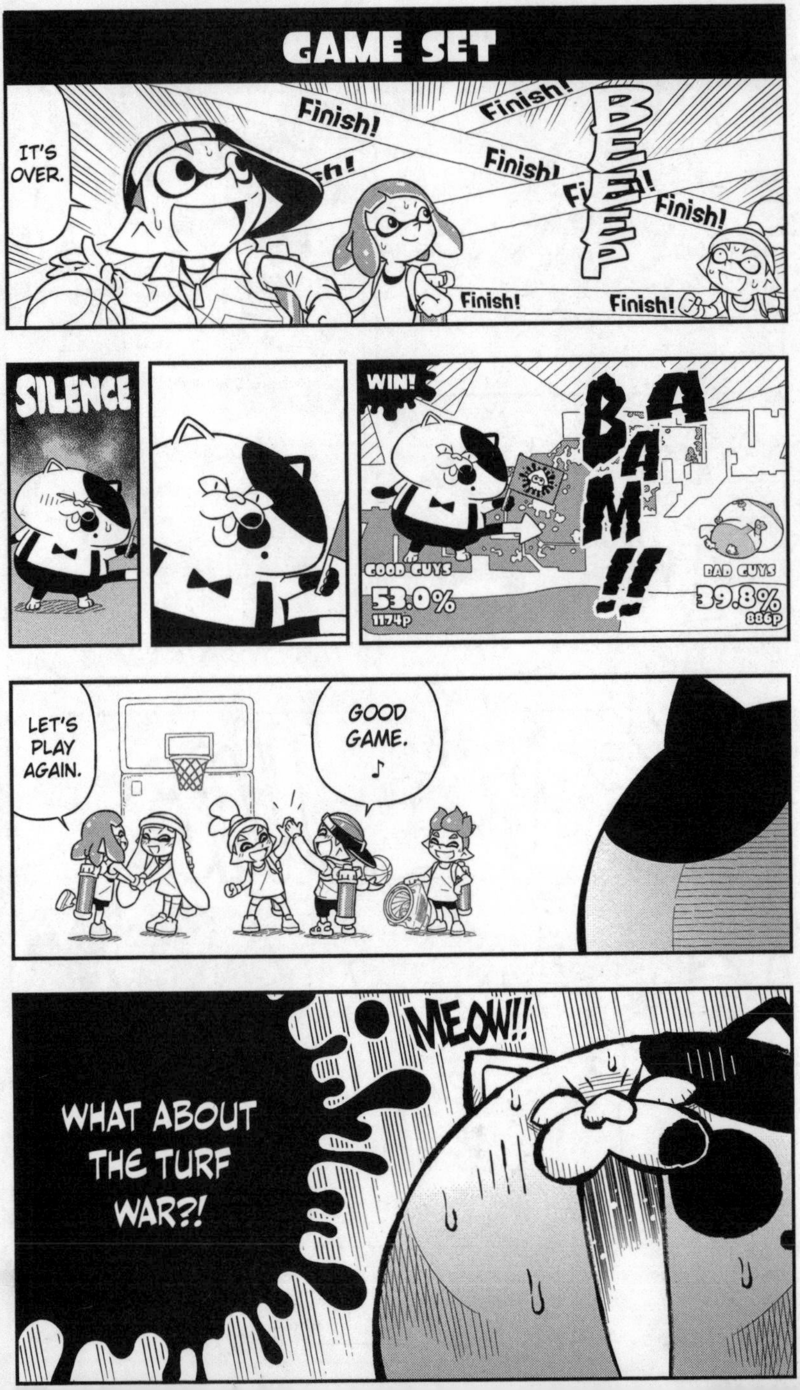
GAME SET
Finish!
Finish!
Finish!
Finish!
Finish!
Finish!
IT'S OVER.
WIN!
BAM!!
GOOD GUYS
53.0%
1174P
BAD GUYS
39.8%
886P
SILENCE
GOOD GAME. ♪
LET'S PLAY AGAIN.
MEOW!!
WHAT ABOUT THE TURF WAR?!

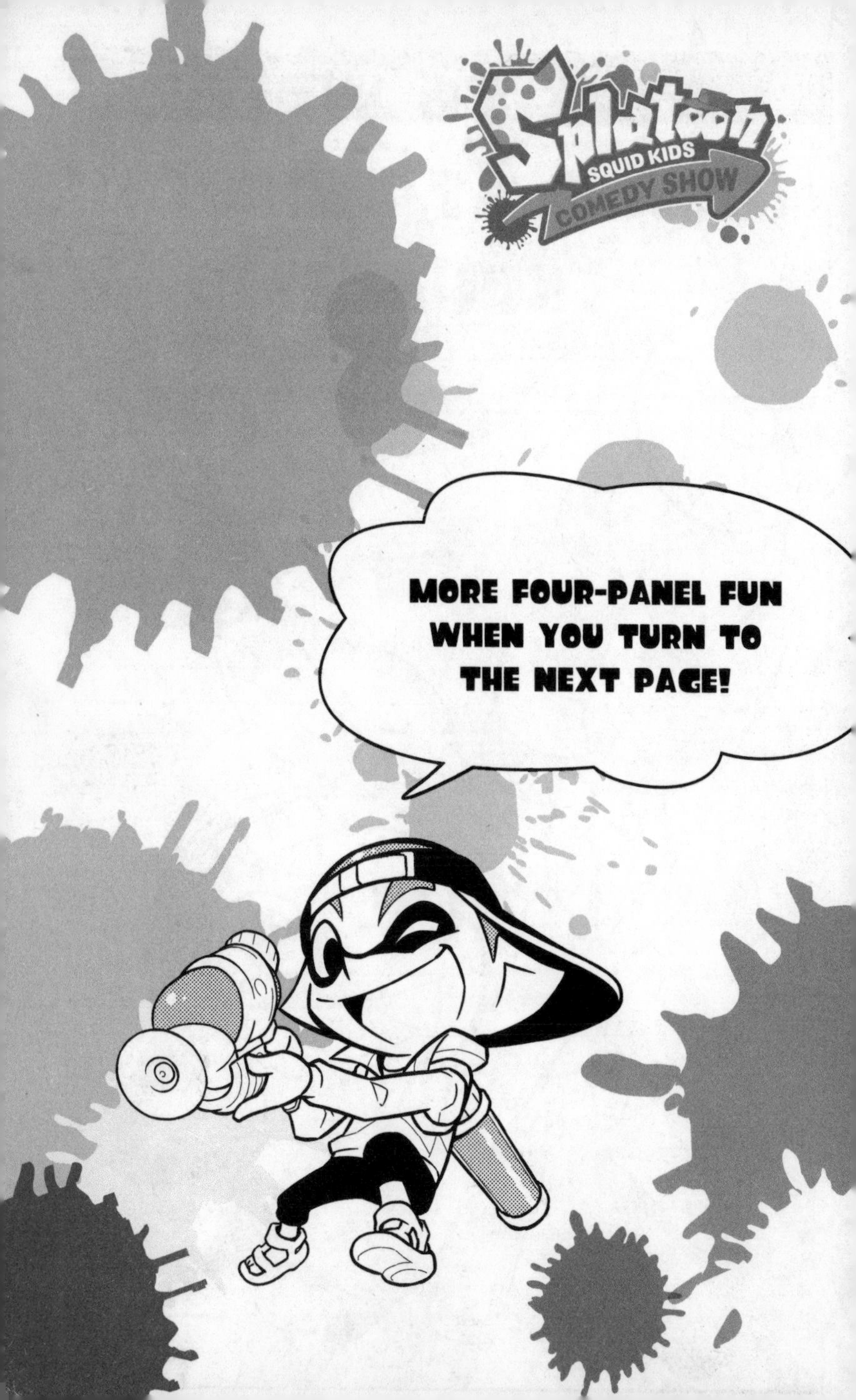
Splatoon
SQUID KIDS
COMEDY SHOW
MORE FOUR-PANEL FUN WHEN YOU TURN TO THE NEXT PAGE!

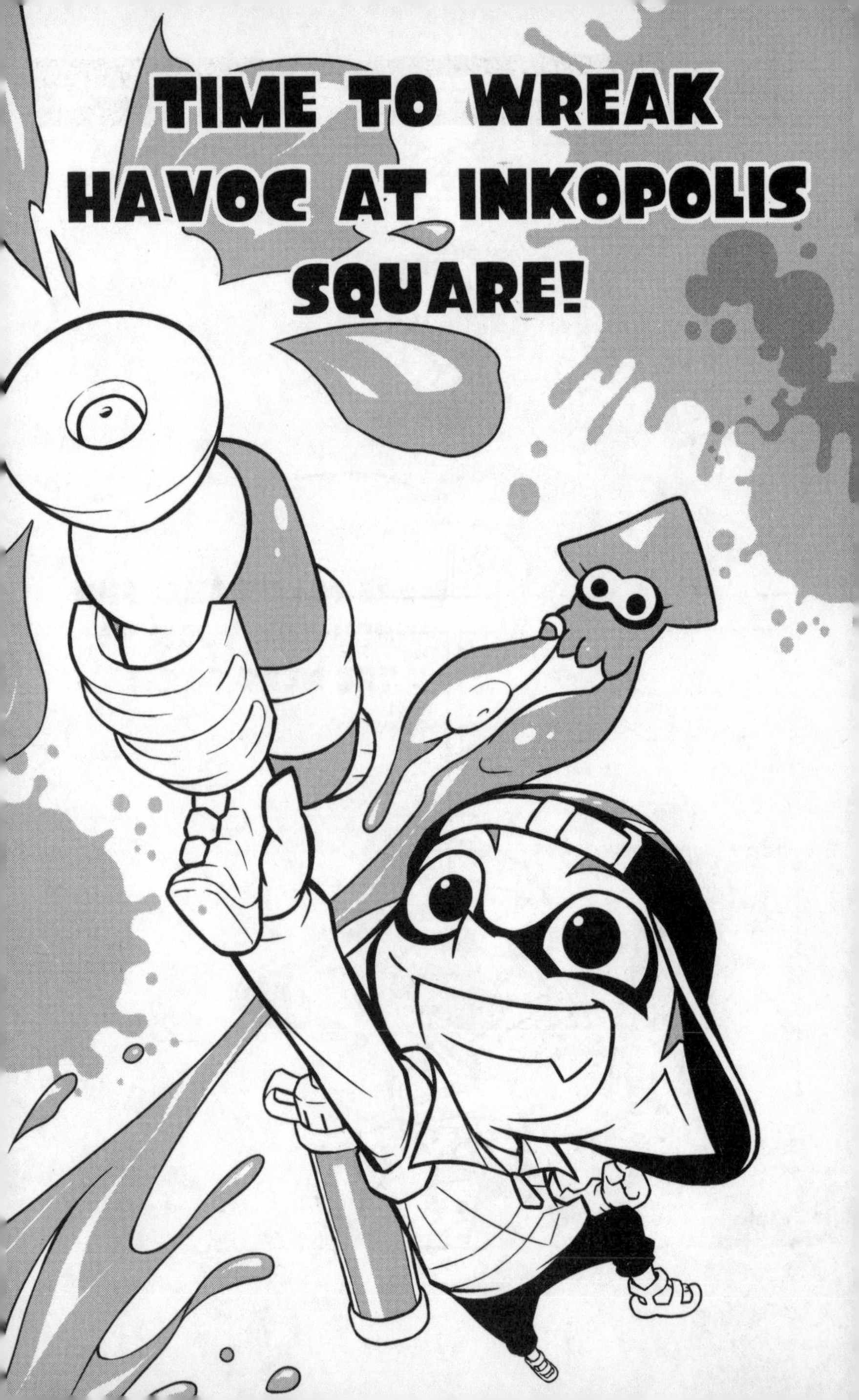
TIME TO WREAK HAVOC AT INKOPOLIS SQUARE!

EVOLVED FROM A SQUID

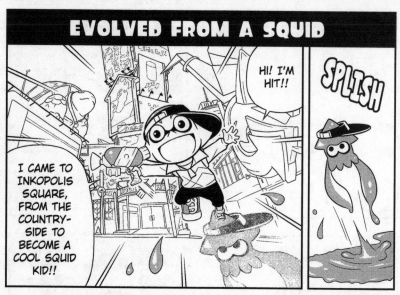

SPLISH
HI! I'M HIT!!
I CAME TO INKOPOLIS SQUARE, FROM THE COUNTRY-SIDE TO BECOME A COOL SQUID KID!!
THAT'S MY FRIEND MAIKA OVER THERE. SHE'S TEACHING ME ALL SORTS OF THINGS.
SPLISH
WE EVOLVED FROM SQUIDS, SO WE CAN TURN INTO SQUIDS.
WHAT'S WRONG, MAIKA?! YOU LOOK SO OLD!
THAT'S A DRIED SQUID...

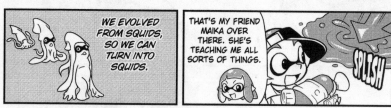

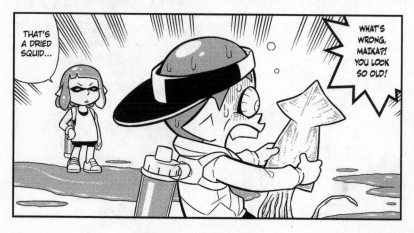

DUAL WEAPON

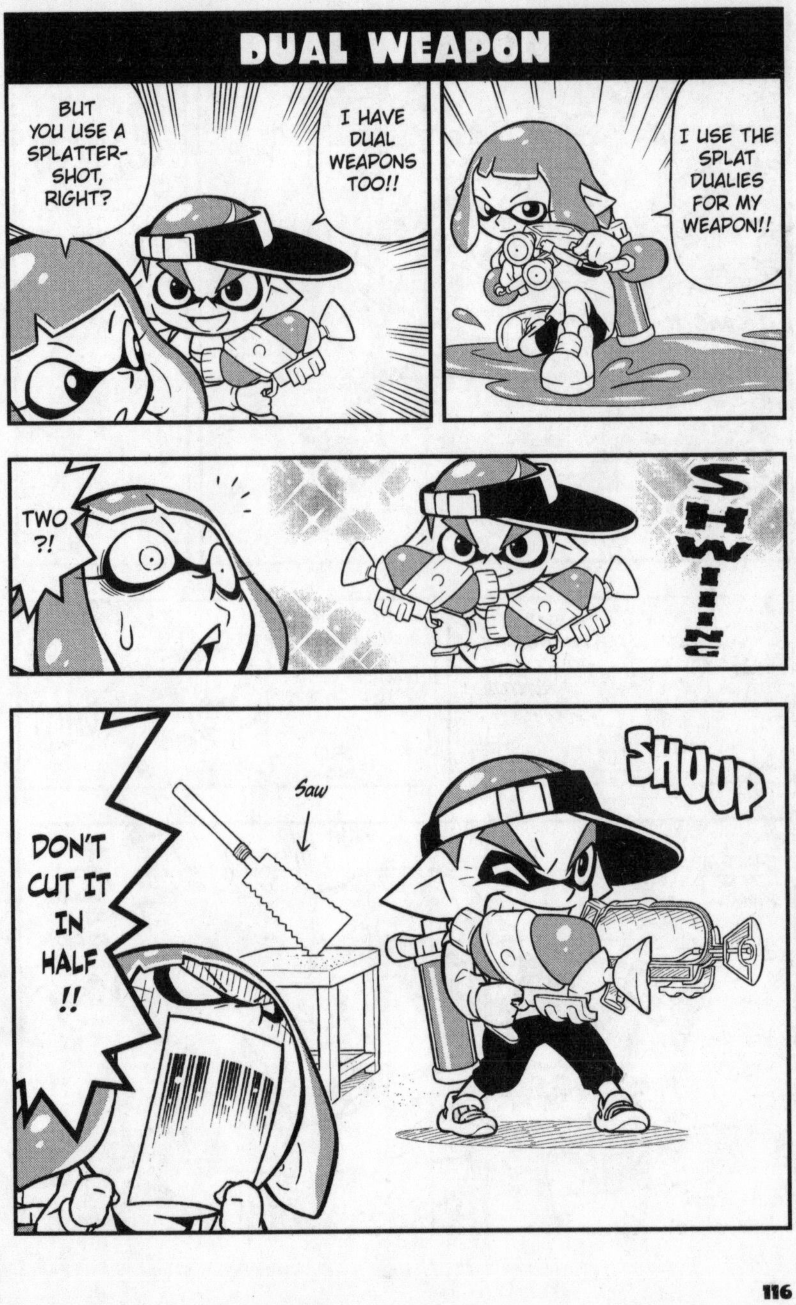
I USE THE SPLAT DUALIES FOR MY WEAPON!!
I HAVE DUAL WEAPONS TOO!!
BUT YOU USE A SPLATTER-SHOT, RIGHT?
SHWIIING
TWO ?!
SHUUP
Saw
DON'T CUT IT IN HALF !!

DODGE ROLL

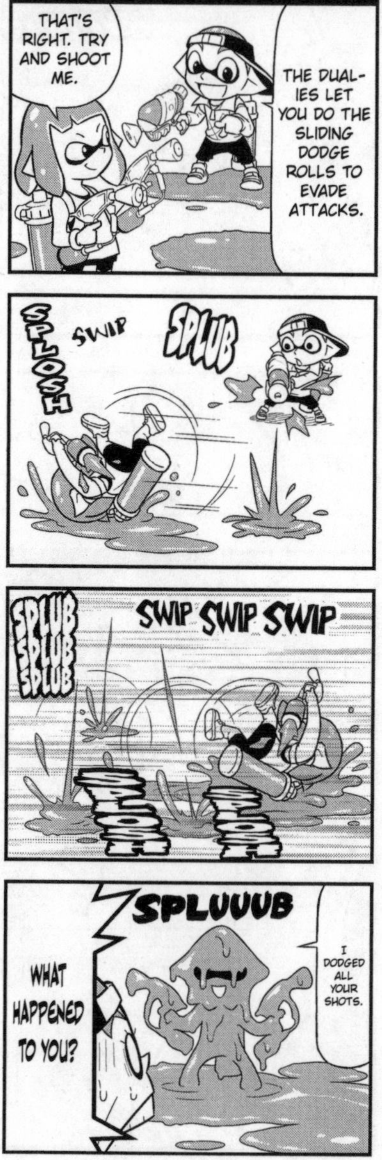
THE DUALIES LET YOU DO THE SLIDING DODGE ROLLS TO EVADE ATTACKS.
THAT'S RIGHT. TRY AND SHOOT ME.
SPLUB
SWIP
SPLOSH
SWIP SWIP SWIP
SPLUB SPLUB SPLUB
SPLUUUB
I DODGED ALL YOUR SHOTS.
WHAT HAPPENED TO YOU?

COLOR

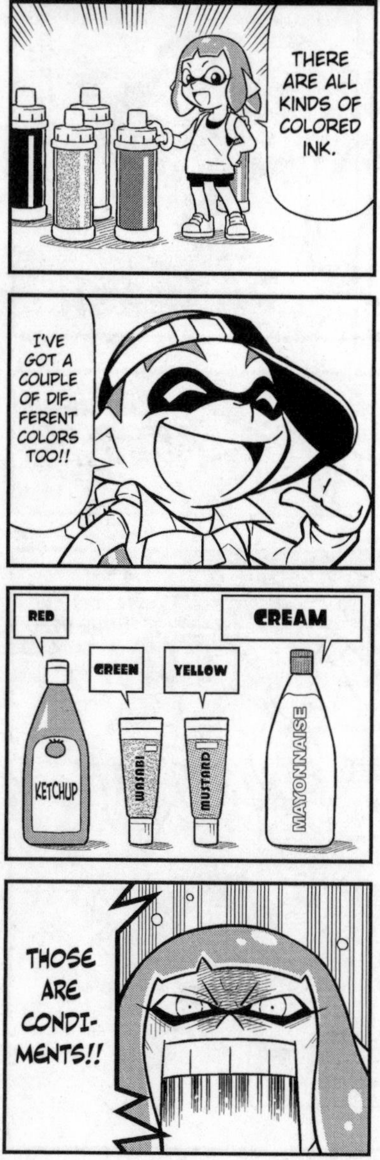
THERE ARE ALL KINDS OF COLORED INK.
I'VE GOT A COUPLE OF DIFFERENT COLORS TOO!!
CREAM
MAYONNAISE
YELLOW
MUSTARD
GREEN
WASABI
RED
KETCHUP
THOSE ARE CONDIMENTS!!

BEES

AHHHHHH!!
DAAAASH
BUZZZZZ
BEES ?!
INK THE GROUND AND DIVE INTO IT!!
HURRY, HIT!!
WHY ARE THE BEES ATTACKING ME?
THAT'S WHY!!
SPLUURB!!!
HONEY

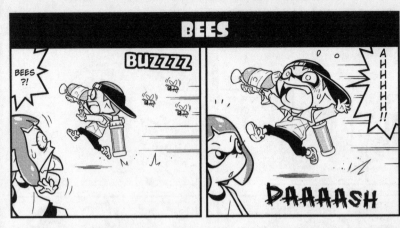

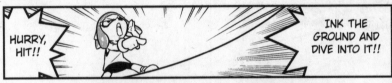

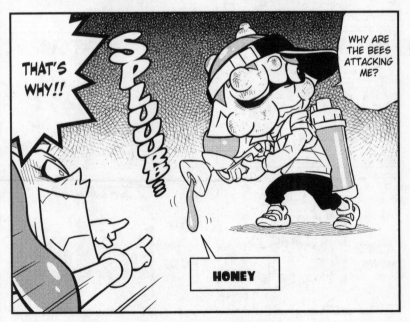

SQUID JUMP

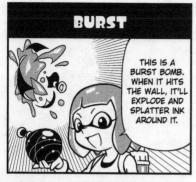

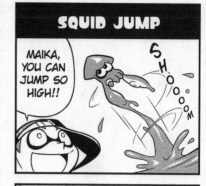

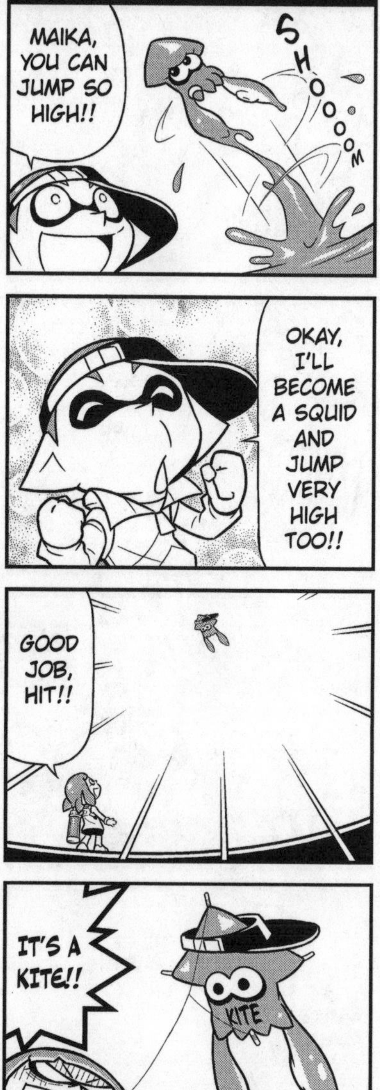
MAIKA, YOU CAN JUMP SO HIGH!!
SHOOOOOM
OKAY, I'LL BECOME A SQUID AND JUMP VERY HIGH TOO!!
GOOD JOB, HIT!!
IT'S A KITE!!
KITE

BURST

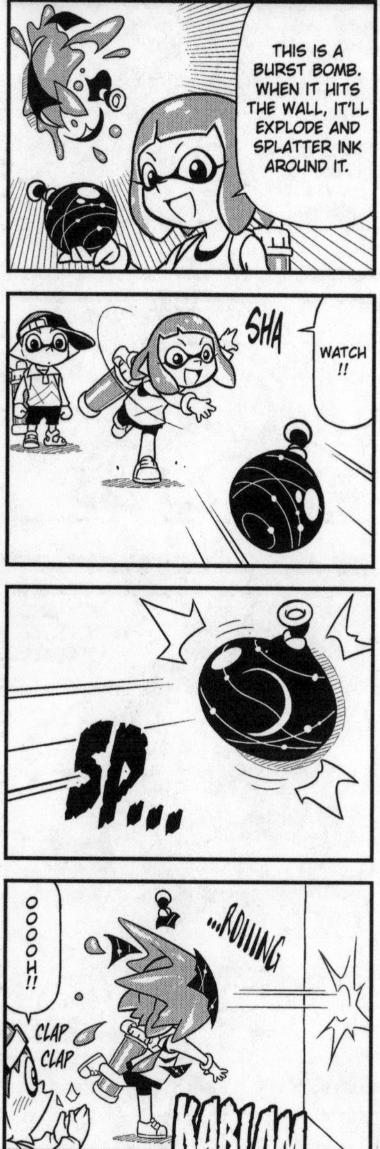
THIS IS A BURST BOMB. WHEN IT HITS THE WALL, IT'LL EXPLODE AND SPLATTER INK AROUND IT.
WATCH!!
SHA
SP...
OOOOOH!!
...ROLLING
CLAP CLAP
KABLAM

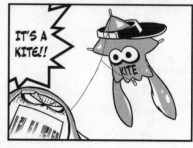

CURLING

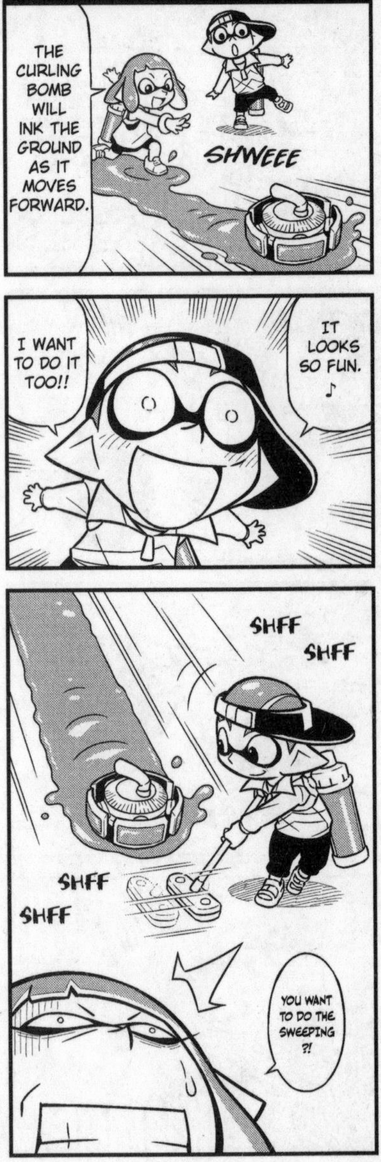
THE CURLING BOMB WILL INK THE GROUND AS IT MOVES FORWARD.
SHWEEE
IT LOOKS SO FUN. ♪
I WANT TO DO IT TOO!!
SHFF
SHFF
SHFF
SHFF
YOU WANT TO DO THE SWEEPING ?!

SUCTION

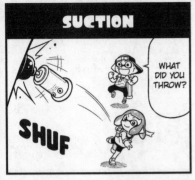

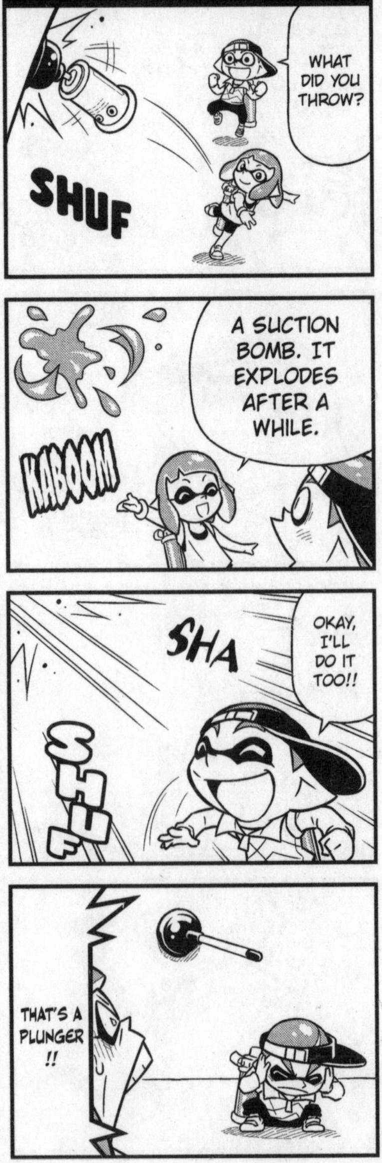
WHAT DID YOU THROW?
SHUF
A SUCTION BOMB. IT EXPLODES AFTER A WHILE.
KABOOM
OKAY, I'LL DO IT TOO!!
SHA
SHUF
THAT'S A PLUNGER !!

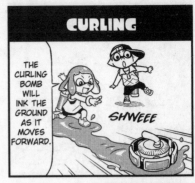

THROWING TENTA MISSILES

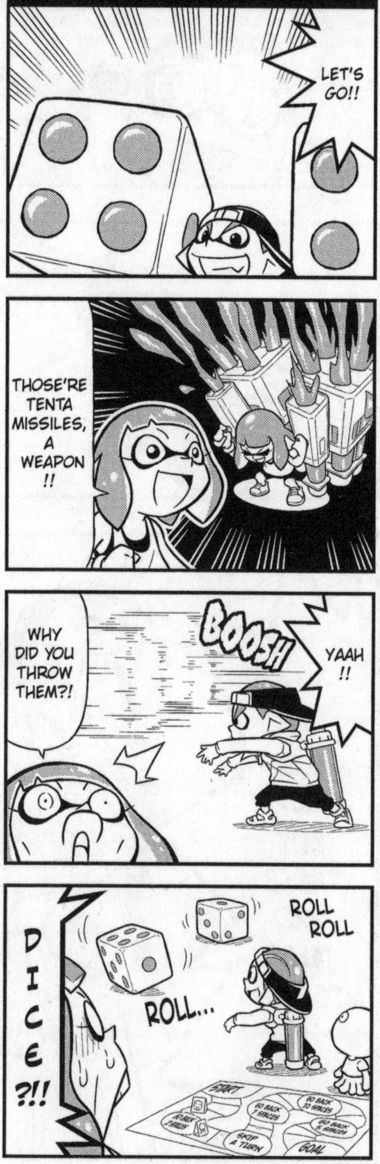
LET'S GO!!
THOSE'RE TENTA MISSILES, A WEAPON !!
YAAH !!
BOOSH
WHY DID YOU THROW THEM?!
ROLL ROLL
ROLL...
DICE ?!!
START
GO BACK 10 SPACES
GO BACK 7 SPACES
GO BACK 5 SPACES
SKIP A TURN
GOAL

PENETRATE

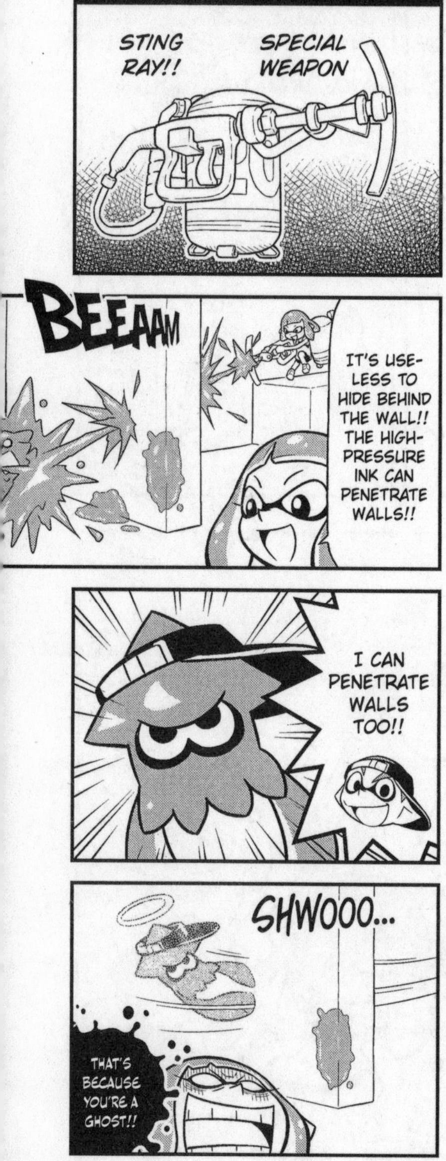
SPECIAL WEAPON
STING RAY!!
IT'S USE-LESS TO HIDE BEHIND THE WALL!! THE HIGH-PRESSURE INK CAN PENETRATE WALLS!!
BEEAAM
I CAN PENETRATE WALLS TOO!!
SHWOOO...
THAT'S BECAUSE YOU'RE A GHOST!!

SKY-HIGH

COO-OOOL!! AN INK-JET!!
BWOOOOSH
I WANT TO FLY TOO!!
OKAY, I'LL LET YOU FLY INTO THE SKY.
HURRAY!!
READY?!
HUUU-UUUUH?! BUT THESE ARE TENTA MISSILES!!

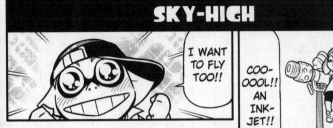

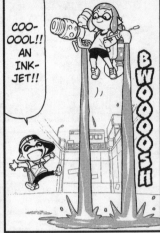

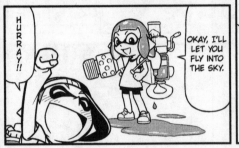

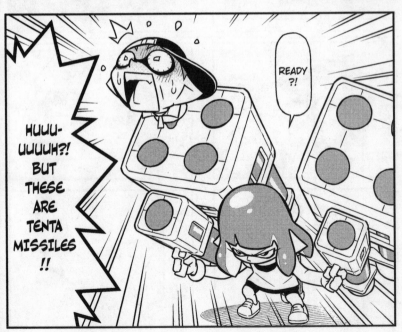

WEAPONS

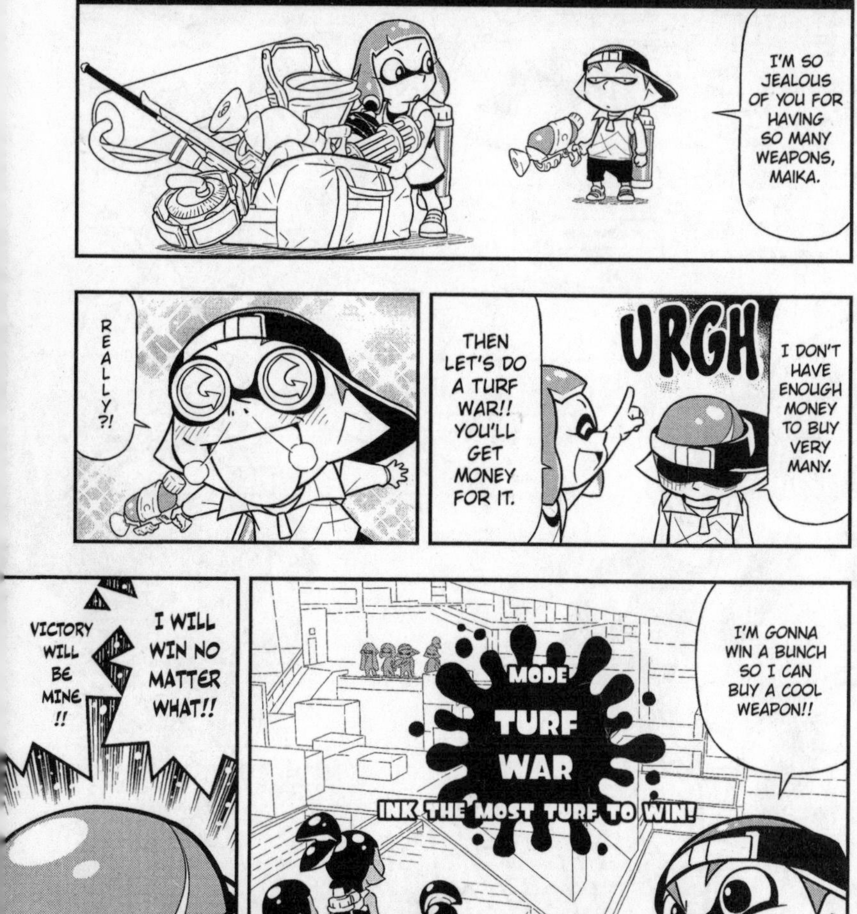

I'M SO JEALOUS OF YOU FOR HAVING SO MANY WEAPONS, MAIKA.
I DON'T HAVE ENOUGH MONEY TO BUY VERY MANY.
URGH
THEN LET'S DO A TURF WAR!! YOU'LL GET MONEY FOR IT.
REALLY?!
I'M GONNA WIN A BUNCH SO I CAN BUY A COOL WEAPON!!
MODE
TURF WAR
INK THE MOST TURF TO WIN!
I WILL WIN NO MATTER WHAT!!
VICTORY WILL BE MINE!!

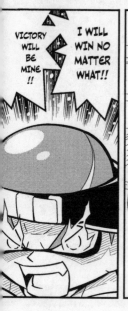

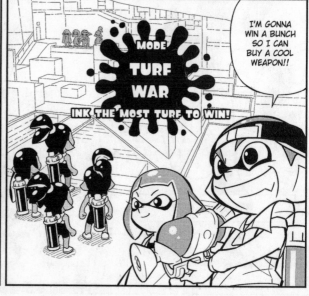

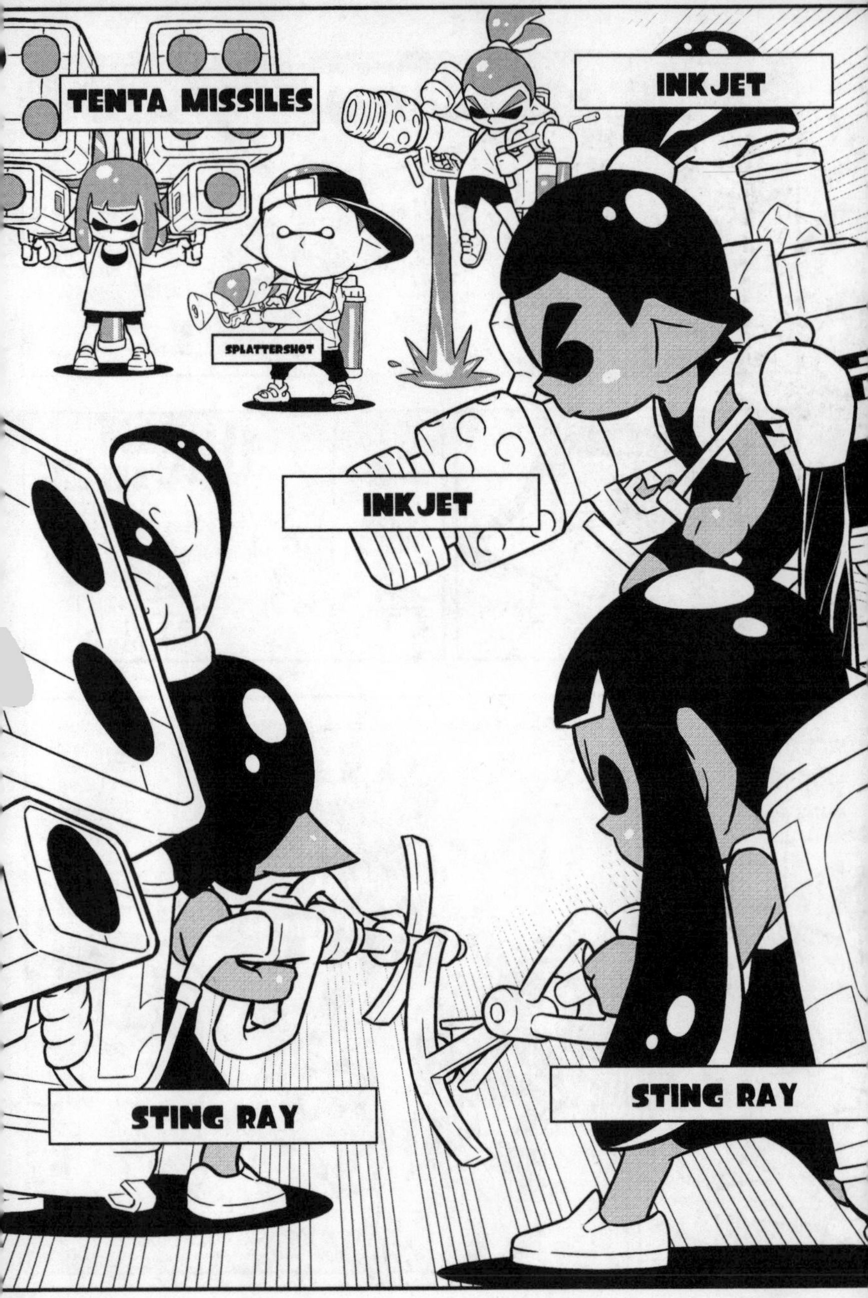
INKJET
TENTA MISSILES
SPLATTERSHOT
INKJET
STING RAY
STING RAY

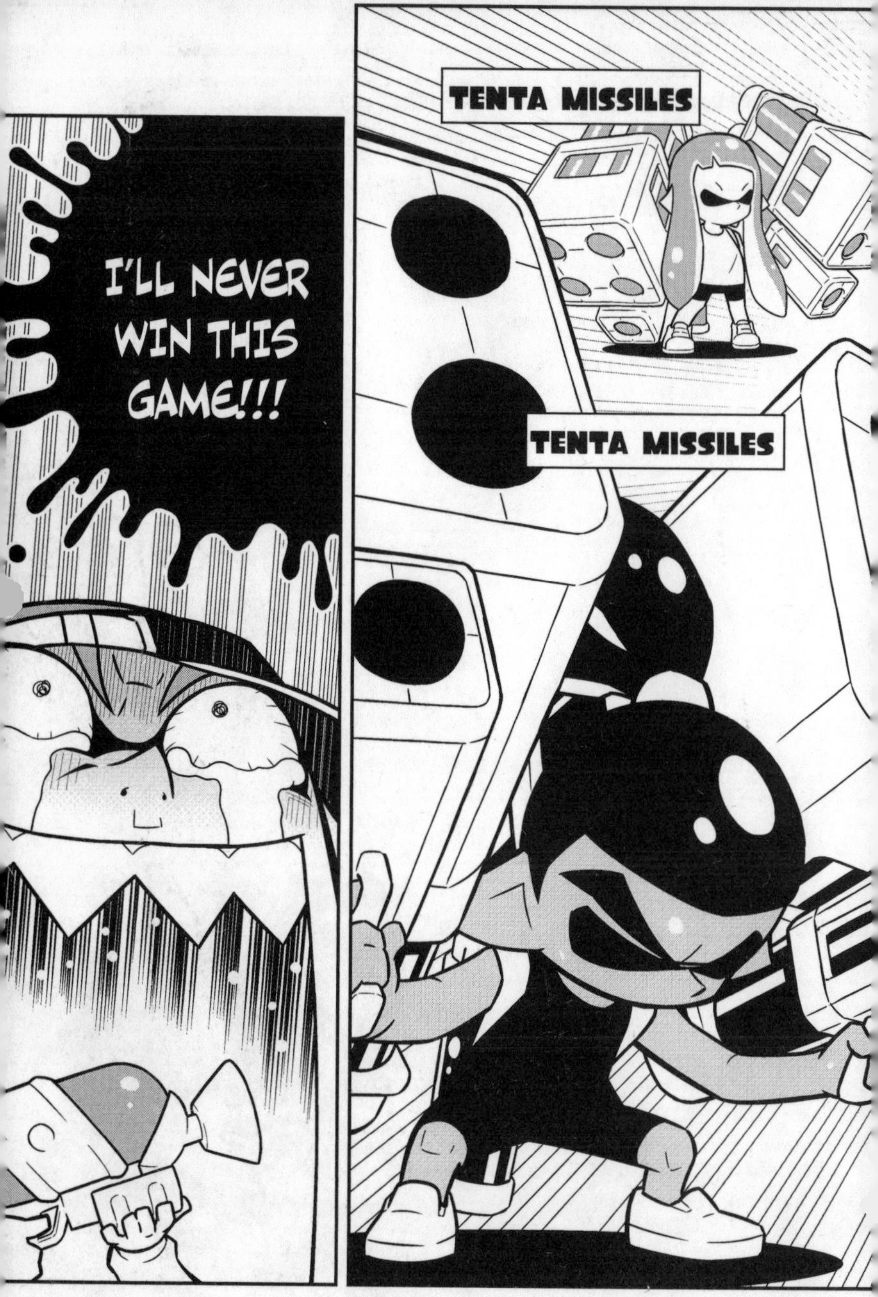
TENTA MISSILES
TENTA MISSILES
I'LL NEVER WIN THIS GAME!!!

HIDEKI GOTO

I love using the N-ZAP '85 in *Splatoon 2*. Its Special Weapon, Ink Armor, is useful too. ♪

Hideki Goto was born in Gifu Prefecture, Japan. He received an honorable mention in the 38th Shogakukan Newcomers' Comic Awards, Kids' Manga Division, in 1996 for his one-shot *Zenryoku Dadada*. His first serialization was *Manga de Hakken Tamagotchi: Bakusho 4-koma Gekijo*, which began in *Monthly Coro Coro Comics* in 1997. *Splatoon: Squid Kids Comedy Show* began its serialization in *Bessatsu Coro Coro Comics* in 2017 and is Goto's first work to be published in English.

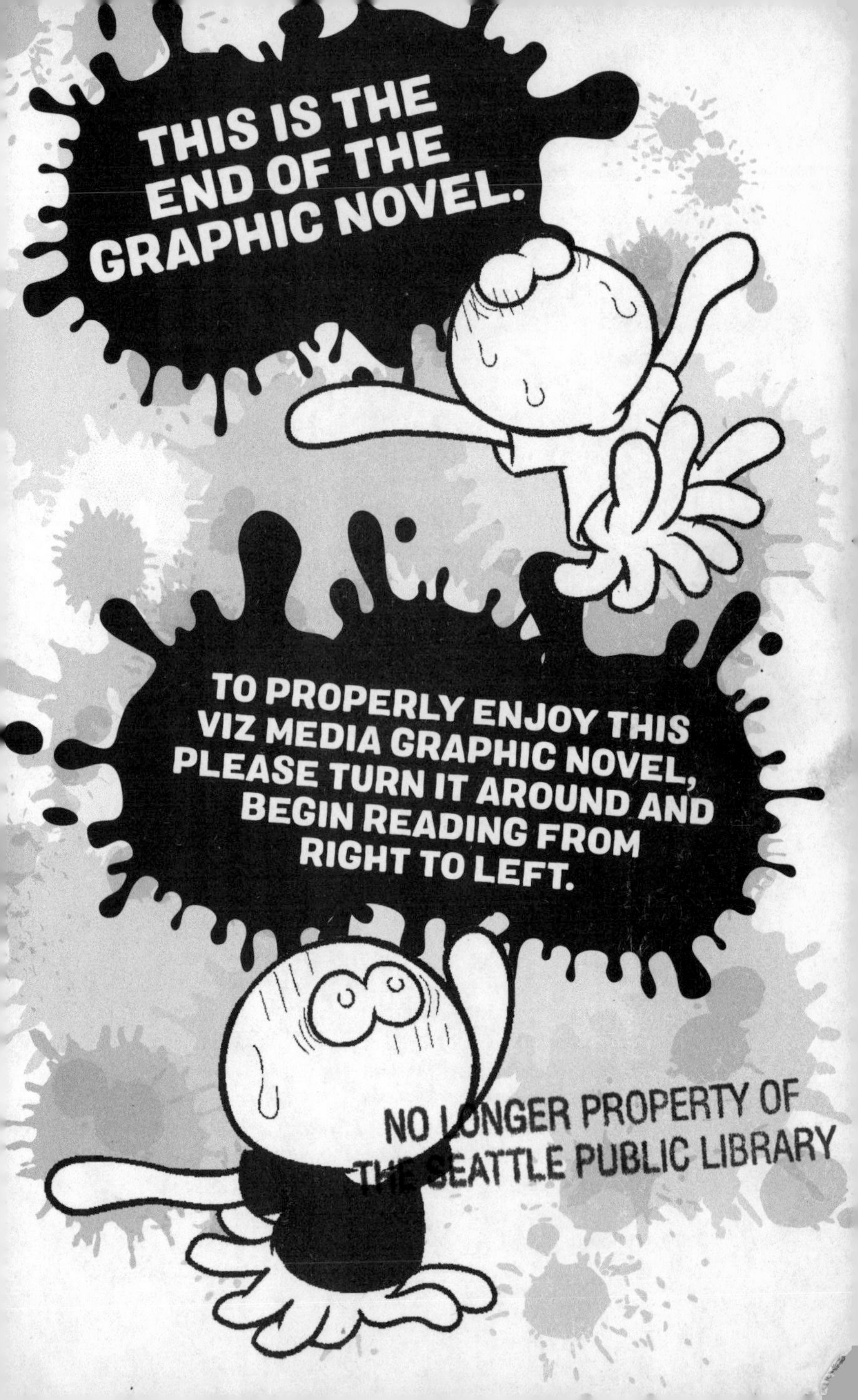
THIS IS THE END OF THE GRAPHIC NOVEL.
TO PROPERLY ENJOY THIS VIZ MEDIA GRAPHIC NOVEL, PLEASE TURN IT AROUND AND BEGIN READING FROM RIGHT TO LEFT.